execution plan

All his life, Patrick Thompson has been inspired by the rolling landscape of tarmac, low-rise concrete slabs and bread queues that is Dudley. He has written for as long as he can remember. His first novel, *Seeing the Wires*, was published in 2002: *Execution Plan* is his second.

execution plan

PATRICK THOMPSON

HarperCollins*Publishers*

HarperCollins*Publishers*
77–85 Fulham Palace Road,
Hammersmith, London W6 8JB
www.fireandwater.com

A Paperback Original 2003
1 3 5 7 9 8 6 4 2

Copyright © Patrick Thompson 2003

The Author asserts the moral right to
be identified as the author of this work

A catalogue record for this book
is available from the British Library

ISBN 0 00 710523 1

Typeset in Sabon by Palimpsest Book Production Limited,
Polmont, Stirlingshire

Printed and bound in Great Britain by
Clays Ltd, St Ives plc

acknowledgements

Thanks to: My agent, Annette Green; my editors, Sarah and Chris, for explaining to me how many days there were in a week (seven, by the way); and to everyone who reads this bit.

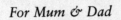
For Mum & Dad

PROLOGUE

Where do I start? Things don't have convenient beginnings, things overlap and collide.

Perhaps it started like this:

Veronica was on her way home, carrying bags of shopping. She was travelling by bus because we are back in the days when families had only one car, if they had one at all. She'd got bags of vegetables and foodstuffs we'd fail to recognize now. She was going to have to make them into something, not just empty one packet or another into the microwave. Microwaves aren't even a rumour. Microwaves are still science fiction. We are back in the early seventies.

The bus was crowded, and people jostled. The young people didn't hand over their seats to young women with heavy bags anymore. Everyone was smoking.

She'd left her son at home, but he'd be fine. He was old enough to look after himself. His father would be at work until six, and then doing office work at home until midnight. She'd be cooking for the three of them.

That was how it was, and it wasn't likely to change. Germaine Greer might not think so, but Germaine Greer wasn't living on housekeeping in the West Midlands. It was

1

easier to be radical when you had enough money to give up the day job. It was no trouble to be a free thinker if you had nothing urgent to think about.

Sometimes she wished she'd taken after her mother, who had been in charge of her own household. The understanding had been that her father had been there to bring in money. He was subservient to the female line. They'd been emancipated before emancipation.

She hadn't, though, and that was all there was to it. There was too much about her mother that was too uncomfortable.

If there was a genetic component to that – which seemed unlikely, as her mother's brand of strangeness was unscientific and didn't sit easily with concepts like genetics – then it might have passed, via her, to her son.

Perhaps it had. Perhaps he'd have abilities of his own. If he had, she hoped they wouldn't hurt him. He didn't need hurting. It'd happen, of course. Life was like that. Damage got done. The innocent came off badly. He'd get damaged.

Knowing that, she tried to prepare him. He wanted a pet. They'd talked about it.

'We can't have anything,' she'd told him. 'We haven't the money for it.'

'I could get a paper round.'

'For how much? A few pence? A couple of shillings? We haven't the room for a dog.'

'We could have a cat.'

'There are too many roads around here,' she'd said, shivering. A cat would never survive.

'A mouse then. In a cage.'

She didn't want mice, or rats, or anything else. Animals cost money. You had to feed them, and clean up after them, and he'd lose interest in it and then it'd be something else she got lumbered with. When the holidays were over and he was back at school he'd forget about it.

The bus driver was in a good mood and stopped short of the stop so that she wouldn't have so far to walk. She thanked him and heaved her bags out into the afternoon air. It was winter, and the air was becoming colourless and frigid. In some houses the Christmas decorations were up. She thought it was too early for that. It was still three weeks until Christmas; too early even to think about it. She wondered what he'd want this year. Everything, probably, and a cat thrown in too.

You couldn't have everything. Not even her mother had everything. Visiting her now, in her dusty old house with the cobwebs clustered wherever she could no longer reach, that was clear. You couldn't have everything. Her father had died, worn out looking after her mother, and her mother lived on in a house she could no longer keep clean. The neighbour's cats popped in for food and a chat. In her mother's trade – if it was a trade – cats were a given. When she dragged her son to visit his grandmother he'd be half afraid, half annoyed. Her husband would not go at all.

It took her a while to rescue her door key from her coat pocket, weighed down as she was by her shopping. Entering the house she knew at once that something was wrong.

Her son's voice, for one thing. It was too lively, too animated, and he shouldn't have been talking at all. There was no one to talk to.

She put the bags on the floor inside the front door, and of course one fell down and unleashed groceries.

Someone answered her son, and the chattering continued.

3

They were in the front room. Perhaps it was the television. She didn't think there was anything on, but they'd watch anything. Everyone said so.

She opened the door and looked in. Her son sat on the sofa, with an orange kitten on his lap. It was sparring with his fingers.

'Where's that from?' she asked, going in.

'I wanted one,' he said. As though that was an answer. 'Gran always says if you want something hard enough you can get it.'

'Gran says a lot of things she doesn't mean,' she said unconvincingly. He was young enough not to notice that. The kitten looked at her. She didn't like the way it looked. It was perhaps too orange. It was perhaps in not quite the right dimensions.

She noticed that there was someone else in the room, a ragged little boy in ragged little clothes. A friend of her son's, she thought, although you'd have thought his mother might have dressed him properly before letting him out.

'Who's this?' she asked.

'Who?' asked her son, and when she turned to look at the new boy there was no one there after all.

She turned back to look at her son.

'You don't want to listen to your Gran,' she said carefully, because this might all be reported back and there were things in that dusty old house of her mother's that were all the worse for being neglected for years. 'She doesn't know everything. You can't have everything you want.'

He looked doubtful at that.

'I mean it,' she said. 'That isn't your cat. Now just take it back where you got it from.'

He looked at her. He looked at the strange orange cat. He

4

did something – and she couldn't even have said what it was – and the kitten vanished, poof, gone.

'And don't do it again,' she said, hoping that he'd take notice. And then she unpacked the groceries and made them a nice stew for tea.

ONE

I

Who is Les Herbie?

The question seemed to answer itself. It was the headline at the top of the page of the issue of the *Pensnett Chronicle* I was reading over the shoulder of the man in the seat in front of me. We were on the 256k bus, Dudley to Birmingham via Christ knows where. The 256k bus has vague timetables and glum drivers.

Les Herbie was a columnist in the *Dudley Star*, not to be confused with the *Express & Star*. Les Herbie wrote a sometimes-irreverent and often-rude column. No one knew who he was. No photograph accompanied his column. He didn't make personal appearances. He didn't do publicity. He'd picked up a readership of young people, bright people, not the usual *Dudley Star* share of the demographic. The *Chronicle* had nothing like him, and so they ran daily articles failing to discredit him.

He was a reporter writing under an assumed name, they'd claim. He was a rich boy slumming it in Dudley. He was the man who wrote the horoscopes expanding his remit.

Execution Plan

The man in front of me turned the page. I didn't want to read any more of his paper; I had one of my own. I was young and bright; I had a copy of the *Dudley Star*. I turned to Les Herbie's column.

They took my car away.

Let's quantify that. Let's pin it down flat and dissect it.

They took my car away. So now I have to flag taxis or walk. Let's not talk about buses. Let's not go near buses. Buses are not an option.

There are some advantages to not having a car. I have time to think, while I'm waiting for the taxi.

They say, they always say, that it'll be there in five minutes. They're liars. That's the only reliable part of the business, the fact that it starts with a lie. After that it's all fiction. Everything – the route, the fare, the language, the glumness with which they take the tip – is subject to change. Only the time the taxi turns up is not subject to change. It is change. It's the thing itself.

While I'm waiting I write my column, which is why it's all about taxis. But not buses. I'm not going near buses.

I do have a car. I'm not dependent on public transport. My car developed a noise, and it's gone to the garage for a few days. Maybe three, maybe six, maybe August, they couldn't narrow it down. It's only what they do for a living. You wouldn't expect them to know how long it'd take.

While I'm waiting, if I'm not writing my column, I'm thinking about costs. A journey by taxi costs me too much a mile. But I save money on not buying a car, or taxing it, or handing out cash to the constables at speed checks. I don't have to take the taxi to the garage. I can have that second drink.

That's not counting the gaps. Time is money. My time has gaps, now. There's the gap between calling the taxi and the taxi turning up. There's a space between wanting to go somewhere and setting out.

It'd be worse if I was going by bus. On the bus, you pay less in cash, but they take the remainder out of your soul. Plus you need to buy new clothes, afterwards.

The gaps add up. I write half a column, and then have to go, and then I don't know where the column was going. You can't write a column in the gaps.

Let's quantify that. Let's pin it down flat and dissect it.

I can't write a column in the gaps. You can't write a column at all.

So, I can't go from A to B at time t. I have to go at t+n. My column suffers. My life becomes gappy. The taxi is late, right now, as I write this. It's taking its time.

When it gets here, it'll parp and toot. It'll flash and honk. Suddenly there will be a need for hurrying.

I want my car back, so that I can hurry on my own terms and in my own time. I want my own time back. I don't like taxis, because of the gaps. I can't use trains, because the nearest station is ten miles away and the trains only go to Coventry and who wants to go to Coventry? How would I get to the station? It's in a bad area. I wouldn't want to go there on foot.

In a tank, maybe. In a Panzer. In an ambulance, more likely.

But not on foot.

And not in a bus.

I don't do buses.

Have you seen the people on buses? Have you? They come in three types. Bus drivers, still learning how to use the gears and the brakes and the road. People too young to drive, although they should be able to hotwire a car. What's wrong with young people these days?

The other type has subtypes. The dead, the doomed, the

dispossessed. They wear bad clothes and don't clean them. They live with their mothers.

I'd hate to see their mothers.

They look like child molesters or serial killers. They look like victims.

So, I'm waiting for the taxi, and writing this to fill in the gap.

If I'm lucky, it won't be a long wait.

If I'm really lucky, this column will cover the fare.

It was a short column for Les. Sometimes he'd have half a page to himself, and sometimes only a paragraph. I folded the paper and looked out of the window. The view was different from the top floor. I didn't usually travel by bus. I had an Audi. But it wasn't well, and it had gone to the garage.

'They'll *rip you off*,' said Dermot, meaning the mechanics. 'They'll have seen you coming a mile off. You can't go on the bus. It's full of *scutters*. They've all got nits. They've all got satchels and scabies. You want your car back.'

■■

I did want my car back. You'd know why, if you'd ever been on the 256k bus. It goes every fifteen minutes on average, apparently managing this by running every two minutes at three in the morning, when there's no one at the bus stops, and once an hour during daylight hours. All bus passengers have a look of despair, forlorn pale things counting their change in the petrol fumes. Women with six children occupy entire decks, men with Elvis haircuts and their hands in their pockets sit next to you and breathe like donkeys. Everyone smokes rollups. At every other stop someone gets on with the wrong change. They go from seat to seat asking if anyone can change fifty pee. No one admits that they can. Everyone looks out of the windows. Everyone puts a bag on the seat next to them.

A boy with cropped ginger hair and an idiot expression sits in front of you, one seat to the left, with his head turned around, staring blankly at you the whole way home.

III

I write small computer applications, using Delphi as a front-end for Oracle databases. Databases are logical, until people get near them and put data in. Then they turn into a mess. I write small applications – applets – to allow users to get at the data and fix it. The trick is not to allow them to do anything. The trick is to give them buttons to click on and primary colours. If it beeps at them from time to time they're delighted. I can program without working at it. It's something that just clicks with me. I pick up computer languages. I read books about them for fun.

'You fucking would, you sad git,' Dermot would say. 'It's the only thing you do pick up. You don't pick up women, that's for bloody certain. What happened to that Julie? Where's she gone to? Let me guess, you told her all about fucking operating systems and she went out for cigarettes and never came back? You sad man. Computers. Sad.'

I had a PC at home, a 500 mhz Pentium III with 128 meg on

board and a 32-meg TNT2 graphics card. State of the art for a couple of months. I wrote applets on it I could have written on a 486.

You can't have a slow PC if you're a programmer. You wouldn't be able to hold your head up in company. You can have horror stories about the Amstrad you learned on, or how long it took to learn the keystrokes for Spectrum Basic. Remember the Spectrum? Little thing that had rubber keys and four colour-coded shift keys; every other key could have four meanings depending on the combination of shift keys you held down as you pressed it. You have to know about them. You need to have experienced them. But you can't have a slow PC now unless it's a spare, wired up as part of your own little LAN or sitting in the corner running an algorithm to find the highest prime number.

My pretty little desktop PC was more powerful than things that filled rooms in the seventies. It could do billions of calculations a second. It could plot millions of points instantly, do four-dimensional trigonometry, produce print-quality images, connect to the Net and kick-start the revolution.

I played games on it.

I have played games on an old ZX Spectrum, and on a Commodore 64, and on an Atari ST and now on a PC that has none of its original components. Everything has been upgraded. Everything has been replaced at least once.

I have also owned a couple of consoles, an old Sega Megadrive with a dodgy converter and a Nintendo 64 that was better than a PC four years ago. I have drawers full of computer games, video games, video-games magazines. I used to read science fiction, all those books about unhelpful robots and alternate universes.

Video games *are* an alternate universe. Each one is a

window onto a new world. They are self-referential like no other art-form, and they started that way. The first widely available game was Pong, marketed by Atari.

Atari – the word – is from a game itself. It's from Go, and it's the state a group of stones is in when it has one liberty left, when it's in imminent danger of capture.

Games are like that. They feed on their own history.

Pong gave you control of a bat; you had to hit a ball with it. The ball was square. Lo-rez was hi-rez at the time. Pong had one control, and three instructions. The best one was:

Avoid missing ball for high score.

Dermot is right.

I am boring about computers.

IV

I met Dermot six or seven years ago. I was on a training course in Birmingham, learning the fundamentals of object-oriented programming. The course was in a small building on a new business park close to the NEC. It was the peak time for new business parks. They were everywhere, and they were all the same. Each one had the small, flat, white building that did computer training, the grey warehouses for furniture companies, the sprawling blocks occupied by new businesses going out of business, the inconvenient out-of-town sorting office. There was a van selling burgers and egg baps. There were signs with arrows in bright primaries. The road names were misleadingly pleasant and rural.

On the first two days of the course, I went to the restaurant for lunch, along with everyone else. It was the usual business park restaurant, with no evening menu and no atmosphere. Secretaries leaned across tables. Men shouted into mobile phones. Nothing meaningful happened. We had scampi that had been constructed from recycled scales, tails and fins. We had French fries made out of anything but potato.

On the third and last day of the course I said I had some work to catch up on at lunchtime. I'd had enough faux scampi. I'd had enough of mobile phones. I went to the burger van. It had been a VW camper once upon a time. It was white under the grime, which was considerable. It was leaning slightly into the road. The tax disc was months out of date. One side of the van had been cut open and brutalized into a serving hatch.

There was no queue. There was no menu.

'What do you have?' I asked.

The proprietor looked down at me from behind the crusted sauce bottles. He had black curly hair and a round nose. He looked like a cartoon Irishman, and as it turned out that summed him up pretty well, apart from his accent. His accent was all over the place, and as I soon discovered, he put heavy emphasis on at least one word in almost every sentence.

'I have fucking *burgers*, what do you *think* I have? Truffles?'

'What sort of burgers?'

'Cheap ones.'

'Do you sell many?'

'Not round *here* I don't. They're all in there, eating *really* cheap burgers.' He nodded towards the restaurant. 'They're all in the fucking *tuck shop*. Have you noticed that? It's like a *campus* here. It's like a *university*. They've all got the *same clothes*. They've got *tie clips*. Fucking tie clips. Jesus.'

He looked at my tie.

'Did you tie that? Was the light on when you did it? You have to be a computer man.'

I told him I was.

'Fucker of a day this is turning out to be. Only one customer and he's a computer man. I'm sick of this. Do you want a drink?'

'I want a burger.'

'I'll *give* you a fucking burger. It's your funeral. Then can we go for a drink? They have a bar in there?'

I nodded.

'Right we are then. Settled. Here.'

He dropped a burger into a bap and passed it to me.

'Sauce is there if you want it.'

He closed the hatch. I heard a door close on the far side of the van, and then he walked around it. He was shorter than me but not by much, and far more alive. He was more alive than anyone I'd ever met. He was all energy.

I took a bite of my burger.

'There's a bin there,' he said, pointing. 'Take my word for it, throw *that* fucking thing into it.'

'I thought it was my funeral.'

'And it's *my* fault. Do they have *beer* in here or is it all wine and shite in bottles?'

'They have beer.'

'In tiny fucking *bottles* or in pints?'

'Both.'

'Fair enough. You had enough of that?'

I had. I dropped it into the next bin.

14

'First sensible thing you've done. For the second one, you can buy the drinks.'

'I'm buying the drinks?'

'Of *course* you are, you cheeky cunt. I bought *lunch*.'

v

If you're old enough to remember a time when there were no video games, then you'll know that the first time you saw Pong it was a vision into a new place. Cyberspace is the place you look into when you look into a monitor, past the screen and into the game world. In there – out there – everything is possible. You can control events there.

In the real world, events control you.

I used to be a student. You don't need to be a student to get into software. Most early coders – the ones on the frontier, the ones on the cutting edge – taught themselves. They had to. There were no landmarks. Now, you need qualifications and experience. I learned how to code from a ZX Spectrum, trying to write games that would make me a millionaire like Matthew Smith. You'd see pictures of him in computer magazines, this long-haired seventeen-year-old said to have a million-plus bank account. This was in the early eighties, when a million was big money. The computer magazines of the time used to have long listings of programs, endless pages of hopeless code for you to type in at the keyboard of your computer. They always contained typos. If you typed them in correctly, they failed to run. You had to interpret and debug the code. You'd spend days typing this stuff in, saving it to a C90 cassette every now and then. Saving took minutes in those days. You had to watch the tape run and listen to a high-pitched electronic squealing.

Sometimes, even now, I hear that sound as I fall asleep.

I corrected the code in magazines and got programs to run. I got jerky stick-men to stroll across the screen. I got fifty bad versions of Space Invaders to run. I got bad eyesight and pale skin.

I gave up on programming games. With games the cutting edge is always somewhere else. In computing the cutting edge is in all directions, and you can't keep up with it. You have to find a wave and ride it. You have to pick a direction and head that way.

I learned computing by myself, and then couldn't get a job. The first wave had gone. The second wave was coming up behind me, schools full of kids learning to program. I didn't have a wave to go with, so I got stuck in the trough. I needed more experience. I had some money in my bank account, left to me thanks to helpful deaths on remote branches of the family tree. I invested it in myself and took a degree course at Borth College. That's where I learned about other worlds. That's where I learned that they're bad places. And then, like all students, I forgot everything I'd learned.

VI

Dermot looked at the interior of the restaurant.

'Look at the *state* of this place. Is this tacky or fucking what?'

A barman in an anonymous black suit watched us nervously. He looked too young to be behind a bar. He looked much too young to deal with Dermot.

'We want beer,' Dermot told him. 'We need beer. We've been having a hard old time. I've been shifting commodities all morning and I'm thirsty. What have you got?'

The barman listed drinks; designer lagers made up most of the options.

'Two pints of lager then,' Dermot said. 'Fizzy piss but you haven't got anything else. You want to talk to the *brewery* about it. I have *friends* in catering. I could put a *word* in. Would you *like* me to do that? Would you *like* me to see what I can do?'

'It's not up to me,' said the barman.

'No, I wouldn't have *thought* so,' said Dermot. 'I'd *imagine* not. We'll have two whiskies to go with them.'

'I'm driving,' I said.

'I'll drink them then. That's two lagers, *two* whiskies, and have one yourself.'

'I'm not really allowed to drink.'

'But I *want* you to have one. I'll be offended. I'd take it as a *rebuff*. Who says you can't have one?'

'It's how it works.'

'Don't say I didn't try. Don't say I didn't offer. Just the lagers and whiskies then, thanks. He's paying.'

I checked my wallet. I didn't know what the prices were like. The training people had paid for all of the meals until then. Which was fair enough as the training was costing thousands of pounds. I checked the room for clues about costs. There was a lot of flimsy wood panelling and acres of flat red cloth. Glass ashtrays the size of dustbin lids held mounds of smouldering butts. The waitresses were teenage girls with the facial expressions of expiring fish apart from one older woman who, on first inspection, appeared to be dead. They wore unmarked uniforms, somewhere between French maids and policewomen. Someone in procurements had overlapping fetishes.

Clusters of men wearing Armani suits they couldn't quite afford or carry off talked about deals they were involved in. Dermot and I were easily the oldest people in the room if you discounted the older waitress. Which, as she seemed to be dead, you could.

'*School holidays*, is it?' asked Dermot. 'Didn't tell you, did I? The name's Dermot. My mother was from Cork, so she used to say. Course she was *off her head*, she could have been from *Mars* for all I know. Didn't know my father, he fucked off to Belgium before I *turned up*. Belgium! Who goes to *Belgium*?' He had a drink and thought about it. 'That's my family history done. Who are you then?'

'Mick Aston.'

'Mick? That's what you'd call a *sheepdog*. We can *work* with it though. Could be Mickey, could be Michael, could be Mike. You're stuck with Aston, though. You not drinking that?'

He pointed at my whisky and I shook my head. He downed the drink.

'Tell you *what*, tell you what I *think*. I think we need to get *out of here*. Out of this fucking *business* park. You up for it? We can go into *town* and have a real drink.'

'I have a course to finish.'

'Well finish it then. Finish it now. You can always do another course. You might not see me again. What have you got to lose?'

'My job. My liver.'

'There are other jobs out there. I can get you a job.'

'Selling burgers?'

'Not fucking likely. You don't have the skill set. You don't have the aptitude. We can use the van to get to town.'

'You're drunk.'

'I've had a drink. There's a difference. Having a drink is sociable. Getting drunk is disgraceful. I don't get drunk.'

The barman eyed him warily.

'I get *rat-arsed*,' Dermot told him. I get *arrested*. Nice place, hope it takes off. You're fucked if it doesn't. You coming?'

Of course I was. I didn't know what to make of him but it'd be an interesting night. You'd have thought that after Dr Morrison I'd know better, but after Dr Morrison I really didn't know what I knew.

'Good man. Fair play. We'll take the van. You'll need to be careful in there.'

'Why? The fat fryer?'

'No, fuck that. We can dump that. You'll have to watch out for the mirrors. There are the wing mirrors, the driving mirror, might even be some shiny surfaces in there somewhere. I doubt it, it's filthy. I honestly doubt it. But there might be some chrome or something.'

'I don't mind mirrors,' I said. Dermot smiled evilly at the barman.

'Oh yes he does,' he said. 'He doesn't like them at all. And now he doesn't know whether he likes me or not, either. Confusing old world isn't it? Come on then.'

I followed him.

19

TWO

I

That afternoon we got ridiculously drunk. I don't remember much about it. I remember abandoning the burger van halfway down Broad Street in Birmingham. Dermot had, as he'd promised, dumped the deep-fat fryer on the pavement at the business park. We'd left it there, leaking grease and steaming.

'Off we fucking *go* then,' said Dermot, scampering gleefully off into the afternoon crowd. We had a few in the first open bar we came to.

After that my memory skips like a vinyl record. I remember a staircase leading down to some toilets far beneath a dingy club. I remember being brightly sick over a flashing fruit machine. I remember it paying out three jackpots in a row in response.

I remember being in a bathroom with a long mirror of polished metal, Dermot beside me, holding my hand out. His small hands were too strong to resist, like the rest of him.

'You can touch it,' he said, meaning the mirror. 'You can touch it.'

Our blurred reflections looked back at us, mine terrified, his delighted.

'Go on,' he urged. 'Touch it.'

A pair of post-punk punks – all polychromatic hair dye and studded leather – arrived in time to hear that. They moved to flank us.

'What's the *problem*?' asked Dermot.

'Pair of queers in the bog,' said one. 'That's the problem.'

'Where?' asked Dermot, looking around theatrically.

Something about him made them leave. He looked for a moment like a werewolf, without any transformation. He was suddenly all violence. They backed off, hands up and palms forward. If they'd been dogs they'd have rolled over. The door dragged itself shut behind them.

'Pair of cunts,' he said. 'Not *going* to touch the mirror, then? Come on. More drinks.'

We had more drinks. How do you become afraid of mirrors? Easily. Here's how it happened for me.

■

In 1983 all sorts of things were changing. There were new sorts of amusement arcades and new sorts of amusements. We were living in the most immoral decade since records began. We were moving into the age of image.

I was moving into the final year of a three-year course in software engineering. This was at a tiny college two miles from Borth, which is a small town on the wet Welsh coast in the middle of nowhere. The campus held a few residential blocks, a blocky little student pub, and a three-storey H-block style building that held everything else. It had been built in the seventies, and designed by an architect with a fondness for the T-square and a big gap in his imagination. The computer rooms held out-of-date green-screen workstations linked to an ancient server. The server was tended by unspeaking drones in lab coats. They gave the impression of depthless knowledge; they never provided evidence of it. The server had its own room, locked with state-of-the-art locks for that time. Large windows with embedded wire mesh let you look in and see the server at work. It was the size of a pair of double wardrobes, with enormous switches and great tangles of cables. Banks of reel-to-reel recorders spooled miles of tape in all directions. The technicians would feed punched cards into slots, pull levers, and run for cover as processing began.

Borth college didn't run many courses, and it didn't attract many students. It didn't attract any good ones. I went there because the entry requirements seemed to consist of turning up. This turned out to be true. It was all subsidised by government handouts and charitable donations, otherwise it would have closed down three weeks after it first opened.

The computer courses were run on the ground floor, and so all of the windows had to be barred. This was Wales in the early eighties and green-screen workstations could fetch a few pounds. On the middle floor they ran hairdressing courses. On the top floor the experimental psychologists watched mice run through mazes. In those days higher education took very little of your time and didn't cost you all that much. I had a lot of spare time on my hands and nowhere to spend it. The campus was situated in a wet wasteland. What seemed to be huge distant mountains were actually small mountains, quite close by. It rained three days out of five. There was a single bus stop, and the bus went between the campus and Borth twice a day each way. If you went there at night you had to get a taxi back, and there were no taxis. Now there are no taxis anywhere in Wales. They were all removed. Now there are only *tacsis*. There's lufli.

I made friends, out of necessity. There was nothing else to do. For three years there was only the company of other students. At night the lecturers drove home in Morris Minors and Volkswagens. The hairdressers vanished. You could try and date them, but you wouldn't get anywhere. They were Welsh and miserably insolent. They were dark-haired, thin, a genotype. They looked like goths, without trying. None of the locals seemed to stay up after eight.

To pass the time, we would go to the student bar. Presumably the college funded it. It didn't seem to do enough trade to stay afloat.

In the first term of my third year, I met Tina McAndrew. We had an affair that didn't do either of us any good, but we got out of the wreckage with our friendship intact. That was just as well, as there were few other people there. You couldn't afford to lose a friend. There were sixteen computer students, the unassailable hairdressers, and the psychologists. Tina was a psychology student. I remember looking out of a window while I was waiting for yet another Cobol program to compile. I saw her walk from one of the residential blocks, wearing one of the long coats that everyone had in those days. She was heavier than the girls I usually fancied. I liked them tiny, and she was my height. She looked as though she'd beat me at arm-wrestling. She had long hair and the Welsh weather was busily fucking it over. I watched her until she walked out of my line of sight.

A couple of nights later I saw her in the student bar and decided to talk to her. I was egged on by Olaf, one of the other computer students. Olaf came from a wealthy family, by early eighties standards. He had a sense of humour that only he understood. You had to decipher him. Olaf wasn't his real name, obviously. His real name was Peter, but he called himself Olaf.

'It's short for "Oh, laugh, for fuck sake",' he once told me.

The night Tina turned up, he watched me watching her. I sometimes thought he should have been with the experimental psychologists. He liked observing. I sometimes wondered if he was an experimental psychologist, sneakily studying the computer students. I knew that was paranoid, which hopefully meant that I was sane.

'Go on then,' he said. 'Talk to the lady.'

There was no point ignoring him. After all, I wanted to talk to her. I managed to get to the bar before she was served.

This wasn't difficult. The student bar had a lone barman, named Sid. He was older than the students and distant in manner. He would strive not to serve people. He would do his best to avoid talking to you.

'Until he gets to know you,' Olaf once said. 'Then he still doesn't talk to you. But at least he knows you.'

Sid could take a long time to pour a simple pint and girls usually chose more complicated drinks. They'd want mixers and ice; that could take him all night. I sidled closer to Tina, whose name I didn't know at the time.

'Hello again,' she said.

I looked around. She was talking to me. What did she mean, 'again'?

'Hello?' I said.

'Who's that you're with? Not one of your crowd. I thought you hung around with a livelier bunch.'

She looked slightly quizzical. Her features managed to be

24

both heavy and delicate; a neat trick, I thought. I didn't know what had compelled me to talk to her. Olaf and drink, perhaps. My usual approach was more circumspect. Still, I did know that I didn't know her. I didn't know anyone who looked that good.

'You must have me mixed up,' I said.

'That sounds about right. Can I get you a drink?'

'I'll get you one.'

'That's a bit old fashioned, isn't it? I'm allowed to buy the drinks. We're in the eighties now, you know.'

'I know.'

'Are you sure we haven't met?'

I said that I was. I'd have remembered her. It wasn't as though I met many girls. Computers didn't attract them.

'I'm Tina,' she said, 'and as I don't know you, you'll need to tell me who you are.'

'Mick Aston,' I said.

'Are you doing anything tomorrow evening, Mick Aston?' she asked. I wasn't. 'Well, you are now,' she said. 'Thanks for the drink.'

▌ ▌ ▌

The next night she took me to Aberystwyth to see a film. I was expecting something French and gloomy, but she chose a noisy extravaganza with car chases and guns. She seemed to be watching me as much as the film. Perhaps it was because she was a psychology student, I thought. On the way back to Borth on the night bus, she edged closer to me across the seat.

'Do you think people always have hidden depths?' she asked. 'Or is what you see what you get?'

'I don't know.'

'I think you've got depths,' she said. She visibly came to a decision and kissed me, as though she'd been wondering whether to or not. I'd already reached the same decision and left her to it.

We had a brief affair, and ended up as friends. That's as good as it gets, I think. Anything longer-term is based on a different emotion. It's still called love, but it's another flavour. Our little affair was all over in a month.

It was obvious early on that we wanted different things from the relationship. I wanted everything. I saw her and became happy.

She, on the other hand, saw some potential in me. She saw something under the surface. She could see a possible me, and it was him that she was after. He stayed hidden, however. She liked me, but not as much as she liked the version of me that I failed to become.

She began to cool. I attempted to woo her. It wasn't something I had a talent for.

I tried to write poems for her, but they came out lifeless. I couldn't get words to do anything good. We'd hold hands and walk the four-mile round trip to Borth and back. We slept together in my tiny student bed. I would find her crying from time to time. By the third week, that was all she was doing.

She told me she was sorry, she'd like to be friends.

We were friends. I didn't have an easy time with that. But hope springs eternal, the vicious little bastard.

IV

Borth is really not much more than a road by the sea. You approach it by way of a long road that follows the estuary of the river Dyfi. The road winds past the college grounds, a thin strip of swampland, and a golf course. The road goes through the middle of the links, splitting the course into two and providing golfers and motorists alike with an extra hazard. A high sloping wall of grey concrete blocks the view out to sea. There are car parking spaces next to the sea wall. Inland, there are mountains and clouds.

A large public toilet, which has won awards, stands between the sea wall and the town. The shops all sell the same things; buckets and spades, strange paperbacks, cheap tat. Behind the main road, reached by way of a track, is a church of dark stone. It's not visible from the town. It's as though they're ashamed of it.

A railway line runs behind the town and there's a station which is not abandoned, despite appearances. Trains stop there at uncertain intervals. Once in a while, if the wind is in the right direction, you hear one clattering off along the estuary, upsetting the seagulls. The town is bookended by two small amusement arcades.

I spent a lot of time in the amusement arcades.

There are two chip shops and one general store. On a high promontory overlooking the town there is a war monument. From there, looking down, you can clearly see that Borth is a straight line of a town, that single road running dead level with the shore. Inland, a great expanse of featureless flat land stretches away to the mountains. It's as though someone decided to try to build a resort on a salt marsh, just to see if it could be done. From this high viewpoint, you can also see the beach.

To get to the beach you have to climb over the sea wall, which is just over six feet high. It's triangular in cross-section, and slopes at about forty-five degrees to the vertical. There are steps, but most people scramble up the flanks. In the lee of the wall you notice a chilling wind. On the top of the wall, it does its level best to throw you miles inland. Families wrapped in flapping cagoules struggle with chip papers. The beach is of fist-sized pebbles that are uncomfortable to walk, lie, or fall on. Either the tide or the bored populace has arranged the pebbles into large steps. Scrambling inelegantly down them, you come to a foot-wide strip of sand and then the heaving grey sea. Someone's dog will shake itself dry next to you. Screeching herring gulls flap out of the surf and are whisked away by the wind.

On bank holidays, people come from most of the Midlands to spend a grim couple of hours struggling along the shore. Children unsuccessfully try to spend their pocket money in the shops. At about five, the town empties. The tourists go home. The wind dies down. The pubs do a miserable trade. In the evening, there's nothing to see in Borth.

We used to go there in the evenings.

V

By midway through our final year, the student bar had lost any attraction it had once had. Instead, I took Tina to the Running Cow. The pubs in Borth were still pubs at the time, and families weren't welcome. The choice of meals consisted of either cheese or ham baps, individually wrapped in cling film and left out on the bar to die. There was a choice of beer or lager and a small selection of shorts. Tina had half a lager. I had a pint.

She was wearing black everything. Her hair had been crimped into crinkly submission. In other circumstances, I wouldn't have found her attractive. In Borth she was the brightest thing around.

We had decided to be friends. Well, she had decided. I was being friends in case it led back to being lovers, which it doesn't. Twenty years later we're still friends.

'How are you for money?' she asked.

'I can afford a round or two.'

'No, you moron. I mean generally.'

Well enough, I thought. I was a little way into debt but not so far that I wouldn't be able to find my way back. By all accounts, computer programming would pay more money than I could handle. I'd be a tax exile inside a decade.

'Fine,' I said.

'It's just that they're paying people for research. They want two people.'

'They? Who are they?'

'Psychology. Dr Morrison is after two volunteers and he's got a research grant. He's paying a hundred apiece. I've volunteered. Which leaves one place free.'

'What do we have to do?'

'He won't say. It'd prejudice the results.'

'Maybe it'd prejudice the volunteers.'

'Perhaps it would. Look, Mick, it's not as though you have anything else to do.'

'Just my course.'

'And how much do you have on at the moment? This is a

single afternoon. You won't miss an afternoon. You can do programming in your sleep.'

'One afternoon? And I get a hundred quid?'

I didn't know why I was quibbling. I had already decided to do it. A hundred would buy new games, with maybe some to spare for pens and paper. I could also buy a couple of floppies to save my work onto. The college computers used a variety of floppy disk that I never saw anywhere else, 7¾-inch things with hardly any capacity. Unlike modern floppy disks with their protective plastic covers, these were genuinely floppy. If you waved them in the air they flapped, and you lost all of your data.

'Cash in hand. Money for next to nothing,' said Tina, still under the impression that I needed persuading. The bar was quiet, as it always was. The locals went to other pubs if they went anywhere at all. Perhaps they all stayed in.

'You're doing it?'

'Yes.'

'I'll do it. But if he asks me about my mother I'm leaving.' She gave me a strange look.

'Is there anything else you'd like to talk about?' she asked.

'Like?'

'Any niggling worries? Anything on your mind?'

'No,' I said, ignoring the niggling worry about the 'just friends' business. I had got used to ignoring that. The only time it became difficult was when I was trying to go to sleep at night.

'Should there be?'

'Not if you don't think so.'

I didn't think so. We drank our drinks and set out for the walk back to the campus. There was no one out, although I knew that if we scrambled up the sea wall there'd be a few people walking dogs along the hostile beach. There was always someone walking a dog along that beach.

'Let's walk on the sea wall,' Tina said suddenly, already well on her way up.

'What for? It's windy up there.'

'We'll be able to see more.'

'More Borth. Who wants to see more Borth?'

'Oh come on,' she said, grabbing my arm and hauling me up after her. 'Look at the sea. Don't you want to swim in it? Don't you just want to throw yourself into the sea?'

'Are you mad? It's night and it's cold. There are things in it.'

'Well do you want to cut through the golf course then?'

What was she getting at? She wasn't planning to seduce me in a dark corner. We were just friends. We'd both agreed to that except for me.

'What are you on about?' I asked her.

'Ask me again next week,' she said, and then, as though it was just a throwaway line:. 'Did I tell you I'd met somebody?'

No, she hadn't. That explained her peculiar mood.

After that, we had a very quiet walk back.

VI

Although I had been at the college for almost three years, I had never been to the third floor until I turned up to earn my quick hundred quid. I had thought about it, and had decided that it couldn't do any harm. I was surprised to see that the stairs continued on up past the third floor, through a locked grille. Presumably they led to an attic or loft. The doors were numbered. I was after 304. It was eleven in the morning and there didn't seem to be anyone around. Didn't they have psychologists in Wales? With all of that research material going free? That seemed a terrible waste.

'I didn't think you'd turn up,' said Tina, trundling round the corner with an armful of brown folders.

'I'm getting paid for this. We *are* still getting paid, aren't we?'

'We are. Don't worry about the money. Now, lets see if he's in.'

She knocked on the door. On the lower floors, the doors had glass panels at head height. Even the door of the server room had one. Up here in the realms of the headshrinkers, the doors were of flimsy but unbroken wood and painted a matte white. She knocked again.

'Come on in,' said someone. Tina opened the door and bundled me in.

'This is him,' she said, meaning me.

'Ah,' said the man in the room. He was a young man, probably no older than twenty, and he was wearing a lab coat. He looked like he might be related or married (or both, this was Borth) to one of the computer technicians from the ground floor.

'Pleased to meet you,' he said in a nervous voice. He gave me a limp, sweaty handshake. It didn't seem like the sort of contact he was used to. There was a good chance that he wasn't used to any at all. He had the sort of sparse ginger hair that shows a lot of scalp without the need for total baldness. His eyebrows were invisible unless he stood at the right angle in strong light. His eyes were a watery blue and he did his best to keep them from looking directly at you. When he spoke, he sounded as though he might stutter. He never did, but there was the feeling that he might. He was always fidgeting with the skin around his fingernails, and from time to time he'd absently bite off a stray strip. To do this he'd bend an arm across his face, turning his hand to the necessary angle for auto-cannibalism.

The top of a black tee-shirt was visible in the V-shaped opening at the throat of his lab coat. There was no writing on it.

'I'm Betts,' he said, letting go of my hand with evident relief. 'I'm the technician. The lab technician, I mean. I'll run you through what we're about, then Dr Morrison will run through the experiment. It won't take long. 'I'll give you some background first. If that's alright?'

We said that it was.

He told us about some tricks you could do with mirrors.

THREE

I

At the time, the technique was new. One or two progressive European clinics were using it. Dr Morrison was a fan of progressive European techniques.

'What's it a technique for?' I asked.

'Whatever,' said Betts. 'It can relax the mind. Sometimes it can provoke reactions. It's all to do with self-image.'

He went into a spiel about the Self while Tina and I sat at a desk. I didn't want my Self getting any ideas so I looked out of the window until it was over. It was like being in a lecture, from what I could remember of them.

'You can try this one,' he said. 'This one shows you what I mean. Here. Put your hand flat on the table. Palm down. Now, watch this.'

I had my hand palm down. He ran his index finger along each of my fingers.

'There, you can see what I'm doing and you can feel it. That makes sense to you. Now, keep your hand flat but hold it under the table.'

I put my hand under the table. He continued to run his

right index finger over my hand, but now he kept his left hand on the table, following his right hand. At first it didn't seem to be doing anything. Someone was tickling my hand and a table. Then he got his hands synchronized. As he touched the back of my index finger – which was out of sight, under the table – with one hand, he touched the same place on the table with the other. Every time he touched me, he also touched the matching place on the table.

My eyes decided that they knew best, and overrode everything else.

I lost my hand.

All of a sudden it wasn't there. I could see my arm going under the table, but the sensations weren't coming from there. They were coming from the table. The table felt as though it was part of me.

'Ah,' said Betts, reclaiming his own hands. 'There. You've remapped. Your hand is mapped to the table. See how easy that was? That's how it works.'

'Let's have your hands where we can see them,' said Tina. I pulled my hand back into view. It didn't feel quite right. It was numb. I patted it with the other hand and it was normal again.

'It's sight that does it,' said Betts. 'If you mix the signals, give a visual stimulus that doesn't match a physical stimulus, the body doesn't know what to do. It can't interpret the signals. You could see me copying what I was doing under the table with my other hand, and because you could only see that one you mapped the sensation of touch to match the vision. Dr Morrison uses mirrors.'

'Nice,' said Tina. 'I could do with a mirror, the rain's played havoc with my hair.'

'How does this help?' I asked.

'It sets you apart from yourself,' Betts explained. 'It lets you see yourself in a different way, without the body getting in the way. I just went through all that. Weren't you listening?'

'No he wasn't,' said Tina. 'He was looking out of the window and thinking about arcade games.'

She was right, as usual.

'It's better with mirrors,' said Betts. He became less nervous as he expanded on his subject. 'We block your view of yourself, and let you see parts of your body reflected. You move your left hand, and see your right hand move. That's the sort of thing. It disassociates you from yourself.'

'And that's all I do for the afternoon? And I get paid?'

'It may be distressing. Some people react to it badly. We're paying you because you might not enjoy yourself.'

'Bring the mirrors on,' I said.

'Dr Morrison is setting things up. We have to get the line of sight right for your height.'

'How do you know how tall I am?'

'You're about my height. Maybe a little taller. A touch less than six feet. Your eyes are level with mine. This isn't rocket science.'

It didn't seem like any sort of science. We were going to stand and look at ourselves in strategically placed mirrors.

'Isn't there a control? You have control subjects in experiments.'

'You're both control subjects. You're both going in there, and neither of you will know when you're the control. It'll switch between you.'

'Fine.'

The three of us ran out of things to talk about. I don't like to provoke conversations. I feel more comfortable joining them once they're underway. Tina seemed preoccupied. Perhaps she had some buried traumas she was worrying about. Betts began to nibble at the skin around his fingernails. He winced and shook his finger as he caught a live bit. I looked back out of the window. The mountains were rendered faint by low clouds or thick sky. I wondered if the rooms across the corridor had a view of the sea.

'I'll see what he's up to,' said Betts, leaving Tina and I alone in the room.

'How's your hand?' she asked.

'It's mine again. That was weird. I could feel it but it felt like the table was my hand. Or my hand was the table. It felt strange. It's an illusion, though. It's not as though my hand became part of the table.'

'Illusions can be enough,' she said. She seemed to be on her way to saying something else, and then stopped and looked out of the window. Between us, we were in danger of using the view up. There wasn't much of it – grey sky, grey mountains, grey fields – and it wouldn't stand up to much more attention.

'What's Dr Morrison like?' I asked.

'What do you think he's like?'

'Are you examining me?'

'All the time. You need it. So, what do you think he's like?'

'Like a movie mad scientist. Mostly bald and with coloured stuff in test tubes. Getting ready to feed us a serum that'll turn us into zombies.'

'He's about thirty, and he has hair. He doesn't have test tubes.'

'Just mirrors?'

'You can be very negative. We'll have to see about knocking that out of you.'

'I'd be careful. Negativity is half of my personality. I don't know if the rest would stand up without it.'

'No,' she said. 'Possibly not.'

She popped her elbows on the table, folded her hands together, and dropped her chin onto them. She looked at the desk.

Neither of us said anything else until Betts came back.

❚❚

At that time video games were everywhere except in the home. In pubs they stood and twittered in corners. There were little tables with video games built in. Player One sat at one side and Player Two sat at the other, and their mates put ashtrays and pints in the middle of the screen and laughed. There were video games in pubs, chip shops, amusement arcades.

Home machines weren't advanced enough to play real arcade games then. The best you got was Pong, and a poor version of that. That'd be on a console with wooden sides and huge silver knobs. To play real video games you had to leave the house.

I would walk into Borth with a pocketful of pound notes. Cars crammed with tourists and their kit – lunch boxes, kites, pets – drove around me. There were no pavements and the verges were of swampy mud beneath a thin veneer of moss. The smell of the estuary would wash over you if the tide was out, a rank stink of rot. On the other side of the estuary, a few miles away by boat but half an hour by car because there was no bridge this side of Machynleth, you could see Llandovery. Llandovery was a town which attracted more tourists than Borth but had less car parking.

Out to sea, you couldn't see anything. There were seldom any boats and never any large ones. There was a harbour over in Llandovery, but the yachts didn't come our way.

I'd walk past the golf course, watching out for stray shots. These were common and not always accidental. Not all of the locals welcomed students.

The amusement arcade at the near end of town was in a wooden building. It might have been a barn at some time. Now it was full of machines calling for attention. There was a single row of six one-armed bandits, the old ones made without software. They took two-pence coins and had jackpots of twenty pence. The one second from the left had an OUT OF ORDER notice on it for three years. It may still be there, out of order, on its own.

There were penny falls with prizes that seemed to have been welded to the spot. There was a betting game with tin horses on sticks racing around a striped track under a glass dome. There were machines with prizes arranged beneath a claw that would touch them and then leave them where they were.

Past all that, at the back, past the booth containing a miserable middle-aged woman and the spare change, were the video games. There were only three, but they were already taking most of the money. They had bright screens and they made more noise than anything else around. Written on them were instructions in a new version of English.

Not to miss shoot for top score!

Tapping button for super jump!

On the left was a classic Space Invaders, one for the retro crowd even then. Next to it was an Asteroids machine, with its simple vector graphics. Finally there was a Missile Command, the one where you controlled the cursor with a trackball. There was a game for the early eighties. Missiles would drop from the sky towards your cities. You'd launch countermeasures, aiming them with that strange trackball. But the missiles would get through, levelling your cities. Nuclear devastation, mass deaths, game over.

If only Ronald Reagan had seen that console. The SDI money could have gone to something useful instead.

I'd change a pound and slowly feed the machines. Missile Command was cheerily nihilistic, but Asteroids almost pointedly demonstrated the futility of working. You controlled a little triangular spaceship which sat in the centre of the screen. Large irregular boulders – the titular asteroids – arrived and began to move across the screen. Two large rocks, moving slowly: no trouble, you'd think. You'd line up your ship and press the fire button.

But after you shot a large rock, it broke into two quite large rocks, which headed off in new directions. Now there were three rocks to avoid. If you shot a rock, it subdivided into smaller rocks, and those into smaller ones, until the screen was a mass of debris.

Once they were very small, shooting them destroyed them. But by this time, you were in trouble because one of them inevitably caught you unaware and you lost a life.

The way to play Asteroids was not to shoot the asteroids. Even in video games, work only leads to more work.

After spending a pound I'd wait and watch the screens. They were still a new enough phenomenon to keep my attention. After half an hour of that I'd change another pound and feed the machines again. I'd repeat this cycle until the pound notes ran out, and then it'd be back out into the drizzle and back to the college.

Those old machines fetch high prices at auctions these days. In the early eighties no one would consider owning one. No one serious even played them. They were a piece of cultural ephemera, a passing fancy. They were the eighties embodied – flashy, expensive, violent, pointless – and no one noticed. In the twenty-first century we can see them for the revolution they were. At the time, it was only adolescents who gathered around them, throwing in the dole money.

There, Tina was right. I really was looking out of the window and thinking about arcade games.

▌▌▌

Dr Morrison didn't join us for the experiment. His presence, Betts told us, wasn't necessary. It might influence the results. He passed on his instructions by way of Betts. That didn't surprise me. Tina had once told me that psychology experiments were eight parts bluff and two parts cruelty. Betts arranged us out of sight of one another in a room with closed blinds and dim lighting. Large mirrors standing on easels were positioned around me. Betts covered them with cloths.

'I'll have to ask you how you're feeling. I have to record it all. I have a cassette recorder, but you'll have to speak clearly. You will need to look where I tell you to look. I will be touching you as part of the experiment. Not all of the time, but I'll need to give you the odd prod. Mick, you'll know what I'm talking about. Remember how I remapped your hand? We're trying to disassociate you from your senses, and map your Self to somewhere else. Are you both ready?'

We said that we were. I was bearing in mind that everything Betts had said might well be part of the experiment. Eight parts bluff and two parts cruelty, Tina had said.

'We've started,' said Betts. He'd positioned himself out of

sight. The experiment consisted of him removing cloths from selected mirrors, so that I saw myself from different angles. On some of the mirrors there were two or more reflections somehow overlaid.

'Look to your left,' he'd say. My reflections would look in all directions. Something would touch me on my left ear, but in the reflected versions it'd be the right ear, or both ears. The thing that had happened with my hand began to happen to my entire body. It began to feel like it wasn't mine. I would raise my right hand and see my left hand move, or both hands.

I wasn't sure which hand was moving.

It began to feel the way I'm told meditation feels, the sense of the body slipping away. I was feeling increasingly relaxed.

'Look to your right,' Betts said. 'Tina, what are you seeing?'

She said something that seemed to come from a great distance. She sounded as though she was outside, in the damp landscape. I could see the landscape in the mirrors, presumably reflected from the window. I hadn't noticed it before.

A tiny figure was running towards the college from the mountains. It seemed to be coalescing from the clouds.

I let myself enjoy the show. No doubt Dr Morrison wanted me to react to the approaching figure, now clearly a human being. Betts would be slyly watching me, waiting to see what I did. So I didn't do anything. I watched it come.

Whoever he was – it was a male figure, I could tell that much – he was coming too quickly to be real. The mountains weren't as far away as they looked, being smaller than you thought they were, but they were still a fair distance away. The running man was already close to the campus.

He looked dwarfish, no more than four feet tall, a grin you could make out at a distance of several miles playing across his coarse features. He wore baggy grey clothes and pointed shoes.

From a long way away, Tina was making a lot of noise.

'I can't see him,' said Betts. 'Are you sure?'

The small man was now so close that I shouldn't have been able to see him. He should have been out of my line of sight, obscured by the angle of the window, but he came straight on.

'Not supposed to,' said Tina. 'Wake him up.'

Not supposed to what? The man was now too close to fit comfortably in the mirrors. He was squashed. He put out a white hand and gripped the edge of the frame.

He said something unintelligible.

I didn't think this was a part of the experiment. This was something else, getting involved. This was an outside complication.

The small man pulled himself free of the mirrors, climbing out of them as though he was stepping through an open window. He didn't look quite human. There was something about the set of his features. He shouted something at me, but it was only a noise and there was no sense in it. I stood up. Tina was standing against the back wall, and Betts was standing in front of her.

There was a sound of breaking glass. Silvered shards flew past me. I watched the small man scamper through the door, grinning nastily at us and emitting sounds that, although unintelligible, sounded anything but pleasant. He ran out of sight and we listened as the sounds of his footsteps – slightly scratchy, because of his long toenails – faded into nothingness. Betts chewed his fingers, shaking. Tina was white. There were only the three of us, standing in a closed room with a few mirrors, some of them broken.

IV

That's why I don't like mirrors. I don't trust them. The small man might have been something I imagined, if Tina and Betts hadn't seen him too. He might have come from the mountains, or the mist, and not the mirror at all. I didn't care. It was mirrors that I became afraid of, and many years later Dermot had somehow picked up on that.

In the toilet of the club, Dermot let me off the hook.

'More drinks,' he said. 'You need more *drinks* and less *mirrors*. Check out the *decor* in this place. Fucking wild. It's like a Bronx *alleyway* down here. It's like a *working men's* club. They still have working men round here? Not that sort of *city* any more, is it. None of them are. Come on then.'

He led me back to the bar. 'Now, drinks. What are we having?'

Pints and chasers, he decided. He saw a machine in a dark corner.

'Look at that,' he said. 'Bargain. That's a Joust. Where have they been *keeping* that then? There are *kids* in here younger than that machine.'

He called the barman over and exchanged notes for coins.

'I used to be good at this,' he said, leading the way to the machine. 'You're a *programmer*, right? That's what you said you did. Can you *program* things like this?'

'I do business stuff,' I said. 'Databases.'

'Fucking wild, that must be a *riot*. Well take the controls then, you're *that* guy over *there*. That's a life you've lost, put the fucking *drinks* down and pay attention.'

He was staring through the screen. I was reminded of the man who'd turned up from nowhere and ruined that experiment, but Dermot looked nothing like him. He didn't feel like him, either. Dermot was merely cheerfully unbalanced, not alien.

He was a lot better at Joust than I was. I was in the low hand-eye co-ordination stage of drunkenness and I couldn't focus properly.

'Oi, watch that one. *That* fucking one,' he'd say as I missed the bad guys completely. 'You *always* this hopeless?'

I had to keep paying for extra lives just to keep up with him. His score was absurd, pinball-table high with half a yard of trailing zeroes. He was smoking a cigarette and drinking two drinks and he was still beating me.

'King of video games, that's me. Can't play pool, can't play darts, but give me one of these things and that's me sorted.'

Finally he lost the last of his lives, and entered his name in the high-score table.

'Right then. That's that done. Now, let's get ourselves something to eat, I'm fucking starving. They still have curries in Birmingham don't they? Fucking must do. Cheers then boss,' he said to the bouncers on the way out. They watched us make our way along Broad Street.

We couldn't get a curry, because it was only four in the afternoon and nowhere was open. In the end we got lukewarm burgers at New Street station while I waited for a train that went my way. Commuters went the long way around us. The station concourse felt like a toilet, all grimy white tiles and headachy echoes. Dermot helped me onto the train when it turned up. The last I saw of him he was running along the platform, following the train as it pulled out, only stopping where the platform sloped down into the sooty Birmingham undergrowth alongside the tracks.

FOUR

I

Of course, that wasn't the last I saw of him. One Saturday a few weeks later I was at home filling in job applications. That wasn't the most fun you could have on a Saturday, even in Dudley, but it was something I needed to do. I'd passed my training courses and I had gained new qualifications and I thought that my salary should reflect all that. I was working for a small software house with offices on the Merry Hill site. They thought that my salary was good enough, or at least as good as it was going to get.

This is why I was filling in job applications. I had qualifications and experience. I should have been able to get into a higher wage band. Perhaps I'd be able to afford to move out of Dudley.

I don't know many people in Dudley. I got a flat there because it was cheap and there seemed to be a lot of programming jobs in the West Midlands, which had just caught on to the idea that making chains and nails wasn't going to bring in much wealth. It was close enough to Birmingham to commute. I had a theory that local industry was going to renew itself, but it didn't. It just got older and more tired. It managed to let go of thirteenth-century jobs – making nails and chains – but never managed to make the leap past the industrial revolution.

As I said, I don't know many people in Dudley. I had friends in other places. I still saw Tina. She'd moved into a cottage in Bewdley, along with her husband Roger. I liked him, although I didn't know him well. She'd kept her maiden name, which helped me to pretend that she was still single and therefore available. I'd go and see them once or twice a week and we'd have a meal or go to a pub.

I'd rather have been in a pub just then. The job application forms were giving me a bad time. I couldn't see why they asked so many extraneous questions. Each form was the size of a first novel, too thick to skim through in case you missed anything but too thin to pay full whack for. They all wanted the answers hand-written so that they could get someone to analyse your script and make sure that you weren't a rapist or a bed-wetter. They wanted to know what other interests you had. I only had other interests. I had no interest at all in filling in forms.

My attention was wandering. I had sworn an oath to myself not to switch my PC on and start playing games instead of doing anything useful.

I turned the PC on. Handwriting was something that had been left behind in the days of chain-making. I would have a quick game of something and then get back to work. I could cope with that. I had self-discipline. I also had writer's cramp.

I had a shareware game called Wolfenstein 3D. In it, you played a prisoner in a Nazi castle. It was in 3D, as the name suggested. You looked down the barrel of a gun and walked around, and you killed everything that moved. If you sent off fifteen dollars, you'd get more of the game. I didn't have any dollars. In Dudley they used pounds, or bartering.

I would just have a quick run through a level or two, I thought.

Two hours later, the doorbell rang. I wasn't expecting anyone, Dermot least of all. Still, it wasn't entirely a surprise when I opened the door and found him there.

'This your *place* then? Bit of a mess. What is all *this* shit? Are you going to get me a *cup of tea* or what?'

He was already past me and sitting on the sofa, shuffling my job applications to one side.

'After another job? It's *all fucking go* in the software world. What's those *magazines*, porn?'

They were computer magazines, mostly about games but with a couple of grown-up ones thrown in.

'You can't get any *good games* on computers,' he said. 'You want to get a Megadrive or something. I've got a Megadrive, *smashing* thing. Where's your computer then?'

It was in the bedroom, on a small table next to the bed. It was a 486DX, whizzy for the time. It was still running Wolfenstein 3D.

'What's this?' Dermot asked.

'It's a 486,' I told him.

'Not the fucking *computer* you dickhead. What's the *game*?'

'Wolfenstein. It's a free one.'

'You're fucking joking. They're *giving* this away?'

'Only the first part. You have to pay to get the rest of it.'

'Where've you had it from?'

'Off a magazine. They have disks on the covers.'

'How do you work it? Where's the *controller*?'

I showed him the keys to use and he took over. He was a little outfaced by the keyboard, but soon learned the game-player's way around it: ignore all of the ones with letters on.

'I haven't seen that *tea* yet,' he said. 'Is this that *virtual reality*, then? Is this what it's like?'

It would be another five years before it turned out that virtual reality hadn't been the next big thing after all.

'No,' I told him. 'In virtual reality you wear goggles. They project an image into each lens, and you see it in real 3D. And they use motion sensors, so when you move in real life you move in the virtual world.'

'So this is what?'

'There isn't a name for it yet.'

'They can name it after *me* then. *Dermot* reality. That's what this is. I know it isn't the real world. Because if it was the real world I'd have had a *cup of fucking tea*.'

I made him a cup of tea. He couldn't control the game one-handed, so he looked around the flat while he drank it.

'Fucking hell, mate,' he said. 'What *is* all this shit? Don't you ever *throw* anything away?'

I didn't, as it happened. The flat was crowded with old clothes, old magazines, books, CDs, and old vinyl albums. I didn't like to throw anything away. I always had the feeling that it'd turn out to be useful sooner or later. I still listened to some of the records. I might reread some of the books.

'I might have to get one of these. How much do they go for?' he asked, back at the keyboard.

'You'd get one for twelve hundred.'

'Fucking hell, they're *paying* you too much. I don't know what you're filling in *job applications* for. You've got a *good enough* job now. I can't afford *twelve hundred* for a fucking computer. You coming out?'

'Where?'

'See the *sights* of Dudley. And bring a coat, it's *fucking* cold out there.'

∎

We went for a walk through Dudley. The market was doing a roaring trade despite not selling anything you'd want to buy. The Merry Hill centre had opened a few miles away, a shiny mall with all of the shops you needed. Dudley had competed by curling up and dying. The strange thing was, Dudley was still crowded on Saturdays. What shops there were, were packed. People gathered around the market stalls, picking up tea towels and misprinted greetings cards.

'What are they all after?' Dermot asked. 'What do they *come* here for? I mean, I came here to see *you* and that's hardly the most *important* thing I could be doing with my day.'

'How did you know where I lived?'

'You *told* me, you piss-head. You were drunk at the time. I said I'd come round. Are there any *real shops* here?'

'Not as such. They're all closing.'

'So what are this lot buying? Scotch fucking mist?'

I shrugged.

'We've got two choices then. As I see it. We can walk around looking at this *fucking market* all afternoon, or we can go to the pub. They still have pubs here don't they? Or, third choice, we can go in the amusements. I'd like to see what amuses these weird fuckers. Public executions? Badger baiting? So, *pub* or amusements?'

'It's a bit early for the pubs.'

'Oh, let's not *wake* the poor sleepy fuckers up, shall we? It's only *half past eleven* and they're still in bed. Shipleys it is then. How much money have you got? Well there's a cashpoint over there look, get yourself another twenty. Call it *thirty*. Amusements don't come cheap these days.'

There was a small queue at the cashpoint, headed by a woman who didn't know which way up her card went. The machine kept rejecting it. She'd look at it, and put it in the wrong way up again.

Dermot had long since got bored and gone into the amusement arcade by the time I got some money. I found him by the video games, which were at the back. There was a booth containing a middle-aged woman, who looked to be the same one that had been in the booth in Borth thirteen years earlier. There was a machine that gave change in exchange for coins and notes, except for all bank notes and most coins. Those it rejected.

There were rows of fruit machines, now mostly in software. One or two still only cost five pence a play and paid out in pocket money. Most took twenty pence pieces and had alleged jackpots around the fifteen pound mark. A handful of young men walked around the machines, clocking the reels, shaking handfuls of loose change. There were small tinfoil ashtrays resting on every level surface.

The video games were much larger than they used to be. They had appendages: steering wheels, guns, skis, periscopes.

You didn't have to go out to play video games any more. You could play them at home. Video games had to do more work to get any attention at all, like old pop stars. Hence the guns and steering wheels.

'Check them out,' said Dermot. 'See why they're called

Space Invaders? Because they're taking up *half* the fucking *space*. Give it another six years and these fuckers will be playing *each other*.'

He picked on the machine with the largest gun.

'Stick a couple of quid in then,' he said. 'Let's mow down a few *innocent bystanders*.'

III

After that, I saw him about once or twice a week. He always came to see me. He lived in a small house on the outskirts of West Bromwich and said that I wouldn't want to meet him there.

'You think Dudley's bad, you should see *West Brom* mate,' he used to say.

After I'd known him for about a year, I invited him to meet Tina and Roger.

'Roger?' he said. 'You mean that's really a name? I thought it had been made up. I don't think I've ever met a Roger. Where do these two live then?'

'Bewdley.'

'What, out in the sticks? Sheepshaggers are they? You used to knock about with this Tina then. What's she like?'

'She's like married. That was all a long time ago.'

'It's about time you got someone else mate. You're pulling in enough money. You want to get yourself a girlfriend before you do your eyesight some permanent damage. How are we getting there? Tractor? Coracle?'

'I'm driving,' I said.

'Count me in. I've always wanted to spend a night with the yokels. Can I dress casual?'

'Do you ever do anything else?'

'Not for your sake mate. I just wouldn't want to give poor old Roger too much of a shock.'

'I think he can cope with you,' I said.

'You never know,' said Dermot, with an evil little grin.

IV

Bewdley is a fairly large town masquerading as a small village. The river Severn runs through it, and over it at some times of year. After crossing the Severn by way of the old narrow bridge I drove around the church. You have to, as the church was built in the middle of the road, with one lane on each side of it. For Bewdley, it's not inconvenient enough to have a river running through the middle of the town. They also have to have a church in the middle of the main road.

Thanks to the river, which allowed goods to be transported from other towns, Bewdley was one of the major English towns until those new-fangled canals were invented. Compared to rivers, canals had the advantages of going to the right destination and not breaking their banks. As canals – and then railways – became the main mode of transporting goods, Bewdley dwindled and Birmingham grew like a tumour.

In response, Bewdley reinvented itself and became picturesque. Now every shop sells antiques, most of them good-quality new ones. The roads are narrow, as they were designed for traffic with hooves, and there are often long queues. When the river floods people come from Kidderminster and Kingswinford to stand and watch water misbehaving. The houses closest to the river are always up for sale.

I left the car on the Pay and Display car park, which was free in the evenings, and Dermot and I walked along the river to Tina and Roger's house. Their house was Georgian and damp, as are most of the riverside houses. It had a step up to the front door, but not a high enough one to avoid the floods. Twice a year they'd have to move everything to the top floor and then spend a week going through the house with the scrubbing brushes and the detergent. Whenever the river Severn visited it brought a lot of things with it, and it left a lot of them when it went. There was a tidemark on the outside wall at about waist height. When it rained heavily in Wales, Tina and Roger would start hauling furniture upstairs.

It often rains heavily in Wales. I know that from my time in Borth. Sometimes there would be more water in the sky than in the estuary.

Dermot was unimpressed with Bewdley.

'I thought it'd be more, you know, more countryside. It's like *Stourbridge*.'

'It's Georgian.'

'It's like Stourbridge but *older*. And what's *with* these fucking shops? They all sell *antiques*. Do they *eat* antiques round here? Or are they all off in the fucking *fields* hunting down *potatoes*? Who *lives* out here?'

'Tina and Roger.'

'I notice you always put them in that order. Here,' he said, alarmed. 'There are ducks in the road.'

'There's a river there,' I said, pointing to it.

'I can *see* the fucking river. Why aren't the ducks *down there* in the water?'

'Maybe they fancied a change.'

'I'm happy for them. Do they *bite*?'

I looked at him.

'Are you scared of them?'

'I'm scared of *nothing*.'

Despite his claim, he gave the ducks – a couple of mallards – a wide berth.

'You're scared of ducks,' I said. 'How are ducks going to hurt you?'

'You're scared of mirrors,' he said. 'That makes *more fucking sense* does it? Where are the trees? We're in the countryside and all I can see is *shops* and a *river*. Where's all the nature?'

'All directions. You have to walk to it.'

'Where are we, the *middle fucking ages*? No one walks anymore. Even *you* don't walk. We're in the nineties now, nature wants to get its arse in gear.'

'This is their house.'

Dermot checked it out.

'Looks alright,' he said.

Tina let us in. She was wearing a loose flowing thing from the Gap. Roger was dressed in a collection from French Connection, as usual. He didn't look anything like a lecturer; all of the other ones I'd encountered were of the leather-elbow-pad variety.

They'd painted the inside of their house the colour of gentlemen's studies in old films. It looked warm and amber, with a density of light you almost had to push your way through. Tina went in for rugs with a lot of dark red in the patterns. Carpets were pointless as you couldn't get them upstairs quickly enough when the river came in unannounced. They seemed to have a lot of dark wood furniture, until you looked more closely and realized how little there was. A table with four ladderback chairs, a cabinet with a small television (they only had terrestrial channels, and only four of those), a small chest of drawers with framed photographs on the top. There was no sofa, no armchairs, nothing that'd take a lot of hoisting up the stairs when the Severn started getting too lively.

I'd seen the kitchen on previous visits and I knew that all of the cupboards were mounted at head height, well above the high-tide mark. They kept the fridge/freezer on the upstairs landing and the washing machine in a spare room upstairs. The small electric oven could be manhandled up the stairs with the help of the neighbours. Even after everything had been moved above the high water mark, the house was uninhabitable until the water level dropped. There would be no electricity until the river stopped having its fun and got itself back where it belonged. The presence of three feet of water dropped the temperature by several degrees, and the water wasn't clean.

In the film *Titanic*, when the sea finally pops in it's a nice fresh shade of blue. It looks chlorinated. The floodwaters in Bewdley were the colour of shit, not without reason.

It all seemed a lot of trouble to put up with for the sake of living somewhere picturesque.

Dermot settled himself into one of the ladderback chairs.

'Nice place,' he said. 'Got a touch of the Sherlock Holmes to it. Sorry, we haven't been introduced, our Mickey doesn't do manners. I'm Dermot, a friend of Mr. Aston here. I know you're Tina and you're Roger, and you knew him when he was a student. Did he have any manners then?'

'No,' said Tina. 'He was hopeless. Wouldn't hold a door open for you, wouldn't offer to carry things.'

'It was 1983,' I said. 'Men weren't allowed to hold doors open. It was sexist. It was politically incorrect.'

'And that died a death, didn't it?' asked Dermot. 'Now we're right back where we were before all that. Still, kept us on our toes for fifteen years.'

'We've had plenty of things doing that,' said Tina. Roger arrived with an open bottle of wine, an aged French one. The name meant nothing to me. No doubt he'd had it breathing somewhere. Roger knew his wines. If they'd lived somewhere less prone to going subaquatic, he'd have had a cellar. As it was, he had racks in the attic.

'What sort of prices do places go for round here?' Dermot asked. Roger told him while Tina set out place mats and cutlery.

'I hope you're not a vegetarian,' Tina said.

'Not fucking *likely*,' said Dermot. Tina smiled genuinely; Roger smiled tolerantly.

She'd done a game terrine with tiny new potatoes and fresh garden peas in some sort of mint dressing.

'This is what the *middle class* have for tea is it then?' asked Dermot. 'Any more wine?'

Roger looked uncomfortable at being tagged as middle class. Tina didn't seem to mind.

'Only the ones with good enough cooks,' she said. 'The rest of them make do with takeaways. What do you have then? Fish and chips? Kebabs? Tripe and onions?'

'Aye, pet. And we have *cabbage* on Saturdays as a treat.'

'What do you do?' Roger asked Dermot.

'Nothing really. I don't have what you'd call a *trade*. I pick up jobs. You can get by like that.'

'Nothing longer term? What about pensions?'

'Bollocks to pensions. I'm too young for pensions. That'll all sort itself out.'

Tina raised one eyebrow, her code for a good point being

made. I was in a private pension scheme because programming jobs weren't lifelong. Sometimes they lasted as long as the project. Sometimes the projects were canned and the programmers got their cards. Besides, there were always people headhunting from other companies.

Roger took a sip of wine to allow him time to compose himself. He couldn't have been five years older than Dermot, but managed to look twice his age. He had grey creeping in at his temples and a touch of middle-age spread at the waist, but it was more his attitude. He was like a father. Dermot was cheerfully playing the part of an unruly child, and Tina and I were the well-behaved children watching the show.

Except that Tina seemed to want to spar with Dermot.

'So you're working class then?' she asked. 'Only we thought that they'd gone. Everyone has an office job now. And if you don't actually have a job, you can hardly be called working class, can you?'

'I was *born* working class,' said Dermot.

'I doubt that,' said Tina. 'I really doubt that. There were lots like you at college, kids who pretended to live on the frontline. What were they doing at college then? Advanced scaffolding techniques? New movements in welding? No, they were doing media studies and art classes.'

'Being working class is a *state of mind*,' said Dermot.

'I thought you were born into it.'

'It's a *state of mind* you're *born into*. It's a way of being.'

'That's Zen Buddhism, I think you'll find. How many of your jobs involve any manual labour? Excluding things like manually writing on paper with a pen, or manually sitting at a desk.'

'Enough. When I met him,' Dermot pointed at me, 'I was

working in a burger van. Cooking burgers. And *kebabs*. That was manual.'

'But it wasn't exactly foundry work. You just come across as a middle class white boy doing lowlife jobs to make yourself more interesting.'

'You don't know *anything* about me. How can you sit there judging me when you live in this fucking cottage? You've never *been* to the real world.'

'I could ask Mick what he knows about you. He's known you for a while, hasn't he?'

'He doesn't take a *blind bit* of interest. As long as he's getting along with his own life, that's all he thinks about. I don't think he's ever *asked* what I do.'

'No,' said Tina. 'He's not like that. Are you, Mick?'

The two of them looked at me.

'I don't like to intrude,' I said. 'I don't like to pry into people's business.'

'You don't want to *know* about them, more like,' said Dermot. 'I mean, you're more remote than these two and they live in a *cottage* in the fucking *sticks*. You live in Dudley. Do you know any of your neighbours?'

'Not to talk to. I've seen them. They're not the sort of people I'd talk to.'

'No? You're a snob mate. They probably don't *want* to talk to you. Any more of this wine then, Roger?'

Roger went to get another bottle from the attic.

'What are we going to do about him?' Tina asked.

'Our Mick?' asked Dermot. 'We'll have to get him to *take an interest*. We'll have to get him a *hobby*. Bring him out of himself.'

'I think he's been out of himself,' said Tina. They exchanged a look.

60

'Then we'll have to sort his life out,' Dermot said.

'There's nothing wrong with my life,' I said. 'Except for my friends.'

Roger returned with another bottle.

'This should stand,' he said.

'Stand it here,' said Dermot.

V

Tina and Dermot got on fine after that. They seemed to have something in common, a shared way of seeing the world. I remembered how Tina had once tried to get me to swim in the frigid Borth sea. She and Dermot shared some sort of adventurous or mischievous gene. They were ready to do something ridiculous, any time.

Whenever the four of us went out, Roger and I would sit and disapprove of them while they talked up a storm.

I suppose I was detached. I didn't have any great interest in other people. I liked them around. I didn't want to know their life stories.

I don't think there's anything wrong with that. Not even now, knowing all that I know. There's nothing wrong with being detached.

Better that than being attached to something dangerous.

FIVE

I

Nothing changed for years. We all kept in touch, I kept getting better jobs, programming moved on and I followed it at a safe distance.

In 1998, my years of staring at monitors did the inevitable damage. Like everyone else, I read the warnings about spending ten minutes an hour away from the monitor. Like everyone else, I ignored them. I was spending most of my time either playing video games or programming, and screen resolutions were getting higher every six months. New graphics cards meant that you could get more dots per inch on the screen, and every time that happened the rez went up and the text got smaller. Ten-point Times New Roman – which used to look like a headline – now looks like it's in the next room.

I was squinting, and getting headaches. I had begun to get strange visual effects, shadows off at the edges of my vision, dots flickering in and out of my field of view.

'Go to the fucking *optician*,' advised Dermot. Tina agreed with him. Roger agreed with both of them.

I went to the optician, and discovered that I was short-sighted. Everything more than a couple of feet away was blurred. He tested me out and gave me a prescription. I went to a big High Street store to get the frames, because they had a better selection. A week later I picked up my spectacles. I tried them on, and everything went from a cheap fuzzy lo-rez to a sharp digital hi-rez.

About that time, Les Herbie did a column about the same sort of thing. I cut it out and kept it. Of course, I kept everything. I didn't like to throw anything away. Perhaps it was something to do with my parents.

||

I have these spots in front of my eyes. I get more of this sort of thing these days. It's because I'm getting old. Things are closing down. Non-essential services are being run down. Manpower is being diverted elsewhere.

Perhaps it's not that. Perhaps it's a brain tumour pushing my eyeballs out of shape.

I go to the doctor. I say I have spots on front of my eyes. He refers me to an optician. Opticians do eyes, he explains. Perhaps it's eyestrain, he tells me.

You didn't think it was a brain tumour, did you? he asks.

No, I tell him. Never even thought about it. Never even crossed my mind.

He knows I'm lying. Everyone lies to him. We don't make anything of it.

I go to see the optician. He makes me read things I can't read. He tries different lenses out.

Suddenly I can read all of the rows on his chart.

He tells me one eye has a focal length half the focal length of the other. One of them is round. The other is egg-shaped. That'll need correcting. He can do that with lenses. That's what he does.

He does me a prescription for lenses. I choose some frames. It's risky doing that before I can see properly, but I don't have a choice. I don't want computer programmer frames. I don't want trainspotter frames. I want to choose good frames, right now.

They'll be ready in a week. In a week I go and get them. I put them on. I can see everything. I don't look a lot like a computer programmer. I don't look much like a trainspotter. I can get away with it. I can carry it off.

I go outside and read things. I read road signs. I read everything, because now I can.

I wonder how one eyeball got egg-shaped. What made it do that? Was it happier that way?

I think about brain tumours. Perhaps a brain tumour has pushed one of my eyeballs out of shape.

I have these spots in front of my eyes.

And now I can see them really clearly.

▌▌▌

I didn't want bifocals. I could see things clearly without my specs if they were close to me. I could see everything within a few feet perfectly with my unaided eyes. I could see the monitor when I programmed or played games. With them on, I could see everything else. Switching from one to the other, just after I put them on or took them off, there would be a moment while my eyes readjusted and focussed. My left eye was more short-sighted than my right eye, and they had to get used to working together.

Sometimes, in the moments while my eyes got their act together, I would see things. Dots crawling up the walls, shadows, nothing substantial. After I blinked once or twice, it'd be gone.

Not long before the end of 1999, with autumn feeling very like winter and a freezing wind blowing through Dudley, getting in through the gaps between door and jamb, I was trying to finish a game I'd been playing. It was the first in what was to become a very successful series, and it had got me frustrated almost to the point of throwing the keyboard through the window.

I kept killing off the lead character. Whatever I tried, she fell to death on one or another of what seemed to be a million sets of spikes. My reactions weren't good enough for that sort of game any more. I turned off the PC two hours later than I'd planned to, having got nowhere. I put on my spectacles and looked out of the window, to give my poor battered eyes some relief.

From the front window of my flat, there's a view down Dudley High Street. I can see about half way down it, as far as Woolworth's and one of the grisly butcher shops. It was about one in the morning and the market was empty. The red and white stripes of the awnings wouldn't settle in my vision. A woman walked into view at the far end of the High Street. She was carrying a pair of guns, one in each hand. She looked cartoonish, and not all that well rendered. She looked a little like the character I'd been unwittingly dropping into spiked pits for the last few hours, but not enough like her to infringe anyone's copyright. I had a very careful imagination, apparently.

She wasn't real. I knew that. She was some sort of hallucination. She walked under the awnings of the market, went out of sight for a moment, and then reappeared close to the statue of Duncan Edwards.

Duncan Edwards was a footballer, and one of Dudley's famous sons. There is a statue of him on the High Street, up on a pedestal, poised on the verge of kicking a metal football. There is a road named after him, too. On one side of the road is a sign saying:

DUNCAN EDWARDS CLOSE.

On the other side is a sign saying:

NO BALL GAMES.

The woman with the guns snuggled up to the statue, having suddenly leapt ten feet up to it from a standing start. Not something most people would be able to manage, but easy enough for a video-game character of course.

She looked woodenly around and then clocked me. She span around the pedestal and down to the floor, hitting the ground running. She was heading for my flat.

My flat is on the second floor, two floors removed from Dudley. Completely removed from Dudley would have suited me fine just then. She vanished from my point of view, being too close to the front of the building for me to get a fix on her. She wasn't real, I reminded myself. Something was going on. I wondered whether it was my eyes or my brain that had broken down.

It all seemed to be over. I couldn't see her.

Then, making me jump about half a mile, she flew to the top of the nearest lamppost, appearing to spring from nowhere. She levelled both of her guns in my general direction and hurled herself at me in a tight somersault. She hit the window firing, her muzzle flashes lighting her but not the surrounding environment.

As she came through the window, which failed to shatter,

she lost integrity, becoming disassociated pixels and stray flashes of light. The pixels faded, the flashes went out. The last to go were the three pairs of pixels which had mapped the centres of her eyes, the barrels of her guns, and the tips of her pointed breasts. Then that strange new constellation also faded and she was gone.

I felt unreal, which seemed unfair. She was the faux video-game character. I had spent too long at the keyboard, I thought. I'd have to give myself a day off. There was no point in overdoing it and risking my health. I took off my glasses and tried to think calmly. I squeezed the bridge of my nose between forefinger and thumb. I tried to be detached and rational.

It was difficult. You can get hallucinations for several reasons. You can get them by taking the right – or the wrong – chemicals. Cheese is mildly hallucinogenic. Bram Stoker is said to have written Dracula after nightmares brought on by too much cheese. Which is apt, as modern vampires are overwhelmingly cheesy. Psylocybin mushrooms are well known for their psychotropic effects in some circles.

The problem was that I didn't do that sort of drug. I smoked the occasional joint, and that was all.

Tiredness could make you see things. I had been tired, after too many late nights trying to finish games. That didn't even feel like a good reason to be tired. It wasn't as though I'd been searching for the cure for cancer. I didn't think that I'd been tired enough to see things that weren't there.

The only other reason I could think of for having hallucinations was that my brain was misfiring. Perhaps some neurones were doing the wrong thing. Perhaps my visual cortex was dissolving. What were the symptoms of brain tumours? From my limited medical knowledge – gathered from all of those drama series about doctors that seemed to light up the lives of the BBC programme planners – there would be headaches and the illusionary smell of roses. I didn't have headaches and the only thing I could smell was the fishmongers. And that was with the windows closed.

I thought about BSE. The government of 1986 had done all that it could to get that as widespread as possible short of actually injecting it into people. I had eaten cheap beef-burgers while I was a student. I'd had kebabs from vans that the UN would have sanctioned for breaching germ warfare regulations. I'd had curries from places the health inspectors only visited under duress.

I didn't know what the symptoms were, other than wobbly cows. I didn't think it was that. Thinking about it, the kebabs and curries were more likely to contain domestic pets and rodents than farm animals.

I didn't feel dizzy or sick. I didn't feel confused. I wasn't suffering from mood swings. It was just that what appeared to be an anonymous video-game character had waltzed along Dudley market and thrown herself at my window, guns blazing.

I wondered whether it might have been a trick, perhaps an image projected onto my window from somewhere. I rejected that theory. She'd stayed in scale with the background. That would have been close to impossible to code. Plus, she'd left a few pixels in my room, like coloured scales from the wings of a butterfly. More convincingly, she was how I'd imagined the character to look. She was my version of a popular myth, something I'd invented rather than something I'd seen.

I put it down to tiredness. I decided to go to bed.

I really didn't feel like playing that game any more.

IV

I tried to keep videogaming to a minimum for a while. I had early nights and took vitamins. I read books instead of playing games. I called Dermot and Tina and arranged to go out as often as I could.

The trouble with my flat was that it was boring. It wasn't that there was nothing to look at. There was plenty of junk. There was everything I'd bought in the last twenty years because I couldn't face throwing any of it away.

'You're a *hoarder*,' Dermot had said on one of his visits. 'The fucking council will come in here with rubber clothes and a *big fucking skip*.'

Most of the space was full of my history. I didn't want to look at any of that, I'd already had to live through it. There were hundreds of books and magazines, but nothing I wanted to read. Like Tina and Roger, I had stuck with the five terrestrial TV channels and there wasn't anything on I wanted to watch. The BBC had limited their output to programmes about people who were:

Detectives.

Doctors.

Vets.

Detectives who were also vets or doctors.

The rest of it was worse. There was nothing to watch and the radio stations played generic dance music. If I sat and read I'd fidget and end up picking skin from around my fingers, which made me think of Betts, which upset me.

I hadn't been in any serious relationships for years and I wasn't in one then. I had no one to distract me.

Dermot had a theory about that.

V

'Your problem is that you're dragging all your ghosts around,' he said. 'You keep your history with you.'

We were in the Slipped Disc, a pub two miles from anywhere. It stood by itself on the long road between Kidderminster and Worcester and there was nothing else nearby. You had to drive there, so a significant proportion of the clientele was always reasonably sober. They did a good trade early in the evenings, mostly catering for unfussy families out for simple meals.

By nine thirty the place was all but deserted. From the outside it looked like a warehouse set in a vast car park. From the inside it looked like a hasty warehouse conversion. The tables seemed dwarfed by the high ceilings, and the small amount of lively atmosphere had a hard time filling the huge rooms. Dermot was delighted with it.

'Fucking *check this out*,' he said. 'Look at this place. What's the *opposite* of cosy? Because this is it. This is the *worst building* I've ever seen made into a pub. What *fucking idiot* thought this'd work? It's *brilliant*.'

He looked at the rows of tables, the families eating their lukewarm, undercooked main courses, the hard-boiled potatoes, the side salads used to fill in the surface area of the oval plates.

'Fucking *scampi*,' he said, examining a menu. 'These poor bastards aren't even middle class. Can you believe it? *Middle class wannabees*. Fucking hell. What sort of *beer* do they do here?'

I followed him to the bar. The bar staff wore red shirts with the name of the pub on the breast pocket, and itchy-looking black trousers. They looked too young to be working in a pub. The bar was twenty yards long and deserted.

'What whiskies have you got?' he asked a youth with the sort of long hair that never seems to become fully unpopular in rural areas.

'Not blended. Malts,' he added.

The boy he'd asked went to ask someone else.

'Ten to one it's Glenfiddich and Glenmorangie and that's your fucking lot. Middle class enough to have malts, not middle class enough to have any *interesting* ones. Can you believe this place?'

'I don't know that drinking malt whisky is a middle class thing.'

'Don't you? It's a fucking good job I'm here to help point these things out to you then. You know what *this* place is?'

'Middle class?'

'*Everywhere's* middle class. It's just that not everyone *knows* about it. Someone designed this place. Someone *wanted* it to look like this. Someone thought that a *big empty room* would do nicely. This is somebody's *bright idea*.'

He looked back to the tables.

'They're all dressed up. Look at them. This is *brilliant*. This is fucking terrific. They're all in their *best fucking clothes* sitting in this *warehouse* eating scampi and having a *fucking awful time*.'

The barman brought back the list of whiskies. Dermot had been right about the available brands.

'Two Glenmorangies then. Doubles. And two pints of Guinness.'

When the drinks arrived he paid with a twenty-pound note and told the barman to have one himself.

'We can't accept drinks,' said the youth.

71

'Who says?' asked Dermot.

'We can take the money for a drink and then we share it out.'

'Share it out? Between *five* of you? It's a drink, not a fucking *timeshare apartment*. Just give me the change.'

He led me away from the bar to a quiet table.

'That's corporations for you,' he told me. 'These minimum wage fuckers don't get anything. Ten to one the manager skims half the tips and gives the rest to the prettiest barmaid. Doesn't that piss you off?'

He looked at me.

'No it doesn't,' he said. 'Nothing pisses you off. You're just *too fucking cool*. Nothing bothers you.'

Not much did. I was worried about my hallucination, but it had been an isolated one. It hadn't happened again. I shook my head.

'Back to you and your ghosts then. All of your friends are people you've known for years. Don't you want to *know* anyone else? Don't you ever see someone and want *to spend some time* with them?'

'Did Tina tell you to say all this?' I asked.

'No she didn't. Why would she?'

'It's the sort of thing she says. It's the sort of thing she always says. Every time I see her I get all of this. There's nothing wrong with my life. It's got enough people in it.'

'There might not be anything wrong with it from where *you* are. From here, it's a *right* state. You ever call old Olaf? Or anyone? If I didn't come and *get* you, would you call me?'

'I called Tina. I called the pair of them and asked to go out.'

'Only because you were going *off your head*. Would you have done it otherwise?'

He saw that I wouldn't. As a rule I don't call people. They can call me if they want. It's up to them. I'm not going to force myself on anyone.

'No, I thought not. You wouldn't call Tina and you still fucking *fancy* her. Jesus wept. I'd walk out and leave you here if you weren't driving. Well drink up and drive me home so that I can *slam the door* then.'

I drank up. The night had gone askew. Dermot changed his mind every twenty or thirty minutes at the best of times. He'd be my friend again before we'd got to Kidderminster. He had two doubles to drink, as I wouldn't be drinking one. I was driving. Four whiskies would calm him down.

On the way out he grabbed the youth who'd served us.

'This is our *secret*,' he said loudly. 'Don't share it with anyone. It's a gift.'

He slipped a folded banknote into the embossed breast pocket and gave the youth a punch on the arm. Then he stalked out, but not before telling the diners:

'And you lot can get your eyes back on your meals. Fucking hell.'

Following him, I felt the disapproval of the diners. What was it with Dermot and gratuities? If he couldn't tip the staff, he took it as a personal insult.

By the time we reached the car park he was back to normal, scampering about and notching up views of the building from all available angles.

'Magic,' he said. 'Brilliant. They wanted a pub and someone built them a warehouse, and they're *going* with it. Excellent place.'

He ran over to the Audi.

'Come on,' he said. 'Get a move on. I don't want to spend *all night* in the car park.'

73

'Where next?'

'Surprise me,' he said. He was full of life again. He was like that, full of enthusiasms that lasted about as long as mayflies.

SIX

I

Dermot was enthusiastic about everything. He was always running at ninety-plus. Whatever he did, he did completely. Any new hobby swallowed him, and he'd spend all of the money he earned at his makeshift jobs on armfuls of supporting materials.

He discovered windsurfing and bought a board and the canary yellow outfit to go with it. He lived in the West Midlands, where the only available water is in canals. There was plenty of wind. There was nowhere to windsurf. He sold the stuff a fortnight after he bought it.

He did the same with paintball, skiing, skateboarding, chess. He was hopeless at all of them. He was always selling off old equipment at car boot sales, out of the boot of my Audi. I used to drive him all over the place in that car. I didn't know that he had a car of his own. He didn't mention it. I suppose that saved him the bother of driving.

▌▐

He began to run out of possible enthusiasms. New ones weren't invented as quickly as he tired of the old ones. He didn't even sign up for some; he decided he was too old for the umpteenth resurgence of skateboarding, and bungee jumping lacked something.

'Not for me,' he said. 'No *skill* in it, is there? It's just *falling off a building*. Anyone can do that.'

'Try getting the length of the rope wrong. Anyway, it's not the skill. It's the rush.'

'Won't be seeing you doing it then, will we? The most fun you have is playing with your computer. Which is a sad thing. That's a very sad thing to be doing.'

'You've never tried it.'

'Oh yes I have, I tried it when you had that Wolfshit thing. It wasn't as good as my Megadrive.'

'Have you still got that?'

'Sold it. Got bored of it.'

'You surprise me. Here, have a look at this.'

We were in my flat. We had been thinking of going out for a drink, but we hadn't been able to decide where to go. I didn't want to drive all the way out to the Slipped Disc, which had become our local in all ways except geographically. I switched on the PC and we waited the usual three minutes for the operating system to wake up. Lights flashed, and the monitor began to glow. I'd got Terminal Velocity, a shoot 'em up which had you flying a spaceship across the surface of a series of planets and shooting everything you met. I loaded it up.

Dermot liked it. His spaceship swooped over the rendered landscapes.

'This is better,' he said. 'This is *more like it*. Are there many games like this now?'

'They're getting there.'

'Nice. Fuck! What's that?'

'It's shooting at you, so we can assume it's not NATO forces.'

'It's not shooting anymore. Another one goes down in flames.'

He ran through the rest of my game collection, ignoring the strategy games in favour of arcade-style ones.

'How are the arcades staying in *business*?' he asked. 'Why am I going to go in there, pay fifty a throw for something I can play for *nothing* at home?'

'You have to pay for the games. And a PC to play them on. You need a fast one for this stuff. You can't just get one at a car boot sale.'

'How much are they asking?'

'Fifteen hundred.'

He thought about it.

'I can't afford that. I don't have that sort of *spare capital* at the moment. I'll have to sort something out.'

After some time he grew bored of the available games. He was hampered by the keyboard.

'I can't play these any more,' he complained.

'I thought you were the arcade king.'

'I *am* the arcade king. This isn't an arcade. They don't have piles of *dirty old socks* in arcades. This is your fucking flat. I'm not the king of this dump. When are you going to throw some of this crap out?'

'I might need it.'

'Oh yeah. There's a *big market* for old computer magazines.'

There might be one day, I thought. Old Dinky toys were going for large sums at the auctions. Crumpled comics were selling for thousands.

At that time, the idea of collectable plates was still inexplicably popular. They appeared in all of the Sunday glossies. Dermot said that they were appearing from the devil's arse. Collectable plates had six characteristics which distinguished them from any other plates.

Firstly, they cost more than ordinary plates.

Secondly, they came in sets, and subsequent plates cost more than the first one.

Thirdly, they were not sold in shops because shops couldn't shift them.

Fourthly, they featured a dismal painting by an unknown artist. The painting would be of the reality-rendered-badly school. The subject matter would be small children doing sickening things, small animals doing sickening things, or American Indians doing fluffy things with feathers rather than skinning their captives alive.

Fifthly, they were in strictly limited editions. The strict limit would tend to be about twenty thousand, which still seemed like a lot of idiots until you compared it to the total population.

Sixthly, and most pertinently, they would never increase in value.

The point was, people did pay for the things. People had them on display, perhaps to make it easier for the men equipped with big nets and syringes full of powerful sedatives to find them.

Computers were becoming part of popular culture. Perhaps one day those magazines would be worth some money. Even the worst of them looked better than a collector's plate.

Dermot began to leaf through the magazines, checking out the small ads.

'Where can I get a cheap computer?' he asked.

'Nowhere legal.'

'Somewhere must sell them. I'm going to get one. I'll see you later.'

'What, you're going? We haven't done anything.'

'I don't want to do anything now. I've got a *mission*. I have a *meaning* to my life. You should try it.'

'I thought you didn't want to play these games anymore.'

He wouldn't be persuaded. He went home, and I went to bed at nine thirty.

■■■

I didn't see him for a fortnight. His home telephone rang out unanswered. His mobile made excuses for him. I went out to meals with Tina and Roger. Tina asked where Dermot was. Roger asked if I was feeling alright. I was. I didn't have any new hallucinations.

Inspired by the code listings in those old magazines, I decided to write a small game of my own. I stayed up late, trying to get the code right. I wanted to write a new type of game. I wanted to get life into the computer, or at least the illusion of life.

I began to put together algorithms.

What isn't widely understood about artificial intelligence – other than the fact that it isn't ever going to happen for real – is that it's what a program shows you, what it tells you it's up to, that tells you how bright a program is. If it puts up messages telling you that it's just going through what you've input and drawing parallels between that and the output of the romantic poets, you'll think it's smart. It might be doing nothing. It might have got into a recursive loop.

If it actually does take your input and compare your sentence structure to that of Byron, but doesn't tell you what it's up to, you'll think it's dumb. Dumb and slow. Artificial intelligence has to make a big noise about being clever, like people on late night arts review shows.

Knowing this, I tried to make a game with a virtual living thing in it. Something that would be perceived as a living thing. Something you could chat with via the keyboard.

I spent two weeks on it before I realized that it wasn't going to be done any time soon. Even getting a program to parse English sentences was a nightmare. Getting it to decode the meaning, and then to respond meaningfully, was worse. And that was only the beginning of what I wanted to do.

I could write code, though. I could write reams of it. I used to do sorting algorithms for fun. I didn't have anything better to do.

I watched films where computers responded to any input. Characters typed in 'Good morning computer, how are we feeling today?' and the computer would respond. Sometimes it'd have a little bit of a talk with them, ask them how the dog was and whether they'd enjoyed the football at the weekend.

I started working on it at work. After all, I wrote programs for a living. It wasn't as though anyone would ever know.

IV

I was working for DataThon, a company with a small set of offices on the edge of Kingswinford. The company employed four full-time programmers. We built small applications for small businesses. People would ask for databases, usually. Stock lists. Billing systems.

We'd build them, and go out and support them when the bugs turned up. DataThon employees didn't wear suits. They dressed casually. I looked fussy in a shirt – without a tie, I never did get the hang of ties – and black trousers.

Clive Pinner, the chief programmer and owner of the business, had several pairs of sandals and a comprehensive knowledge of Windows architecture. He was in his fifties and had been interested in computers since encountering one the size of a caravan at his Cambridge college in the early seventies. He would reminisce about the days of punched cards and paper tape. He'd fiddle with system registries when he was bored. Andy Worsthorne was a young programmer who dressed in black. He had been a hacker back when you still needed to be able to write code to be a hacker. He'd been about twelve at the time. He'd been into the Pentagon's computers, but then, everyone got into those. Tim Winters was in his early thirties and wrote machine code. Sometimes he spoke in it. The four of us were able to write small applications quickly and look after them well. We weren't going to be driving Ferraris around Dudley anytime soon. But then, neither was anyone else.

The company also employed Tracy Brady, a woman from Brierley Hill with the bubble perm endemic to that area and seventies footballers. She was a secretary, receptionist, and everything else that required any skills other than typing code into a PC. She interfaced between the coders and the physical world. She was in her fifties, had been divorced a couple of times and had enough grandchildren to populate Stourbridge twice over. She mothered us, which was necessary.

Clive had been a programmer early enough to catch the first big wave, but didn't have the business sense to do what Bill Gates did. He just noodled around with software, assimilating knowledge and amassing a good-sized collection of woolly jumpers. He had the last vestiges of an upper class accent, but the nasal West Midland voice – like that of a duck with brain damage – was close to swamping it.

We did well enough. I was taking home more than twenty thousand a year before adding in bonuses. We got bonuses for completing projects. When we sold a package, the money went five ways. The company got a fifth to pay for new equipment, and the rest of it was split between the human beings, excluding Tracy. She'd get a box of chocolates and a thank-you card.

I had a fast PC at work.

We were between projects. I took in my sample code and began to work on my artificial intelligence project in the office. After thinking about things – like, being sacked – I told Clive what I was doing just to keep everything above board. I didn't want any trouble at work.

'You won't get it working,' he said. 'you'll never do it. But if you get the Turing prize, I want half of it.'

v

After some time spent elsewhere, Dermot returned to the human world. He arrived at my flat with a large bag.

'You've got to see this,' he said. 'This'll blow you away.'

He unpacked a PlayStation and unplugged my PC so that he could plug it in. He connected it to the television and swore as he tried to tune it in.

'Where's this telly from? The *antiques fucking roadshow*? Does it run on *coal*? What the fuck does it *mean*, automatic level adjust?'

I took the controls and got my TV tuned to his new machine. He popped a CD into the PlayStation and switched it on.

'I've got a Nintendo as well,' he said. 'I didn't want to bring the pair of them.'

He'd finally found a hobby he could cope with. He'd got bored with his Megadrive long ago, but the new consoles delighted him. It was his dream hobby. He could throw money at it. There was always new kit to buy. There were always new titles. There were books about the games, books of tips for people who didn't know how to play them, books of hidden secrets. There were CDs of the soundtracks of the games. There were new consoles every few years.

He would turn up with new hardware. He added in lightguns and steering wheels. He had joypads in different colours, and joypads that fought you back.

'Still having fun with the PC then?' he'd ask. 'Get me a cup of tea then.'

We started to stay in more. He'd bring one or other of his consoles and perhaps some drinks from the off-licence. I'd supply the television and provide cups of tea, and fetch extra drinks from the off-licence.

My job was fine, my life was even, I was coming to terms with just being friends with Tina.

If that hallucination had been a one-off, I had nothing to worry about.

SEVEN

I

The next hallucination turned up a week later. Dermot was excitedly demonstrating his new steering-wheel-and-pedals combination.

'Look at this,' he said. 'It's a *brake pedal*. Watch the car.'

I watched the car on the screen as he drove it into everything in sight.

'Your chairs are the wrong height,' he said. 'How can I *control* anything in this chair? How are we doing for beer?'

We were doing badly. We had a lot of empty cans.

'You can go and get us some then,' he said. 'Pop to the off-licence and get six cans. No, twelve. There's some money in my wallet.'

'Where is it?'

'At home. I don't bring it out in case I get mugged. You're the computer programmer, you can afford it. You're all on fucking *millions*. And get some crisps or something.'

I could afford it, as it happened. I was well-off by Dudley standards. I told him I'd be back soon and walked to the off-licence.

It was cold outside, but unseasonably dry. Looking down the length of the High Street I could see the castle silhouetted against the grey evening sky. One or two lost stars were out early, making their slow way to the end of the universe. Looking at Dudley, it was hard to believe it hadn't already happened. A handful of Asian girls shouted at one another excitedly next to the closed post office, comparing mobile phones.

A square yellow street sweeper was being driven under the market awnings, shoving the litter out into the street. Its driver aimed it at pedestrians when any strayed nearby. A group of three lads looked at me, waiting for me to look back at them so that they could talk it up into a fight. I looked at the castle instead. The chairlifts were running, carrying the zoo visitors over open-topped enclosures holding some of the less dangerous animals.

Distorted jukebox music came from the pubs, and through their windows I could see fruit machines and quiz machines in attract mode, lighting up in patterns.

The off-licence was close to the far end of the High Street, close enough to the zoo to hear the animals when they cried out at night. Entry to the zoo was by way of a row of turnstiles set under a long concrete roof shaped into a series of gentle waves. On the same road were two old cinema buildings, long since converted into bingo halls or convention centres. Cinemas are out of town these days. Dudley is out of town, these days.

Inside the off-licence, students from the residential halls looked for the cheapest drinks.

'Where's the blackcurrant?' one asked. 'We need blackcurrant for the girls.'

It was more of a general store than an off-licence. It sold

everything, all day. Thanks to the nearby student housing it concentrated on cigarette papers and cider but there were also shelves of videos to rent, racks of paperbacks, toiletries, fresh vegetables and spices. It didn't have opening hours because it didn't close. It was open all hours, forever.

I bought twelve cans of cheap strong lager and a few bags of crisps. They did a line in crisps with strange flavours – hedgehog, roast parsnip, seafood medley – and I tried to get a good varied selection. Dermot always wanted to try the weirdest flavours.

'Check them out,' he'd say. 'Dandelion and cowslip. Cajun catfish! Just try these.'

The assistant put everything into a bag very slowly. He operated the till as though he'd never seen one before, and puzzled over the change.

'Thanks,' I said. He ignored me. He was on a different wavelength, not quite aligned with the human world.

As I left the off-licence I saw a car sneak across the junction down by the ex-cinemas. The traffic lights down there were on red, as usual. The car ignored the lights and drove quickly across the junction, heading up past the entrance to the zoo. There wasn't much other traffic. I was reminded of Dermot demonstrating his new set of pedals.

The car continued on up the road. It was a strange colour, a bright sunburst orange that hadn't been seen on cars since seventies US cop shows. It didn't look right. It was reflecting streetlights where there weren't streetlights. It had a number plate but there were no real letters or numbers, just that squiggle that lazy cartoonists use to represent writing. The windscreen was a flat grey panel.

It wasn't any particular make of car. It was just a car, vaguely sporty. It didn't sound like a car. It sounded like a bee in a jar. The wheels weren't turning. It had no windscreen wipers.

I realized that I was picking up all of these details because it was heading towards me. It was aimed at me, and it was going to run me down if I didn't move. It crossed a lane and drove through a couple of real cars without anyone else noticing. I knew it was after me. There was no other reason for it to be there. I knew it wasn't real, but I didn't want it driving into me. I didn't know what might happen. I ran towards the bus station, where cars weren't allowed.

I wasn't thinking straight, but I did know that if you're chased by a car you should get off the road. In films, people being chased by cars run down the white lines.

I ran up the wide flight of stone stairs that led to the bus terminus. From there I'd be able to loop back to the High Street and get home. It wasn't going to be able to drive upstairs to my flat. It'd have a hard time getting to me now, I thought.

The car came right on after me. It simply drove up the stairs. It didn't bother with real-world physics. It let out a couple of badly animated showers of sparks as it scraped against the wall of the public toilet and then did an impossible turn and faced me. The stairs hadn't even slowed it down.

The bus terminus has long stands for people to wait in while the buses make their weary way home. They're long tunnels of Perspex and green tubular metal, with far fewer seats than prospective passengers. For most of the time they're occupied by the living dead, who can't drive. At that time of night there were only a few people, standing glumly, waiting for amusement.

Because the car was my own private hallucination and none of them could see it, they got the fun of watching me run from

88

side to side down the length of the central stand, leaping over barriers and looking behind me in panic at nothing. I dodged sideways into another stand and ran across the road and around the corner onto the High Street. The amplified angry-mosquito sound of the pursuing motor followed me. I ran past the Asian girls, who stopped comparing mobiles to watch me run past. I didn't do a lot of running. Computer programming involves sitting still. Some programmers thought that was too energetic, and slouched. There wasn't much physical exercise involved except for typing. Clive didn't even do much of that, he had keystroke macros recorded for words he used a lot – loop, while, exception – and got by on shortcuts.

The illusory car pursued me, following me wherever I dodged, maintaining enough speed to keep me running.

I ran in and out of the empty market stalls, did a quick semicircle around the statue of Duncan Edwards and got through my front door just ahead of the tinny whine of the car. I raced up one flight of stairs and looked around. The car had come into the hallway, going through the front door without in any way affecting it. It had got itself stuck, not having room to exist. The space was too small and the car was having trouble sorting out its co-ordinates. It tried to squeeze into the available space but it was loosing integrity. It couldn't fit into that amount of reality. It exploded into separate polygons, and vanished.

I took the shopping upstairs.

■■

Dermot was still trying out his pedals.

'Let's have a drink then,' he said. 'You're breathing a lot there mate. Those stairs getting *too much* for you are they? Shall we get you a *bungalow* instead?'

I passed him a can. I didn't want to tell him what had happened.

He opened the can and of course it covered him, the chair, and a good part of the room with spray.

'Have you had this in the *spin dryer*?' he asked. 'Look at that, I've missed the *time bonus* now. And I'll reek of fucking beer all night. What's wrong with you?'

He had turned away from the screen for a moment. Something about the way I looked was unsettling him. I imagined that I looked quite shocked. I certainly felt it.

'You're the whitest person I've ever seen,' he said. 'What happened to you? Muggers? Terrorists? Dinosaurs?' He looked out of the window. 'Those girls down there was it? Did they call you something *naughty*? I could go and give them a slap.'

I sat in a chair.

'I was chased by a car,' I said. I sounded very calm, all things considered.

'Why?'

'I don't know.'

'Well what did you *do* to it? Cross in front of it or something?'

'No. It just chased me. It nearly hit me.'

He let go of his steering wheel. I had his full attention, although knowing him I wouldn't have it for long.

'Where did it happen?'

'All the way home.'

'What, you *outran* it? What was it, a fucking *milk float*?'

I didn't answer him because my lower lip had started to quake. I tried to open a can but the ring-pull was too difficult for me. I wasn't very calm after all. Dermot took it from me, opened it, said 'fuck' as the spray drenched him all over again, and handed me what was left.

'Calm down,' he said. 'Sit quietly. You're in *shock*. You need *brandy*. Do we have brandy in the building?'

I shook my head. He'd finished the brandy off months ago, along with all of the other spirits.

'Well I'm not going and buying any, there's a mad fucker out there running down innocent pedestrians. Oh look, it's *smiling*. We have a *connection* with Mr. Aston. What make was it?'

I shook my head.

'He doesn't know. He doesn't know one car from another. Well what *colour* was it?'

'Orange.'

'What? No one has an orange car mate. At least the witnesses will have noticed it. Did you clock the number plate?'

'It had one but there was nothing on it. There were no numbers on it. And no one else saw it.'

'Are you shitting me here? What was it, the fucking *mystery* car? It came from nowhere, did something or other and then *fucked off*? All unseen by human eye? What happened to it?'

'It followed me into the hall downstairs and then it exploded.'

He sat back. He had developed a wary look.

'Oh yes,' he said. 'I heard that. I remember wondering

91

what it was. That had *slipped my mind*. Is your telephone working?'

'It wasn't real,' I said. 'I'm not mad. It was a hallucination. I know that, but it doesn't help. I imagined it, but it felt real. That's why you didn't hear anything.'

'Right, that's not mad. That's *normal*. What do you mean, it was a hallucination? What the fuck are you on? And why didn't I get any of it?'

'I'm not on anything. I had another one a few weeks ago.'

I told him about the non-specific video-game bint who had flown in through my window spraying the room with bullets.

'She was the same,' I told Dermot. 'She was a video-game thing. I thought I'd been playing too many games too much of the time and I gave it a rest for a few days. Spent quality time with the real world, started on a new idea for a game myself. Then this car turns up and chases me home.'

'Have you seen anyone?'

'Only the girl with the guns.'

'No, have you seen anyone medical? Have you sought *medical attention* for your *condition*?'

'Not yet. I thought it might just be that one time. I'd been working a lot and I was tired.'

'Well I think you should see someone. You have a doctor?'

'I used to. When I was little.'

'Well you need one now you're all grown up. Fucking hell, you could have a *brain tumour* or something. Did you used to get a lot of burgers from Scratto or anything? Any of those *big bags* of minced hooves they do in there?'

I shook my head.

'You're not being very comforting,' I told him.

'Well I'm not a fucking *nurse*, am I? You had a burger off me a few years ago. I told you not to. I *warned* you about it. Don't eat the burger, I said. Did you eat many burgers?'

Of course I did. I was a computer programmer. Convenience food was convenient. Of course, British fast food joints had never got the hang of 'fast', or indeed 'food'. There would always be a queue waiting while the dazed staff warmed up more roundels of mashed livestock.

'It's just a couple of hallucinations,' I said. 'Everyone gets those.'

'Everyone at fucking *Woodstock*, maybe. The rest of us mostly get by without them. You need to see someone. You might be right, too much time staring at the screen, not enough sleep. You might be wrong, your brain could be melting or your eyes could be going mad. Best to do something about it now, before it gets any worse.'

'I'll go to the doctor.'

'Good man. And don't worry about it. I'm sure they can fix it, whatever it is. Now, pass another can.'

III

I didn't know how you went about getting to see a doctor. They were protected by receptionists who didn't want to let you into the practice. I looked in the Yellow Pages and that got me nowhere. The numbers I called rang out unanswered, when they weren't engaged.

The next day at work, I asked Tracy. She would know. She knew everything.

'I can get you an appointment,' she said. 'My ex-husband's sister is a receptionist at the Keys Place clinic, she'll get you

93

in. Will this afternoon do? They're usually full but she can get someone else moved, they only ever have colds. They only go in to get doctors' notes.'

I said that would be fine, and spent the rest of the morning working on my artificial intelligence project, which was showing no signs of intelligence at all. I'd christened it Boris.

I'd have to draw up an execution plan for him. That'd tell the code what order to do things in, and where its priorities lay. Without a good execution plan, it's difficult to write decent software. I hardly ever used them. Perhaps if I did, I'd be able to move somewhere nicer one day.

I told Clive that I had an appointment at the doctors that afternoon and he told me to take all the time I needed. I'd been hoping that he wouldn't let me go. Going to the doctor might only confirm that my brain was turning into Swiss cheese and that I'd be spending the first half of the year walking backwards and talking to people who weren't there, and the second half in a coma as my systems shut down.

Perhaps it would be better not to know something like that.

At one thirty I saved everything, powered down the PC, and left.

I felt as though I was going to my own execution.

EIGHT

I

The Keys Place clinic had been built in the early sixties in an attempt to cater for the increasing population of the Dudley area. More and more people were moving to Dudley, for no good reason. The people already there were breeding like rabbits because there was little else to do that didn't involve going down a mine shaft. The existing medical practices soon were overrun with people with measles, colds and warts.

In an attempt to reverse the spread of unsightly disorders, the Health Authority reluctantly stumped up the cash for Keys Place. It was build with that sixties flair for characterless cuboid concrete constructions, and it sat next to the Broken Egg café until the Broken Egg was demolished in 1970 along with the surrounding streets. The area was unsafe due to mine workings. After that, Keys Place clinic stood by itself, a mile out of town, with nothing else nearby. It couldn't be demolished because it couldn't be replaced.

On the plus side, it was easy to park nearby.

I looked at the clinic. It didn't cheer me up. The concrete was grey under the soot. The windows were narrow and barred. A security camera watched the world. It looked more like a correctional facility than anything medical. It looked like a castle. A door with powerful springs holding it closed led into the clinic.

Inside, after battling the door, I found myself in a small anteroom. Another door led on, but it was locked. A handwritten faded note was taped to the door.

'Check in at Reception,' it said.

There was a Perspex screen set into one wall of the small room. Behind it, three middle-aged women with variously coloured and elaborately coiffured hair ignored me. They each wore spectacles with thin gold chains attached, and a pen on a string around their necks. They were having a nice chat, and couldn't see me, obscured as I was by being in plain view of them. I looked for a bell to ring but there wasn't one.

I knocked on the Perspex screen.

They looked at me. They looked at each other.

The largest one approached the window.

'Do you have an appointment here?' she asked.

'Yes. Doctor Phipps at three.'

'Oh,' she said, evidently disappointed. 'Take a seat in the waiting room. Doctor will see you when he can.'

She pressed a button and the inner door shifted in its frame with a loud click.

I carried on through to the waiting room.

∎∎

The waiting room was large. It was twice the size of my living room, and full of long red benches with padded seats which were spilling yellow foam from flesh wounds. The walls were painted pale green and the floor was coated in linoleum so that it could be wiped clean. No one had taken advantage of the feature. A Perspex screen allowed the receptionists to ignore patients in that room too. In one corner a small area held battered toys. Another door led to the doctors. On the walls posters gave health tips:

'If your skin begins to slough, stop what you are doing and call . . .'

'Rat bites can be nasty if left untreated . . .'

'Incontinence can be difficult to talk about . . .'

On the benches rows of ill people sat, most of them appearing to be at death's door. Some had made it to the hallway. One actually was dead, as far as I could tell.

I tried not to look at anyone's rashes or boils. I found a space between a young woman who was apparently suffering from a deficit of shampoo and an old man holding a wadded handkerchief against one eye. There was a distinct smell of urine from somewhere. It was so strong that I checked my own lap. There was a hint of dampness from the bench beneath me.

Someone sneezed wetly, filling the air with a cloud of droplets. God knew what was in them, it could have been anything from the common cold to Dengue fever. People sneezed, snuffled and scratched. I felt less healthy by the second. I wanted to bathe in antiseptic.

The old man took the handkerchief away from his eye,

held it out, wrung it out with both hands and replaced it. It left a yellowish pool on the floor. I was in danger of doing something similar.

The young woman with the shampoo problem shouted 'Tiff' at the top of her voice. A little girl in a shell suit arrived from somewhere, holding a length of discoloured bandage.

'Give that back to the man,' said the young woman. 'He needs that. Naughty girl, aren't you? Bad thing.'

The little girl, Tiff, offered me the bandage.

I didn't want it. I wanted to go to the centre for tropical diseases in Atlanta, Georgia, where they only had Ebola and Lassa to worry about. I was trying to make myself as small as possible so that the germs would overlook me.

'Not this man. The one with the finger. Go on, give it back to him.'

Tiff toddled off.

'She's a one,' said the young woman. 'She's always up to something. That's how she got the nits, if you ask me. Spending time with the wrong people.'

I nodded. Another sodden sneeze released another cloud of microbes.

The final door opened. A man came out of it with a small bottle and a worried expression.

One of the receptionists gave up on her knitting pattern for long enough to call a name out. Another man stood and walked through the door, followed by Tiff.

'Oi,' shouted the young woman next to me. 'Don't you go through there.'

The door closed.

'Oh well,' she said. 'She can't get up to a lot in there. They're trained to deal with children, aren't they? I've just got her and her brother, he's no trouble.'

She looked at my clothes.

'Are you married at all?' she asked. 'Do you get on with children?'

The old man emptied his handkerchief again.

▌▌▌

By the time they called my name out, hallucinations were the least of my worries. I wanted immunising against everything. I wanted a full blood transfusion.

I sat in the chair Dr Phipps offered me. He looked about as tired as a person can get without keeling over. He wore the traditional white coat and kindly expression. He looked like someone's favourite uncle.

I told him about my hallucinations.

'That's a relief,' he said. 'That's the first case today that hasn't involved excessive dampness. Well, you survived the waiting room so there can't be much wrong with you. How many fingers am I holding up?'

I told him. He shone lights into my eyes.

'Hmm,' he said. 'Do you have any other symptoms? Do you find it difficult to balance at all? How's your attention span?'

They were fine, I told him.

'Well it's not likely to be anything too awful. You'd be having more symptoms if there was anything terribly amiss. Did you think you had a brain tumour?'

I nodded.

'Yes. Most people do. Well, most people that I see. They have a headache, bang, it's a brain tumour. That's not awfully likely to be the case. I do want to send you for a scan, but to be honest I don't think there's anything to worry about. Try to steer clear of computers for a while, to give your eyes a chance to relax.

'Are you feeling stressed at all? Is anything playing on your mind?'

'Nothing,' I said. It was true. I had a decent job, I had gadgets to occupy my time. Apart from the hallucinations I had no troubles at all.

'Stress can cause that sort of thing sometimes. I suppose you've read all of the stuff in the newspapers about BSE?'

I nodded.

'Well try not to worry about that. It's not likely to be that. We'll be picking up the real fallout from that one in about 2010. But try not to worry about it. I try not to. I'll get you an appointment for a scan. Give this to the receptionists and they'll arrange it. You can get back to me if they find anything. I'm sure that they won't. Thank you, Mr. Aston.'

I handed the note to one of the receptionists on the way out, after waiting the obligatory quarter of an hour while she determinedly failed to notice me. She told me the hospital would be in touch with a date for my scan.

Tiff's mother gave me a little wave on my way out.

IV

A month later, I went to the hospital. They didn't do the sort of scan they wanted to give me in Dudley, so I had to go to a small unit outside Arley, a tiny village on the banks of the River Severn.

It was a bright new building on one floor, on a plot of land surrounded by nicely arranged shrubbery. It looked like a Pizza Hut from outside. From inside, it looked like a lost set from *2001: A Space Odyssey*.

Chirpy young staff sent me to a cubicle to swap my clothes for a gown so that everyone would be better able to see my bare arse. All of the staff looked like they'd escaped from an Australian soap opera. They were all young and lively and optimistic and tanned. They wore loose-fitting uniforms in various pastel shades. A pair of young nurses, one male and one female, led me to a white room holding an enormous cylindrical machine.

'I'm Brooke and this is Paul,' said the female one. 'We'll be looking after you. All you have to do is lie in there for a while and the machine will do the rest. We build up an image of the inside of your head.'

They arranged me on a bench. It glided inside the machinery.

They built up an image of the inside of my head.

Sadly, there was nothing wrong with it.

v

They were certain. They were positive and the results were negative. My brain was physically intact, no unexplained lumps or unusual holes.

Whatever had caused my hallucinations wasn't in my head. They told me that some foodstuffs might cause visions, like the ergot-infested grain that gave rise to many of the religious visions of past centuries. Cheese could cause nightmares, as I knew. Some antidepressants could trip you out, as though being depressed wasn't enough to cope with.

I didn't think it was anything I'd eaten. I was reassured but

I'd wanted an answer. If I'd lost half a lobe of cranial matter, that would have been that. I'd have learned to live with it. Or without it.

There could still be crossed wires somewhere. Something that didn't show up. Sometimes that happened, and you'd end up hearing the colour blue or seeing the smell of frying fish. I tried not to think about what I might not be thinking about, the possible gaps in my mind. I wanted to play video games but they were bad for me. According to intermittent reports in the dumber tabloids, they were bad for everyone.

I got bored, sitting at home doing nothing. It was the evenings that were getting to me. In the day, I was at work, and that kept me occupied.

After work, I was on my own. I decided that I needed some company.

I didn't feel like seeing Dermot. He was too lively. I needed more restful companions. I called Tina and arranged to go round for tea the following night.

VI

Bewdley was unusually quiet. Most weekends, it was crowded with tourists. If it was flooded even more would turn up. That evening, midweek and out of season, it was like a ghost town. A few couples walked along the riverbanks. Ducks – also in couples – stood sleepily and watched them pass. The sky was making its way towards night.

I parked in the long-stay car park and didn't pay. I walked along the river to Tina's house, dodging couples. Ducks eyed me beadily. A flying V of Canada geese hissed out of the sky and landed noisily on the water, looking at the world with the expressions of hitmen. Ducks would accept bread from you. Geese would knock you down and rifle your pockets.

It was a warm evening, and Roger had set up a table and chairs in the tiny back garden. It was surrounded by a tall wall of local stone, and felt isolated and peaceful. It wasn't overlooked by anything. Tina had done a salad and Roger had made crab cakes and potato wedges. He was still kitted out in French Connection clothes. Perhaps they were sponsoring him. The interior of their house still had the amber glow. Perhaps they'd bought that, too. Perhaps it came in buckets and you topped the room up if it ran low.

'Tina is just getting herself ready,' said Roger. 'Can you drink, or are you driving?'

I said I could have a little drink, and he poured me a hefty measure of his latest red.

'Not sure we should be having this with fish,' he said. 'Do crabs count as fish? More like insects really, aren't they? All legs and feelers.'

Tina arrived, in a white peasant blouson and unlabelled blue jeans. She'd had her hair cut into layers so that it looked natural, except that hair didn't naturally look that good. You needed to pay a good stylist to get it to look as though no one had been near it for weeks.

'No Dermot?' she asked. 'I thought you two were inseparable.'

'Hardly,' said Roger. 'What do you drink with insects?'

'Depends what they ask for,' she said. 'I'll have a glass of that red, if you don't mind.'

He poured her half a glass. She took it and sipped, nodded, said 'mmm'.

We sat around the table. It was a cheap white plastic one from an out-of-town garden centre, and the chairs gave under you. It still felt like being at the Henley regatta. It was some sort of emanation the two of them gave out. Roger seemed elegant and expensive, Tina rich and mysterious. They were comfortably off, and you could feel it. It wasn't a matter of money. I was earning a lot, by Dudley standards, but my flat wasn't going to get an amber glow unless it caught fire.

As we ate, they interrogated me.

'So, how are things?' asked Roger. 'Still single?'

'At the moment.'

'Perhaps you'll meet someone at work,' said Tina. 'I read that seventy per cent of relationships start at the workplace.'

'Not my workplace,' I said, thinking of Tracy Brady and her bubble perm.

'Not enough material there?' asked Roger. 'Perhaps you could try a dating agency.'

'I'm fine,' I insisted. 'I'm happy by myself.'

Tina hid her down-turned mouth by pouring wine into it. Roger put an arm on the back of his chair so that he could study me more directly.

'Any other problems?'

'That's not a problem,' I said, and then, thinking that perhaps they might have some useful advice, 'but there has been something. I've been to the doctors.'

Tina put her glass on the table but kept hold of it. Roger continued to pick at his food with his fork while I told them about my hallucinations. By the time I'd finished, Tina was also facing me, one arm on the back of her chair.

'So the tests didn't find anything,' Roger said. 'So you think it's you going off the rails, yes?'

I nodded.

'It might be something else,' said Tina. 'No one else saw these things, you said? And they were things you'd seen while you were playing games? Perhaps you're manifesting them as signs of something else. Perhaps you have something buried in there that you can't get at.'

'Such as?'

'I wouldn't know,' she said. 'Unless it was that business at Borth. You still don't like mirrors, do you?'

'Do you?'

'Not much, no. But you're afraid of them. We do have them in the house. And I don't think you have any in your flat, do you?'

Roger was beginning to look uncomfortable with the conversation. I could understand that. Suddenly he was the only sane person at the table, outnumbered two to one.

'Have you thought,' she asked, 'have you ever *considered* going back to Borth?'

NINE

I

I had never thought of going back. After the experiment ended I went downstairs while Betts and Tina were still talking about clearing up the mess.

What did they know about mess? I was the one in a mess. I had lost half of of my past. A hole had been driven into my memory. When the mirrors crashed, at the end of the experiment, I ran to the halls of residence with my hands over my ears, afraid of what I might hear. I looked only forward, knowing that something was out there in the damp air.

I went to my room and grabbed as much as I could force into a bag. I walked across the marshes and fields to Borth, under the drizzle. Every ten paces I had to look around to assure myself that no goblins were scampering down from the mountains to worry me. I didn't want to use the road because I knew Tina would try to find me there, if she tried to find me at all.

I didn't want to see her. I didn't want to see anyone. The Welsh rain crawled into my clothes. The whole landscape was the colour of wet cement. Water from the drenched fields got into my shoes. The wind was blowing in off the sea; I had to turn away from it to breathe. It was like swimming. It was like drowning.

I reached the first half of the golf course and walked onto it, because the grass was shorter there. I didn't want a golf ball catching me on the head, but I didn't want to stay near the college. Another world had stuck its nose into our world. I wanted to get back to the West Midlands, where there was only the one world.

I darted across the road to the other half of the golf course, and ran over that to the sea wall. When I climbed to the top of that, I looked around. Nothing was coming after me. The only cars were on their way inland, as was the sky, propelled by the wind. I could only see the tops of the college buildings through the hanging drizzle. I slithered down the seaward side of the wall and onto the beach, which is longer than the town. Gulls dangled in the sky like scraps of bad weather. Where the sea hit the pebbles it was battered into a greyish foam which flew at me in grubby-looking clumps.

I walked along the beach in the direction of town. The sea wall hid most of it. I could see chimneys and television antennae picking up both available channels. I walked along the beach behind the houses until I was level with the railway station, and then crossed the sea wall back into the town.

It was empty. No one was around. Out of season, the town closed itself up. The tat in the shops went back into storage, the number of jobs dropped by nine-tenths, the locals sat indoors and waited for next spring.

The railway station is just behind the town. The town is a single long road with houses and shops on each side, and the station sits behind the inner line of houses, as far from the sea as you can get in Borth. A single poster pinned to a notice board on one of the platforms flapped in the salty wind. It was too faded to read. There was a small ticket office, which was closed. I was alone there, looking at the rails. I looked behind the flapping poster and found the timetable. There would be a train in about another three hours, heading out to Aberystwyth.

Why hadn't I gone there instead? They had a real University there. They didn't get nightmares to step out of mirrors and spoil your day. They had a pier. They had amusements.

Borth had amusements. I could occupy myself for three hours, with an amusement arcade. They didn't close out of season because there were always enough students with enough money to keep them in business.

I went to the amusement arcade.

I found the future in there.

∎

I didn't mention any of that to Tina as she sat in the back garden of her country house, eating crab cakes and potato wedges and laying into Roger's wine collection. There was nothing back in Borth for me. I'd left my course unfinished and I didn't bother to finish it later. I could program, and I got jobs without anyone ever asking to see a certificate. I told Tina that I had never thought of going back.

'Perhaps you should,' she said. 'I think most of your problems started at Borth.'

Well, she would know, I thought. After all, she'd been there with me. I hadn't looked her up, afterwards. I'd avoided her. She would occasionally send me letters, which I would ignore. She'd finally tracked me down – two years later – by pestering my parents until they gave her my latest address. I had been flattered that she'd made the effort. She didn't phone, just turned up one day and hugged me. I misinterpreted that, but she didn't hold it against me.

So, she thought that my problems started at Borth.

'I think they did,' I said. It was true. Perhaps my hallucinations were fallout from the experiment.

'I'd be careful, digging things up,' said Roger.

'He can be careful,' said Tina. 'He can go right on being careful until he gets one of these things while he's driving home, and then he can be carefully cut out of the wreckage. I think he needs to get to the bottom of this. Going back to the source of it might help. I did *pass* my course, you know.'

'I know that,' said Roger.

'So let's help him along. I still think that these things might be manifestations, things that you're dragging out of your imagination. What do you want to do about it?'

'I don't want to do anything,' I said. 'I'm frightened to go back to Borth.'

'Perhaps we won't need to,' said Tina. 'Perhaps we could talk to Betts. He helped to set the whole thing up, so he might be able to tell you what to do. I could try calling the college for you.'

'There won't be anyone there at this time of night.'

'I'll call tomorrow then. I'll let you know what I find out.'

I wasn't at all sure that I wanted her to find Betts. I'd spent a lot of time getting safely away from Borth. Perhaps it would be sensible to let sleeping dogs lie. By that time the crab cakes were cold and the wine seemed to have partially congealed. It was no longer very pleasant. It felt too thick and heavy. So did my head.

Tina started to clear things away to the kitchen.

'What has she told you?' I asked Roger when she was out of earshot. 'About Borth?'

'She's told me quite enough,' he said. 'I know about the business with the mirrors. Haven't you ever wondered why she got you to do that?'

'We got paid for it.'

'Did you really?'

Of course not. I was off to the West Midlands before anyone could give me any money.

'Well, Tina did. I ran off.'

'Yes, she did. Which is why I asked you whether you ever wondered why she got you involved in it?'

Tina returned before I could ask him what he was talking about.

'Been chatting?' she asked. 'Good, I like to see everyone getting along. I didn't get anything for afters, there was a queue at the co-op. I think we've got some biscuits, if you're still hungry at all?'

I shook my head.

'Come on,' she said. 'Cheer up. It won't be that bad. At least you'll get things sorted.'

'I suppose so.'

'Good. Well, let's have another glass of wine. And I'd quite like a full one this time.'

III

After that, the evening was uncomfortable. Tina and Roger were quietly but palpably at loggerheads about something. I was worried about tracking down the source of my problems. I was also worried about what Roger had said about Tina.

For an hour or two I tried to get him away from her, but wherever we went she'd turn up with an imaginary job to do. In the end I said that I had to go and left them to the washing up. Tina gave me a light hug, Roger gave me a heavy look. As the door closed I could hear them beginning to discuss me.

Away from the amber glow of their house, the sky had turned darker than the river. Night was well on its way. There were no stars and the moon was half-cut and blurred, sitting behind a skein of thin cloud. The ducks had all left the water to stand on the river bank with their heads turned back to front. The chip-shop windows had been turned opaque by steam; inside, indistinct forms queued. The antique shops were all closed, the pubs were all open. There was no traffic, and even with the streetlights glowing it felt as though Bewdley was still in the early eighteenth century. It felt as though I was in a different time.

I didn't hear the footsteps at first. They were in time with my own, trailing me. When I heard them I stopped, and they stopped a step or two later.

I walked on again. On my right the river crawled along. It looked shallow enough to wade across, and slow enough to swim in. Neither of those was true. Every summer one or two swimmers would learn that there was an undercurrent; their bloated bodies would end up tangled in the branches of fallen trees miles downstream. It was deeper and faster than it looked.

On my left were houses with solid stone walls and firmly closed doors. If I had to knock, they might not answer in time.

Someone slithered around the corner by the chip shop, looked my way and edged out of sight.

I thought of the game Dermot had turned up with a few nights earlier. He'd been very pleased with it.

'You're the Ripper,' he'd said. 'You follow them through the alleyways and wait until they're somewhere quiet and then wallop! Can you believe that? Can you believe they've *done* that?'

I could believe it. I thought about what Tina had said earlier. She'd said that I might be manifesting things, not imagining them.

The figure slid back into view, sliding close to the houses so as to be in their shadows and coming on.

I wondered how far it was to the car. The long-stay car park filled the gap between the main road and the river. I'd get there faster along the river, but I would be alone. There would be no one around. If that was the Ripper, manifested out of a video game, then I didn't want to be alone with him. Up into the back of the town, I might see someone walking their dog.

I walked backwards until I reached the corner and then sprinted up a thin alley between waterlogged houses. Over the noise of my own splashing and nervous breathing I heard someone running towards me. They sounded fitter than I did. I ran up to the main road, and at the corner came close to running into a small group of teenagers.

'Watch where you're going, man,' said one.

'Who dis ofay motherfucker?' said another, forgetting that he lived in a small English village.

'Sorry,' I said. I couldn't think of an excuse. I could see the car park, which was almost empty. My Audi was parked close to the river.

I'd parked it there so that it wouldn't attract car thieves, as though Bewdley had any. After all of my running away from the river bank, I'd still have to go most of the way back to it.

There were lights in the car park, I reassured myself. There were other cars. I'd be in plain view of anyone passing, and safely out in the open. I walked to the car the way people walk across contested ground in war films. A wood pigeon threw itself out of a nearby tree with the usual wood pigeon clatter and commotion, and I didn't jump more than a foot.

I reached the car without being murdered. I'd seen enough tacky horror films to check the back seat thoroughly before I got in.

No one was in there. Perhaps there hadn't been anyone following me.

I drove back to Dudley.

IV

There was a note from Dermot on the floor inside my front door.

'Where have you been, you arsehole?' it said. 'I'll be in the Skinned Mule until closing time. Pop down and buy me a drink.'

I popped down. The Mule was at the top of the High Street, opposite a late-night chemists that was closed. It was only ten thirty. It felt as though it should be later. I'd done a lot for a weekday evening – gone out for a meal, heard weird intimations, been stalked by something I'd imagined – and it felt as though it should be midnight. There was still time for a drink or two. The Mule had a late licence because it had entertainment.

That night, the blackboard by the door said, the entertainment was a night of sitar music from the Shiva Brothers.

It was easy to find Dermot. Not many other people were there.

'Where have you fucking been?' he asked. 'Hang on, tell me after you get the drinks in. And get a few shorts too, they won't stay open late for *these* tuneless bastards.'

On the tiny stage at one end of the room, two Asian teenagers played instruments like hyperthyroid guitars with thousands of strings. No one was paying much attention to them. Most of the people in the bar watched me buying drinks.

I took them back to the table in instalments and then sat down.

'Cheers,' said Dermot. 'And where have you *been* all night?'

'I went to see Tina and Roger.'

'Did you now? And I suppose you had a *nice meal* by the river while I was stuck here with this pair of tuneless wankers.'

'How long does it take to tune those things?' I asked, looking at the masses of pegs at the ends of the strings.

'Too fucking long, and that's why they *don't bother*. They just play them *out of tune*, which is why they sound like two spring mattresses having a fucking *wrestling match*. All notes, no tune.'

He had a point.

'What's the story, then? Why this journey to Bewdley? Did you want to see the fair Tina? Or is there a *sheep* out there with your name on it?'

'I'm going to try and find some people I used to know,' I said.

'And who are these mystery men? Have you found the

missing Shiva brother, the one with the fucking tune? And you're off to Bombay on the first flight to knock the shit out of him?'

'It's about Borth,' I said.

'It's about fucking time. You've been moping about that for as long as I've known you. You can't go on being frightened of *mirrors*. That's unreasonable. So how are you going to do it? Go back there and see who's around?'

'I can't go back there. Tina's going to call them and see if we can find Betts.'

'Who's Betts? You can't just drop *names* on me. I'm not *psychic*.'

He gave me his evil grin. I ignored it.

'Betts was the lab assistant. He's the one who did most of the work in the experiment.'

'He might still be there. Then if you find him, you'd have to *go there* to see him.'

'He didn't live there. He used to drive off somewhere. I don't need to go to the college. I can go to his house.'

'Not by yourself you can't. *Look* at you. You need someone to *help* you on the way. I'm not doing much these days. There are *gaps* in the *market* and I'm in one of them.'

I knocked back a whisky. I thought about it. I'd rather have someone with me. I didn't want to be anywhere near Borth by myself. Dermot was irrational but he was good company, most of the time. He was lively. I had the feeling he'd protect me.

'You can come along,' I said. 'But you'll have to behave.'

'On my *honour*,' he said. 'On my dear old mother's *grave* in lovely old Kilkenny.'

'I thought it was Cork,' I said.

'That's where she *came from*,' he said. 'And she *went to*

earth in Kilkenny. You're getting very suspicious all of a sudden. Hey! You two!'

He was shouting at the Shiva twins. At first, engrossed in playing the most unbalanced musical scales I'd ever heard, they didn't hear him. That wasn't about to deter him. I recognized his expression. He'd reached boiling point.

'Are you two *fuckers* going to stop *fucking* about and give us a proper bloody song? Do you know any *Black Sabbath* there kids? Go on, give us "Paranoid". For me old friend Mick here. It's his *theme tune* this week. He used to like "Hobby For a Day" by The Wall, but he hasn't listened to that in *twenty years*.'

He gave everyone a look at his evil grin. Most of the other patrons were smiling. The bar staff had backed away from the bar and had their hands out of sight. They'd be reaching for handily placed chair legs or snooker cues or baseball bats.

The Shiva Brothers ignored him and ran through another number. They'd have sounded better running a tractor over corrugated iron sheets.

'I *told* you two to *stop it*,' said Dermot, standing at the centre of attention. 'I wouldn't ever want to offend anyone's *own taste* in music. So I can tell you two to *fucking stop it* with impunity because *no one* likes that fucking racket. At Monterey they had to fill people with LS fucking D and cannabis pasties just so that they wouldn't all fuck off when Ravi Shankar did his fucking set. No one *likes* that stuff. *I* don't like it, *they* don't like it, I don't even think *you two* like it so will you for the love of Mary *just fucking stop it* once and for all?'

A couple by the cigarette machine applauded him. So did one of the bar staff.

The Shiva Brothers left the stage in a huff.

'There,' said Dermot, sitting down and acknowledging his admirers. 'What did I tell you? You need me along. You'd have listened to that *all night*.'

'I said you could come along.'

'Then I will. I'll call you tomorrow. Now, that deserves a celebration. Drinks all round. Can you afford that?'

'Do I have a choice?'

'I can get them back on stage if you want. If you'd *prefer* that.'

'I'll get the drinks.'

'Good man,' said Dermot. 'And tomorrow we can start our *little adventure*.'

TEN

I

The next day at work, I tried to clear my mind. Usually work was a good place for that. Normally I could lose myself in code, watch it growing into subroutines, think of ways to make it neater and more elegant. Code nowadays is in tiers. At the front end, where the user sits, are the pretty boxes and buttons. Behind those is a layer of code, shaping the screen. Behind that, there's the operating system of the host PC. Behind that, there's the database on its server somewhere, and then the operating system of the server.

All I have to do at work is get the back layer visible to the front layer without it being apparent that there are any layers at all. All I have to do is make a series of layered realities work together.

In my side project, all I had to do was get the computer to respond like a living thing. I wasn't trying to get it to learn. Neural nets stopped being the next big thing the year before last. All I wanted was something that appeared to be paying attention.

Boris was growing at an alarming rate. There were many

screens of code. There were nested routines inside nested routines. There were loops and conditions and functions. For all of that, it still made no more sense than someone at a call centre.

'Hello Boris,' you'd type. 'How are you?'

'I am fine,' it would print, then give you a cursor to type with.

'I'm fine too,' you'd reply.

'That is nice,' it would say. But it'd say that if you told it you were feeling awful. If you typed 'I was bitten by a rabid dog on the way here, if I don't get medical attention I'm in for a long and unpleasant death' it would say 'How is the weather?'

It wasn't possible to teach it a response to every possible input. I needed to teach it to interpret what it was told. I needed to get it to spot strands in conversations.

I saved Boris and scrapped most of the code. To pass for human, he'd need a personality. To avoid difficulties, it needed to be a one-dimensional one. He wasn't going to be moody. He was going to have a single mood and stick to it.

I decided he could be grumpy. I liked the idea of a misanthropic computer.

Besides, that way he could ignore most of the input. It'd look like he was being rude, rather than stupid.

With that decided, many of the more complex routines became unnecessary. I got lost in the code, as I do. Everything beyond the monitor blurred and vanished. My peripheral vision shut down.

It's almost like meditation, except that it produces something useful. I find video games serve the same function.

■■

This is what Les Herbie had to say about video games:

I don't make much money at this. This job barely pays the rent. I have a few pounds spare at the end of the week.

Could be worse. I could be dead, or Welsh. In Merthyr Tydfil, a few pounds is millions. A few pounds gets you the freedom of the valley.

I get my pounds switched for smaller denomination cash. I prefer it.

Neat. I have bulging pockets. I have holes in my pockets too. Change destroys pockets. Sometimes all of my change gets out and runs down my leg.

This happens where it's crowded. This happens in the middle of the High Street. This happens as I pick up the Pulitzer.

I take what change I keep to the amusement arcades. You need to go to those places. They're where the future used to be. Now the future is in cyberspace, which is in your bedroom if you're an adolescent boy. Cyberspace is full of naked chicks. So is Merthyr Tydfil, if you have paper money.

The difference is that the future has never been near Merthyr Tydfil.

I play arcade machines. Fifteen years ago arcades were crowded places. That's where the adolescent boys were at, fifteen years ago. Now they're at home, jacked in, all jacked out. Now I get the places to myself. The machines are huge now. You used to stand in front of them. Now you get into them. They're exoskeletons. They're wardrobes. You get in and find the screen and there are rows of buttons.

The instructions don't help. They're not in words. Words are the future the same way that Merthyr Tydfil is the future. Words are over and done with. The instructions are in pictographs.

Next to a red button is a sketch of a man crouching. This is the crouch button.

Next to a blue button is a sketch of a man with one arm outstretched. I have to guess what this one is. This may be the button for saluting. It may be the button for waving. It may be the button for throwing.

I get out of the machine. I check the name. That might clue me in.

The name is all trademarks, piled on top of each other. Every corporation in the world has a slice of this thing.

I read between the trademarks. This game is a representation of communist art.

I make most of this up. That part is true. I can't give you the name, because it's owned by six corporations.

What you do is, control a character on the screen. You always do that. This one is different. You have to make the character stand in that Soviet artworks way, one arm outstretched, staring off into the distance. The usual nuisances try to shake him out of it.

It's a dumb game. I spend eight pounds on it. I get the hang of it. I get my guy staring off into the distance.

Why are the characters in Soviet art always staring off into the distance? Because they don't like it where they are. Because there are worse things than corporations, like not having any money and not having anything to spend it on.

Ask anyone in Merthyr Tydfil, next time you're there.

But don't give them my name.

III

I was finding the neatest way to get Boris to store threads –
in a good old-fashioned multidimensional array, I'd decided
– when Tracy butted in.

'Telephone for you,' she said. 'Tina somebody. She says she
has some news for you.'

'What?' I asked Tracy.

'A call for you,' she said. 'Do you want me to put it through
to your desk?'

'Yes. Please.'

She put the call through.

'Hello?' I said to Tina.

'Morning,' she said. 'I've been on to that old college of
ours. They need to get someone better on the switchboard,
I can tell you. It's been like talking to the sphinx, all riddles
and obfuscation. But the main thing is that neither of our
men stayed there. The girl who eventually answered the
phone didn't even remember Morrison. She only sounded
about twelve, and we were there a fair while ago. She probably wasn't even born then. She remembered Betts though.
God knows why. Perhaps he tried it on with her or something. Anyway, he left too. He went to work at a college in
Herefordshire. It was near a place called Monkland, if you
can believe it. I've checked on our motoring atlas and it's a
real place. I thought she'd made it up. It's a tiny place, so this
college should be easy to spot.'

'Didn't she have the name of it?'

'She couldn't find the records. The girl who finds the
records was out. You could get to Hereford in about an
hour, couldn't you?'

'I could do. Wouldn't it be easier to just call them?'

'It would if we knew what the place was called. I've tried to ask Directory Enquiries, but all of their girls were out. I had to talk to machinery. Have you ever tried talking to software?'

'You'd be surprised.'

'Not very. I know what you do for a living. Anyway, Directory Enquiries couldn't help me. You could go to the college. Wouldn't it be better to talk to him directly?'

'Better than what?'

'Well, better than being chased home by imaginary vehicles.'

'I don't know whether I want to go near a college,' I told her.

'Take Dermot with you. He'd be glad to go along. He's never got anything to do.'

'When am I going to go? I have to work for a living. There won't be anyone around at the weekend.'

'It's a college, there'll be people there night and day. If you're really lucky they'll have computers. They might even have a mainframe for you to make friends with. All you need to do is find a lab, and you'll find Betts. Where else would he be?'

'Couldn't he have got a job somewhere else? Moved again?'

'He's a lab assistant. That narrows down the employment opportunities. It's either colleges or Porton Down. Which would you choose?'

'It'd be a close thing.'

'Look, it's up to you. Phone if you want, you should be able to get the number from Directory Enquiries if you have long enough. The name of the place was Monkland.'

She spelled it out for me.

'A college near there, that should narrow it down.'

'I'll try calling them. You really think that finding Betts will help?'

'He was there, wasn't he?'

'He was. That's what worries me. He was there.'

'So was I, and that doesn't worry you.'

I didn't tell her, but it did. It was playing on my mind. We said goodbye and I put the phone down.

I had the feeling that she was pushing me, aiming me at something. But what other choices did I have? When I got home, I decided, I'd have a look at the motoring atlas.

IV

A quick check of the AA Road Atlas revealed that I needed to buy a new copy. Mine was twelve years old, and missing a few pages. I'd torn out Borth and the surrounding area myself. Others had gone their own way.

Looking at the street layout for Dudley, I could see that it was hopelessly out of date. The new traffic islands that the council were so fond of, the bypass that had allowed the traffic jam to queue with a different view, the six hundred sets of unsynchronized traffic lights; none of them were there.

Dudley used to allow small businesses to sponsor traffic islands. Small companies learned the error of their ways and went back to using single-frame adverts shown at local cinemas before the real trailers started.

For a while the traffic islands of Dudley stood bare. Then, unannounced, art started to appear on them. Big heavy art, cast in metal, high on weight, low on definition. On one island there are three huge red triangles, symbolising huge red triangles; on another, a mysterious lion/monkey hybrid cut out of sheet metal stands next to a giant bell topped with enormous pincers. None of it makes sense. None of it was on my map.

Hereford would surely be different, I thought. The roads wouldn't have changed since the Middle Ages. In Hereford they still told the time using notched candles, and locked menstruating women in a hut outside the village. I mentioned this to Dermot.

'What, Pizza Hut?' he asked.

He'd turned up almost as soon as I'd got home, armed with his latest console.

'Not Pizza Hut. Just a hut. A small one, well out of the way.'

'They've got some *smart ideas* in Hereford. That could catch on.'

'Hopefully they don't have any new roads. This should still be alright,' I said, waving the road atlas. Some pages dangled precariously from it.

'Don't ask me, I've never been that good with maps.'

'You'll be navigating.'

'I can't read maps. I'll drive, you navigate. You drive like an *old woman* anyway. You should have a fucking *Metro*. That car of yours is *wasted* on you.'

'Well you're not driving it. You're not insured.'

'I wasn't planning on *crashing* the fucking thing. If it'll make you feel better I'll be sure to put on *clean under-wear*, in case we have to go to casualty. Or we could take *my* car, then you could read what's *left* of the fucking map.'

'You haven't got a car.'

'Of course I've got a car. What do you think I *am*, a fucking tramp? How do you think I *get* here?'

'I thought you walked. You're too drunk to drive, most nights.'

'I'm *never* too drunk to drive. What, are you telling me you always drive sober?'

He looked almost shocked.

'Of course I do. That's how you drive. Sober.'

'I take it back, you don't drive like an old lady. Even old ladies go out for a tootle round the lanes after a *couple of sherries*. Have you ever thought about being an *undertaker*, they drive at the sort of speeds you like?'

I ignored that.

'I've never seen your car,' I said.

'You've never *asked* to see it. It's outside, on the corner. I always park it there. Besides, I was driving a bloody great van the first time we met. Didn't that *suggest* to you that I might be able to drive?'

I'd forgotten that, somehow. Drunkenness, more than likely.

'Where do you live?' I asked him.

'West fucking Bromwich, the land that time ignored. I've fucking *told* you that before. You know, you've never even *asked* me where I lived before? How long have I known you?'

'I don't like to ask people things.'

'You can't be bothered, more like. Most nights I drive here and then I drive back and you do the driving *in between*. That sounds fair to me.'

'So do you want to drive to Hereford then?'

'No, *you* can drive. But you'll have to *colour in* the roads on the map so I can follow them. Fair?'

'Fair. And it's not Hereford. It's Monkland.'

'Monkeyland? Like in the song?'

'What song?'

'"Monkeyland", what fucking song did you think? So where's Monkeyland then? Twycross Zoo?'

'It's Monkland. As in monks. As in monasteries.'

'Is there a monastery there?'

'Just a college, as far as I know.'

'That'll have to do then. When are we going to go?'

'Tina thinks we can go on a Saturday.'

'I think we *can't*. There'll be no one there. We should go in the week. There'll be no fucking *students* there, but we might see your lab assistant.'

'When are you free?'

'Whenever. I have a *flexible arrangement* as far as jobs go.'

'I'll try to get Friday off.'

'I can manage that,' he said, turning his attention to his latest video-game acquisition, an old-school platformer with nu-skool graphics.

I had decided that Tina was right. I'd be better off going to see Betts. He could avoid telephone calls, or flat-out lie to me. It'd be more difficult for him to do that if I was with him at the time. Dermot would add a touch of menace. From what I remembered of Betts, he'd be highly susceptible to menace. If I was lucky, he might even have some answers for me.

v

I spent most of the next day working on Boris. He was getting to be quite curmudgeonly. I thought that was the right feel for an English operating system. I wanted it to seem like a waiter in a middling good restaurant, all knowing sneers and long waits for service.

If it caught on, I could do different personalities for different countries. A laconic Australian one:'Your file's ready there, mate.' A therapeutic American one: 'Your file is ready, and please be sure not to forget that you made it yourself, and that it – just like you – is a thing of worth.' A steam-driven Welsh one. The possibilities were endless.

I asked Clive whether I could take Friday as annual leave, and he said it would be fine.

'How's your little project coming along?' he asked. 'I did look into AI for a while, once upon a time, and I thought I could help with the logic. We've got a bit of spare time at the moment. I could do with a bit of real coding.'

He rubbed his hands together enthusiastically.

'I haven't got far with it,' I said. 'It looks a bit over-ambitious now. I think I should start on something smaller and then work my way up.'

'Shame,' he said. 'So I'm not in line for half the Turing prize money, then? Probably just as well. I've tendered for a job doing work on the traffic monitoring system.'

'The council?'

That would be good. Most town councils didn't know anything about IT, and would pay far more than the going rates for just about anything.

'No, it's an independent firm working for the council. So there won't be a lot of spare cash floating about. If we get it, we'll need to start putting a demo together in the next couple of weeks. Flow modelling, mostly. Not something I've done before, but I can't imagine it's all that difficult. We could do our own graphics engine for it, that'd liven it up. Might be able to license the engine out afterwards.'

We chatted about the pros and cons of using someone else's graphics engine for a while, and then I went back to Boris. I wasn't going to have him in any sort of useable state in a week. It'd be difficult to work on him at home. My home PC was ludicrously powerful, but all of its power was aimed at running games.

I'd have to save him and get back to him later. That was the good thing about computers, you could get back to your saved position. That would be so helpful in real life. I thought about Dermot, driving home drunk. If he was a simulation run by a computer, you'd save the conditions, send him on his way, and if he came a cropper on a country crossroads you'd just load back in the starting parameters and set him off a different way.

In real life it wasn't like that. Car crashes couldn't be erased. People could, of course.

Perhaps it was Clive's talk about modelling traffic flows, or Dermot's chat about drunk driving, but I seemed to have developed a car-crash fixation.

I was, I realized, thinking about a specific car crash. I was thinking about a small red car, overturned and crumpled, rudely reshaped along new lines. Inside the car, something red and wrecked dangled upside down, held in place by a seatbelt, dripping heavily and struggling feebly. I could almost see the wreckage. I could all but smell the smoke. There had been a car crash and a girl had died, caught in the wreckage on a quiet road with the sound of the waves washing her away. I'd known her, although I couldn't remember her name.

In Borth, I'd lost six months of my memory.

I had a terrible feeling that part of it had just come back.

ELEVEN

I

We started out early on Friday. Dermot turned up while I was still getting dressed. I'd had time to think about my car-crash fixation, and it would have to wait. I had enough to think about, and besides, finding Betts might help.

'Come on then,' Dermot said. 'We've just got to sort your *whole life* out, then this afternoon we'll have a go at the Aegean stables, I hear they're in a *right* fucking state. Are you going like that?'

'Like what?'

'Never mind. Did you colour in the route for me?'

'I did.'

Outside it was brightly cold, with the clear sky promising a warm day.

'Did you turn off the gas and cancel the milk?' asked Dermot. He pointed to a low blue Meriden 733t parked on the kerb outside the newsagents. 'Since you've decided to show an interest, that's my car,' he said.

It was low, wide, and obviously powerful. It sloped inexorably down from the oversized rear spoiler to the minimal front bumper. I'd heard of the make. It gave the Top Gear crew palpitations and had a top speed around that of an F15. It was in the same price range, too. The Meriden production line was based in a tiny factory somewhere in Kent, turning out hand-tooled vehicles designed chiefly for speed. The 733t was known to be near-lethal to drive. Dermot had parked his on double yellow lines.

'You can't leave it there. That's a no-parking zone. That's what the yellow lines are for.'

'Don't be fucking stupid, of course I can leave it here. It's worth more than the *houses* round here. The fucking *property values* will go up. They should *pay* me for parking it there.'

We got into my car.

'Here we go then,' said Dermot. 'Hold on tight, he's going to let it rip. Monkeyland, here we come.'

As I turned the ignition, he said 'Hold it!'

'What?'

'Are you *sure* you turned the gas off?' he asked.

■

Monkland didn't look big enough to support a primary school, let alone a college. There were three houses that looked to have been built about the time Robin Hood had first been doing the rounds, and a church approximately twice their age. We passed though the village – all four buildings of it – in fifteen seconds.

'I told you it was Monkeyland you were after,' said Dermot. 'There's *nothing at all* here. They're all inside practising playing the fucking *banjo*.'

I pulled up in front of a farm's gate and checked the atlas.

'It's here somewhere,' I said.

'Maybe it's in someone's loft. Perhaps they don't want *outsiders* getting a glimpse of it.'

'Must be further on. We didn't pass any turnings.'

Things were looking distinctly rural. There was a line of mud down the middle of the road, and straw everywhere. Pheasants with all the brainpower of pot plants wandered into the road. There and elsewhere, people shot at them for sport; that must have been difficult. They had all the manoeuvrability of oil tankers but none of the cunning. I saw a tractor approaching. It was the first vehicle I'd seen for some time, but I didn't want to see it from the back. I pulled out in front of it.

'Good man, well fucking done, pulling out in front of the tractor,' said Dermot. 'Now they hate us. They'll *feed us* to the pigs.'

Because I was looking out for the college, I slowed down. The tractor – red, with a clinging mud motif – began to catch up.

'Get a fucking move on,' said Dermot. 'He'll tie us up with *baling twine* and rape the living shit out of us. And I'm prettier than you so I'll get it *twice* as bad.'

'I'm looking for this college.'

'Well look faster. What's that?'

He pointed to a sign, almost hidden in a bulging hedge.

'That's it,' I said. I saw a gap in the hedge large enough to drive through, with a small track leading off. I drove the Audi through the hedge, and we saw the college. It was a little two-storey building in the modern flat-pack style, with car parking opportunities in a small adjacent field. As we turned in, the tractor passed us. The driver shouted something earthy and rural.

'What a charming man,' said Dermot. 'I hope all your fucking cows melt. I hope your sister marries someone *outside the immediate family*.'

He looked at the college.

'What do they *teach* out here?' he asked. 'Incest?'

'Only one way to find out. Are you coming in, or waiting out here?'

'I've seen *Deliverance*, I'm coming with you. If we split up we're *fucked*. There aren't many cars here.'

There weren't. I counted four, not including my Audi. It was a small building, but even so it must have been all but empty.

'Come on then, let's see what they've got in here.'

Dermot trailed me to reception. It felt as though I'd been seeing a lot of receptionists recently. It seemed to be becoming a theme. Little did I know I'd be seeing more still before much longer. This one was a girl who looked fifteen and bored. She was decked out in black clothes bearing names like Slipknot and Filter and the usual pictures of men with white faces, shouting. She was wearing more eyeliner than Cleopatra and had black hair. She had bare arms with Celtic tattoos, the Celts of course being well known for their office work.

'Hello,' I said. 'We're looking for someone.'

She looked at me with all of the excitement and curiosity of someone seeing a new cattle grid.

'Do you know who's here?' I asked.

'I've not been on long,' she said. 'I don't do the mornings. The girl who does has gone home.'

'Well, is there a register or something?'

'It's not a school,' she said, further communicating her disdain by looking briefly at the ceiling.

133

'Do you have a list of the people who work here? I'm after someone called Betts.'

'What's he do?'

'He's a laboratory assistant.'

'Labs are back there. Don't think anyone's in though.'

'Is it OK if we have a look around?'

'Up to you.'

'Thanks,' I said.

When we'd got far enough away from her, Dermot asked me why I'd thanked her, given her generally unhelpful demeanour and glum manner.

'You should have *twatted* her,' he said. 'You should have *decked* her. So why did you *thank* her?'

'I don't know.'

'Good job I'm here to tell you then. Because you're *middle class*, that's why. You're *brought up* to thank people. You thank them if they tell you to fuck off. You thank them if they steal your *kidneys* and then fuck your dog to death on the *kitchen table*.'

'There's a point to this?'

'The point is, you're *fucked* by being middle class.'

'I'm happy to be middle class. I can settle for getting the good houses and the good jobs. You working class heroes can man the burger vans and building sites and kid yourselves that you're still needed.'

'I'm proud of being working class.'

'Horseshit. You're middle class and embarrassed about it. I'm middle class and resigned to it. At least I'm not pretending to be something I'm not.'

'Truer than you *think*,' said Dermot. 'Here we go, the laboratories.'

I knocked on the door of the first one and went in. It

was empty. It looked the same as the laboratories at school, decades ago. There were the same rows of workbenches with large arching black taps poised over stained sinks, the same quartets of gas taps set at regular intervals, the same stacks of dented tripods. There was a poster of the periodic table on one wall. It looked to have gained a couple of elements since I'd last seen it. That didn't worry me. New elements were never of any use.

Of course, there had been a lot of changes since my schooldays. We'd been allowed to play with all sorts of lethal substances. I remembered our physics teacher letting us play around with mercury. Mercury was fun. You could flick it at other pupils or drink it. I remembered him opening small heavy boxes marked with black and yellow radiation symbols.

'This is giving off gamma rays,' he'd say, informatively. We'd sit around, soaking them up, sneaking looks at the girls' bra straps and paying no attention to him whatsoever.

I had another few thoughts about tumours.

'There's no one in,' said Dermot. 'Well, it's been a *nice day out.*'

'There's another lab,' I said. 'I saw it from the corridor.'

It, too, was abandoned. It was much like the first, but it also had a fume cupboard, if that's what they call them nowadays. It was a little enclosure with an extractor fan so that dangerous fumes would be whisked outside, poisoning the entire village rather than a single room. The number and type of fumes considered dangerous had increased in the last couple of decades. I'd expected that. The substances we were allowed – encouraged, really – to handle in our science classes were now known to be actively nasty. I wondered how much damage I'd incurred.

My cancerous thoughts were growing like the thing itself. I was surely doomed.

'There's no one here,' said Dermot.

'There might be someone in there,' I said. There was a door marked PREP ROOM. 'That's where lab assistants would hang out.'

'Making LSD from *leftovers*,' said Dermot. 'After you. It's your manhunt.'

I knocked on the door, and Betts answered it.

■■■

Without much wanting to, I remembered the experiment. I'd been unable to see Tina and Betts during it. I'd always assumed that Tina was undergoing the same treatment as me, looking into mirrors and being prodded by Betts. I realized that she might not have been. Until Roger had started to ask me about her, I'd never questioned it. Of course she was going through the same thing. I'd brought something out of the sodden Welsh air, something that had broken in and wrecked the room and then . . . and then what? What had it done? Run off again, vanished the same way it had come? Got a job in Eastenders, even then known to be a good home for the ugly and misshapen?

Tina hadn't done anything like that. Tina hadn't produced anything at all. What had she been doing? I'd known that psychology experiments were eight-tenths bluff. She'd told me that, and she'd asked me to take part. Psychology was all double-bluff and double-blind.

Perhaps she'd led me along. Perhaps she'd always led me along. Perhaps she'd been in on something. Perhaps I was her third-year project.

I tried to remember the thing that had come skipping in from the mountains, covering miles in seconds. I'd only seen it in the mirrors, running along. Perhaps it had only been in the mirrors and I'd imagined the rest. Light is a wave or a particle depending on the circumstances, according to quantum physics. Perception affects reality.

My imagination was certainly affecting my reality. It was populating it with video-game offcuts. Betts had been involved in that, or at least in the genesis of it.

He stood in the doorway to the prep room, and I saw that he'd changed a lot. He was thinner, for one thing. And apart from that, he was someone else.

IV

I realized that the lab assistant didn't look much like Betts after all. I'd been expecting to see him and my mind had filled in the rest of the details itself. This was a younger man, with a shaved head with the shadow of black hair under the skin. He looked at the two of us.

'Yes?' he asked.

'We were after someone,' I said. 'We think he came to work here. He was called Betts.'

'You'll mean Josh,' said the assistant. 'He was here for a while, but he left. You have to, really. This place has been closing down since it opened. There aren't many job opportunities here.'

'We noticed you weren't all that crowded,' said Dermot.

'We thought they might be out getting the sheep in from *top field* or something.'

'It's a ridiculous place for a college,' said the assistant. 'I'm Dan,' he said, offering his hand. We took turns shaking it.

'So where is everyone?'

'No one ever turned up. There was a landowner who lived somewhere round here, and he owned this land. Nice work if you can get it. He left his money to the local community, as long as they built a college with some of it.'

He looked around the lab.

'I don't think they wasted much of it on this place. Still, it keeps me in a job.'

'What did Betts do?'

I couldn't get used to Betts having a forename. For some reason, I'd never thought of him with one. And if he had to have one, it should have been a more fitting one than Josh. That didn't suit him at all.

'He got bored,' said Dan. 'I avoid that. I read a lot. We do get students from time to time, too.'

'Where did he go?'

'He went to a pharmaceutical company somewhere. Not one of the majors, some tiny place that does independent research. The sort of independent research that discovers what you pay them to discover. You know what I mean? If a brewery asks them to, and hands over the readies, they find scientific evidence that drinking makes you thin and brilliant. He wanted to get out of college work. He never seemed settled here.'

'You seem settled.'

'You can always sell things to students,' Dan said. 'Especially if you have access to chemicals. LSD from leftovers isn't far off the mark.'

He winked at Dermot.

'I didn't think you'd heard us out there,' said Dermot.

'It pays to keep an ear open. I don't know how they'd take to me knocking out barndance Es.'

'Have you got any samples?' asked Dermot. 'Only reality is *wearing us down*. My friend here is suffering from too much of it. I feel it's my duty as his *guardian* to get him out of it.'

'I do have some homebrewed acid,' said Dan. 'It's not as good as stuff you'd buy. I don't have access to much equipment here.'

He searched through a crowded cupboard, found something, and handed Dermot a few small squares of coloured paper.

'Keep out of reach of children,' said Dan, 'and don't operate any heavy machinery while under the influence. Now, you were after Josh Betts. He went to this little pharmaceutical company called, let me think, it was something to do with Neil Young. Bright Harvest Research Laboratory, that was it. Made me think of Neil Young, anyway. It's a little place near Stourbridge. In the West Midlands.'

'We're from there,' I said. 'Or near there.'

'I thought so,' said Dan. 'It was either that or you had to blow your noses. You should be able to get hold of him there. They don't encourage visitors, though.'

We thanked him and left. Dermot sniffed his newly acquired pieces of paper.

'The wonders of science,' he said, opening his wallet and slipping the little coloured squares inside. 'What's for *lunch*, then?'

'We haven't got anything. You know, I really thought he'd be there. I would have bet on it.'

'All bets are off,' said Dermot. 'As is our man Betts himself.'

There was a silent pause.

'You *can* laugh you know,' said Dermot, huffily stamping off to the car.

V

On the way home, he insisted that we stop for cider.

'These fucking yokels have *real cider*, stuff that stops you feeling your *teeth*. We need to get some. We need to get *as much as we can*.'

'What's wrong with you? You've suddenly turned into Hunter S. Thompson.'

'It's real cider,' he said. 'Come on, we only get *supermarket cider* at home. That's a fucking girl's drink. We need this *backwoods* stuff. Stop at the next place that sells it. It's not like we're buying *crack cocaine*. It's only cider.'

'The stuff in your wallet isn't just cider. That's a class-A drug.'

'I don't bother with the *lower classes* when it comes to drugs. I only do class A. I'm a drugs snob.'

'You're mad enough without drugs.'

'Cheers,' he said. 'Pull over here, they've got a sign up. This is the *very place*.'

Jutting from a bulbous hedge was a hand-written sign advertising cider. A badly drawn arrow apparently pointed at the hedge. As we passed, I saw that there was a stile set into the hedge. Beyond it a muddy path led off into greenery. I pulled over and looked again. There was no sign of a farmhouse.

'Are you sure?' I asked him. 'There isn't anything here.'

'There's a sign,' he said. 'They have cider for sale. If they didn't have *cider* they wouldn't have a *sign*.'

'We could get some from somewhere else. Anywhere else, really. All the farms down here sell it.'

'I want it from this farm,' he said. 'This is the one for me. The next one might be *closed*.'

He'd made his mind up. I knew that it'd probably take longer to dissuade him than to walk to the farm. It couldn't be too far away. We got out of the Audi and I bleeped it shut as we crossed the road. I climbed over the stile and put a foot gingerly onto the ground. It had been muddy not long ago, but had since dried into solid ruts and ridges.

Dermot followed me.

'This is a field,' he said accusingly. 'You've *brought me* into a field.'

'You told me to bring you. You insisted.'

'Well I'm hardly to be trusted, am I?' asked Dermot. 'What are *these*?'

They were buttercups. The field had been left to its own devices. It was full of buttercups, dandelions and thistles nestling in what looked like long grass. The thin trail led across the field, to another stile in another hedge.

'These are flowers,' I said. 'They won't hurt you.'

'You ever heard of *nettles*? Those are flowers and they *fucking hurt*.'

'Come on,' I said, walking ahead of him.

The day was still hot, but it had become hazy. The air felt like a warm flannel. I began to sweat. Hefty bees visited flowers and filled their knees with pollen. Dermot swatted at them, missing them completely. I was sweating; he looked as though he'd been in a shower. His little wild face was dripping, his tight curly hair was plastered to his scalp. I watched him flailing inaccurately at the bees and climbed over the next stile. The path crossed a small stream by way of a bridge made

141

out of two narrow planks. Dermot made his way across it as though it lay over a deep ravine. There were scrubby bushes on either side of the stream. A butterfly flew from a bush and passed me at close range. It was a bright blue, and when it passed me it became invisible for a moment. It was as though it had vanished. It reappeared on its way to Dermot so that he could flap his hands at it, which was his response to all insects.

I realized that it had vanished because it had been a two-dimensional sprite, rather than a polygon figure. It had dimensions in x and y, but not z. No one wastes polygons on background details like butterflies. They're lucky if they get animation, let alone polygons. As it passed me I had been on its plane of origin. My line of sight had matched its z-axis position.

I also realized that it must be another hallucination. Reality is in 3D. Reality doesn't include sprites.

'Dermot,' I said.

'What?'

'Can you see that butterfly?'

'Where?' he asked, looking where I was pointing. He clearly couldn't see it. He squinted.

'Doesn't matter,' I said, as it didn't seem to. It was only a butterfly, after all. It wasn't about to savage us.

The path led up an incline away from the stream and into a little plantation of pine trees, set neatly at the corners of imaginary squares. After we walked a little way through the neat plantation, we saw that there was a house with white-painted walls visible between the trees. The paint obscured any detail, the house looking at that distance like a white space with a red roof. There was a door and two windows.

'Who lives here?' asked Dermot. 'Hansel and fucking *Gretel*?'

The house stood in a regular rectangle of garden. A fat barrel stood by the door. I looked in it, on impulse. There might be something useful in there, I thought. There wasn't. There was only water, which failed to give my reflection.

Dermot knocked on the door. It opened towards us. A man stood there, looking like a farmer from a BBC drama about the eighteenth century. He rolled his large eyes. Like the water, they didn't hold any reflections. Reflections take too much work.

'What can I do for you gents?' he asked. 'Not seen you before.'

His accent was awful, way off the mark. Dermot didn't notice. Behind the man, I could see the dark walls of his hallway stretching back perhaps four feet. After that, they fell into a strange black fog. There were no other details.

'We saw the sign,' said Dermot. 'For cider.'

'I'm not with you,' said the man.

'Can we buy cider here?' I asked.

'I'm not with you,' said the man.

'Do you have cider for sale?'

'I'm not with you,' said the man.

'Do you sell cider?' I asked.

'Of course we do! Never heard a question like it. I'll just get you some.'

He retreated into the hallway, vanishing into the fog after he'd gone a few feet. Dermot was looking nervous.

'What the *buttery fuck* is going on?' he asked.

'You have to ask exactly the right question,' I said. 'There's not much detail here. It's very old-school. You need to ask exactly what it wants you to ask. Otherwise you don't get a response.'

'What?'

143

'This is one of my hallucinations. Look at it. This looks like a scene from a 16-bit adventure game. We're standing in it.'

He shook his head.

'You're the one with the hallucinations, you can't drag me into one with you,' he said. 'I don't drag you into my dreams. I wouldn't fucking *allow* you in my dreams.'

'You're here. You saw this house, it popped up when we were about twenty feet away. That's a terrible draw distance. You saw those pine trees. They weren't just regularly spaced. They were the same tree, lots of times. Lazy coding.'

'It's your lazy fucking *imagination*. You've got me into this mess. So now what are we supposed to do? Jump on fucking mushrooms?'

I didn't have time to reply, as the man returned carrying an absurd flagon. It was large and stone coloured but with a flat texture. CIDER was written on it in a common font. He offered it to us.

'Here we are gents,' he said. 'Cider.' He stood in the doorway, head on one side, expectant.

'Thanks,' said Dermot. He reached out and took the flagon. 'We'll be on our *merry way* then.'

Dermot began to back across the lawn. That too was lazily rendered, apparently only using a small texture map copied several hundred times. I followed Dermot's example, backing away so that I could keep an eye on things. Before we got far, I hit a bad point of view. We caught a bad angle, and I saw a seam open along the junction between the wall and the ceiling of the hall. A neutral white light shone through the gap. The man looked around.

'Bother,' he said, noticing the mistake. He stepped to one side in his agitation. He came to a rest halfway through the door. Not the doorway, the door. One of his shoulders, plus the accompanying arm, were on one side. The rest of him was on the other. Either the door went through the middle of him, or he went through the middle of the door.

'Bother,' he said again. Now that he'd got himself caught in the door he couldn't get back out of it. He began to struggle.

'Bother,' he said, with some vehemence. I began to follow Dermot towards the thin stand of pine trees, or rather pine tree. The door began to shudder on its hinges as the man's struggles became increasingly violent.

Dermot fled down the path towards the small stream. It had gone. On the way there Dermot had crossed the stream as though it had been a ravine. As if to upset him, it had now become one. The stream was suddenly at the bottom of a deep crevice two feet across and thousands of feet deep.

'Now what do we do?' Dermot asked, unnerved.

'Jump over it,' I said. 'Think games.'

'Horseshit.'

'It can't really be there,' I said. 'Think about it. We're imagining it. It wasn't there ten minutes ago, so it can't be there now. It's a little stream, jump over it.'

'*You* fucking jump over it.'

I looked down. A small pebble rolled over the edge and fell cinematically for what felt like minutes. There was a commotion behind us.

'He's got dogs,' said Dermot, looking round to see what was happening. 'Really fucking big ones.'

I closed my eyes and jumped, landing a moment later. I looked round to see what Dermot was doing. He was taking a short run-up. Not far behind him, two enormous black dogs were prowling through the trees, glaring around with the help of glowing red eyes. They hadn't yet seen us, or scented us, or whatever it is that dogs do.

'Go on then boys!' shouted the man, rattling the door against its hinges. 'Tear them up!'

Dermot landed next to me.

'I'd *fucking run* if I was you,' he said.

The dogs halted. They turned towards us, having heard Dermot's voice. Dermot was already heading for the stile. I ran after him. He jumped over it and turned round. I could tell by his face that I was in trouble. Something was very close behind me. The sound of my breath filled my ears, along with the sound of my heartbeat. Neither of them sounded all that stable. Through those sounds I heard the snuffling and panting of the dogs as they closed on me. Dermot closed his eyes. I jumped and felt something snag the leg of my trousers and then I was over the stile and in the field. I landed badly and fell. I lay on the ground and waited for the dogs to pounce.

They didn't. When I looked up they were gone. They didn't belong on this side of the fence. I'd imagined them on the other side. We were back in the real world.

Dermot was white and shaking. He was still holding the flagon, which had made it out of the hallucination.

'That's it,' I said, standing. 'It's finished.'

He looked at the flagon. It was now of the more usual white plastic variety, and it held a cloudy yellowish liquid. He unscrewed the cap and sniffed it.

'Cider,' he said, surprised. 'It's *really* cider.'

He looked at his fingers.

'That Dan sold us some really good shit,' he said. He gave me a look, inviting me to contradict him. I didn't. I knew how difficult it was to deal with my hallucinations. It seemed unfair that Dermot should get caught up in one.

He tramped off across the field.

After that, the journey home was uneventful.

TWELVE

I

When we got to my flat I dialled 1471 on the phone and discovered that Tina had been calling me while I wasn't there. I rang her back and asked what she wanted.

'I just wanted to ask whether you and Dermot would like to come out for tea,' she said. 'The weather reports say it's getting stormy in Wales and we could use some extra bodies around in case we need to get everything upstairs in a hurry.'

I said we'd be there as soon as we could manage it. I didn't feel like going but I couldn't think of an excuse. Perhaps it would do me good to get out. It'd keep me from spending the night moping. Dermot was still hanging around by the door, waiting to see who I was talking to. I told him we had an invitation.

'Well we've had a wasted day so far,' he said. 'Might as well go out for tea. At least she usually puts a good spread on. What did you have the other day?'

'Crab cakes.'

'Didn't know crabs ate cakes, the *crusty little fuckers*. Come on. If we go now we'll be in time for a drink or two. You're driving. You never have a drink when you're driving. You wouldn't fucking *dare*. You won't even have your *mobile phone* switched on while you're driving.'

'I can manage one or two drinks.'

'Is that a bit of *danger* coming to the surface there? Is that a hint of *risk*? Holy mother of Mary the man's turning human.'

We went back out again and got back into the Audi. As we passed Kingswinford for the umpteenth time that day, Dermot asked:

'Are you *sure* you cancelled the milk?'

▌▐

That morning, the sky had been clear. During the day it had turned hazy, and with evening coming on it had turned grey. Enormous dark blue smudges were crawling over the horizon and heading towards us. There were faint grumbles and rumblings from the air. Dermot held onto his flagon of cider as though it contained nitro-glycerine. As we crossed the bridge over the Severn fat raindrops began to speckle the windscreen. The barrage continued as we turned left towards the car park. The sky crackled like a speaker with a loose wire, and what seemed to be most of the water in Christendom fell on the area all at once.

'Looks like *rain*,' said Dermot. 'I may have to wind the window up if this *inclement weather* persists.'

The range of vision closed around the car. I switched on the headlights and managed to gain another few feet of visibility. The windscreen wipers were overwhelmed and thrashed about in the water like swimmers with cramp. I wondered what state the river was in. It tended to get too lively for comfort in wet conditions.

'What's the river look like?' I asked.

'Fucking *wet*,' said Dermot. 'Like everything else.'

I parked as close to the edge of the car park as I could manage. That way we'd only have to run through three hundred yards of drenching downpour. There wasn't anywhere else to park. Not many houses in Bewdley come equipped with garages, as the town was built centuries before the internal combustion engine was invented. The locals park in the streets, along both sides of the road.

'We could wait for it to pass,' I said.

Dermot shook his head.

'It's not *going* to pass,' he said. 'It's going to make a *night of it*. We'll have to run for it. I'll bring the cider, you bring you. On three.'

He counted us out into the weather. By the time I'd beeped the locks shut – all of two seconds – the rain had penetrated through to my underwear. Neither of us had brought coats. It had seemed hot and muggy, and we'd thought that we might be sitting outside drinking Dermot's farmhouse cider. Now, the outside had become waterlogged. The Severn was getting set to burst its banks and make everything wetter. Dermot had turned his shirt collar up, which did him no good at all. He was walking hunched over his cider, in case water got into it and diluted the impurities. Confused ducks wandered past, trying to find the main body of water.

'The *ducks* are drier than we are,' complained Dermot. 'The fucking *river* is drier than we are.'

The sky roared and flashed. We reached the house and

Dermot hammered on the door, hanging on to his cider with one hand. Roger opened it and looked at us.

'What are you two doing here?' he asked, nonplussed.

'Tina asked us round for tea,' I said.

'Well you're out of luck there. Tea's off. But you can help us carry the furniture upstairs, while you're passing. I suspect that was somewhere close to the top of her agenda.'

He let us in.

'Don't bother wiping your shoes,' he said. 'There'll be two feet of water in here by midnight. According to the weather reports it's been like this for most of the afternoon in Wales.'

III

The lower floor was looking empty. The rugs had gone upstairs, along with some of the furniture. Even the amber glow had been taken out of harm's reach. A large, bearded, placid-looking man was helping Tina to get one of the chairs upstairs.

'This is Martin, from next door,' said Roger. 'We've already lugged his stuff to the top floor. Can you two get everything out of the kitchen?'

Dermot and I began to empty the kitchen while Tina and Martin dragged furniture up the narrow winding staircase and Roger stood nearby looking elegant but bemused. He had the air of an Englishman in India as the Raj fell to pieces, locked in place by manners while his wife was savaged in the billiard room. In half an hour, we'd got everything moved to the spare room upstairs. That left the bathroom, the bedroom, and what Roger liked to call 'the secondary living area' free. That was a small upstairs room with a pair of armchairs and a few dark wood cupboards in it, along with a sideboard under the window. Tina had placed candles on all available surfaces.

'I've turned off the gas,' she said. Martin attempted to sneak quietly out, with a shy wave.

'See you then Mart,' shouted Dermot. '*Nice work* with that table.'

He looked around, searching for something.

'Who's got my cider?' he asked. 'We had to walk *miles* for that. You wouldn't fucking *believe* what we had to go through to get that.'

Tina handed him his flagon, which had been sitting under a chair.

'There might not be much for tea,' she said. 'As the cooker's off. And so is the gas, and I'll be switching the electricity off any time now. Would someone like to go for a Chinese?'

'I'll go,' said Dermot. 'I can't get any *wetter*, can I? Mick can help me carry stuff. Will they be open?'

'They're up above the high-tide mark,' said Tina. 'They do a roaring trade when this happens. I'll phone the order through. What do we want?'

There was the usual process of negotiation, making the Northern Ireland peace talks look rushed by comparison. Dermot put in bids for extra portions of rice and all the starters, Tina wanted crispy duck, and Roger tried to find something that no one else had tried before. I asked for anything with noodles and waited for everyone else to sort themselves out. Tina phoned the order through when we eventually settled on it.

'They say it'll be ready in about ten minutes,' she said. 'If you two go and get it, I'll light up some candles and try and get cutlery organized. We've got some up here somewhere.'

'Come on then,' said Dermot. 'Otherwise all of the *candles* will have burned down. Then we'll have to sit in the fucking *dark*.'

We went back out into the weather. The sky had settled on a black and purple motif.

'Looks like someone *beat the shit* out of it,' said Dermot, looking up. 'Serves it fucking right.'

The rain had eased, but the river was already reaching over the pavement with pudgy brown fingers. Lightning flashed in the distance, and a rumble of thunder went running past us, rattling windows in their panes. When we reached it the Chinese was a mass of steam contained by a plate glass window. From the middle of the cloud a smiling woman handed over two huge bags of cartons. I paid.

'I'll pay my share,' said Dermot. 'When I get paid.'

Taking a bag each, we made our third trip along the river in the rain.

IV

Tina had pushed the furniture in Roger's secondary living area back against the walls. She had also spread a tablecloth on the floor. She'd put out plates and cutlery, including a few pairs of chopsticks, and there were glasses. Roger had been to the attic and had brought back a selection of bottles. The flagon of cider that Dermot had somehow managed to bring back from my hallucination stood on one side. No one had tried it while we were out. Most of the candles were lit. I realized that Tina would have the electricity off by now. The river would be up to the level of the front door before much longer.

'Bung all of the cartons down here,' said Tina, indicating

the centre of the cloth. 'We'll just grab whatever we want from there. We'll have to squat. I hope your knees can cope with it.'

She settled down, folding her legs tidily underneath herself. Roger assumed the lotus position. No doubt he'd be using chopsticks, too. Dermot collapsed gracelessly, ending up with one leg sprawled across the cloth and the other somewhere underneath him. I made my way slowly to a squatting position. Computer programming doesn't do much for suppleness or poise. By the time I got myself into a suitable position, Dermot was tearing foil lids from containers and helping himself to large portions of everything.

'Chopsticks,' he said. 'I can *use* those. It's a *knack*.'

He began to spread rice over quite an area. Roger looked on archly. Tina had half a smile, which I didn't trust. To tell the truth, I didn't trust her. At least with Roger you knew what you were getting. He thought that he was better than you, and there was a fair chance that he was right. He didn't so much look down on you as get you to look up to him. He was permanently unruffled. Every time he began to speak, I thought he was about to say, 'of course, dear boy . . .' Dermot was a storm of energy. He looked as though he'd been to a wedding where they'd used fried rice for confetti. Despite that, he also appeared unruffled. I seemed to be the only ruffled person there. I drank another glass of wine. I'd heard rumours that you could sip wine. I'd have to try that one day.

'These are *out of whack*,' Dermot complained, waving the chopsticks. 'They're different lengths.'

He up-ended another couple of cartons onto his plate.

'I don't like prawns,' he said. 'They're like *woodlice*. They've got *legs*. And feelers.'

I felt calmer. Perhaps that was because Roger kept refilling our glasses.

'Here you go,' he'd say. 'A little bit of white in there won't hurt.'

Once we'd finished the meal, Dermot cleared up by bundling everything into a carrier bag and knotting the handles together. He folded the tablecloth unevenly and put the bag on top of it.

'There's some rice down here,' he said. 'Someone's a *messy eater*.'

Tina looked at the carpet.

'Somebody is a spectacularly messy eater,' she said. 'I'll have to get the hoover at that when we have the power back on.'

'When will that be?' I asked.

'Days, probably. The water will come up another few feet tonight, some more tomorrow, then start to go down. The weather reports say a warm front hits Wales tomorrow afternoon. This is all run-off from the mountains, you know.'

As she said *run-off from the mountains* she looked at me. I wasn't happy about that.

'How deep is it now?' I asked.

'Have a look,' said Roger. 'Your guess is as good as mine.'

I went to the landing and looked down. The hall floor had vanished under water. In the darkness it looked heavy and cold. A smell rose from it, of damp and dirt. I knew that was nothing compared to the smell it'd leave when the water receded. I tried to remember how many stairs there were on their staircase. I couldn't decide whether one or two were underwater. If it was two, the water was more than a foot deep already, and the house was a good few feet above the riverbank. It had risen a foot while we'd been watching

Dermot demonstrating the incorrect use of chopsticks. There must be water across half the town. We'd have to wade to the car park.

I hoped the Audi was above the water level.

I wondered how we were going to get back to Dudley.

Tina joined me.

'We're filling up,' she said. 'You're going to have to stay here tonight.'

I shook my head.

'Come on,' she said. 'You can't go out there in this. And you've had about a litre of wine.'

'I can't have,' I said, sounding unpleasantly like a sulky child. 'I haven't had that much.'

'Roger's getting through it tonight,' she said. 'So is Dermot, which isn't surprising. But you've had plenty too. Come on, we're opening that cider next. Where did you get it from?'

I didn't know. It had come out of my imagination.

'A farm,' I told her.

'Rough cider,' she said. 'It's like being a student again. What's bothering you?'

'Nothing.'

She set her head at an angle and looked quizzical, but when she didn't get a response she shrugged and went back to the others. I looked down at the water for a little longer, the river imposing its will on the building. It had imposed itself into the usual world, like the cider that we were all about to drink.

I went in and drank some. It wasn't as though I had any other choices.

v

It had a flavour somewhere between apples and surgical spirit, and it was real enough. It had flakes floating in it. It might well have had twigs in it. After Roger's wines it tasted very sweet.

I was already drunk, but so wound up about being in the house that I didn't feel it. Dermot, on the other hand, was visibly plastered. This was something new. He could outdrink me, and I had the feeling that he could out-drink anyone. He was slurring. Drunk, he became more like a squirrel than ever, all bright eyes and sharp movements.

'Why not *write off* the bottom floor?' he asked. 'Just live up here, and *convert* the loft.'

'The wine's in the loft,' said Roger, looking pained.

'Move it *downstairs*. Above the water level. Then that's a *cellar*, this is the *first floor*, put the bedrooms *in the loft*. That's easier than carrying everything up and down the stairs, surely.'

'We like the exercise,' said Roger. 'Anyway, you can't live here while it's flooded.'

'Some people do,' said Tina.

'Yes they do,' said Roger. 'They stay here with no power, no heating, and no running water.'

'There's all the running water you could want,' said Dermot. 'Your living room is *full* of the fucking stuff.'

'You can't drink it,' said Roger. 'It's cloudier than this cider, which is saying something. Where did you get it from?'

'A farm,' said Tina.

'Oh yes,' said Dermot, 'a *farm*. Nothing strange about that, except that it wasn't real.'

156

Tina and Roger ignored him.

'I mean it,' he said, now in the stage of drunkenness where it becomes important to explain exactly what you're talking about to everyone unfortunate enough to be trapped with you. 'It's a fact. We went through this field and then we were in one of his fucking *visions*. I was there too. It wasn't a real house. It wasn't a real farmer, either, and we got this *cider* and had to run off. From dogs. Across this chasm that was a *stream* before. We got the cider there.'

'Are you telling me,' asked Roger carefully, 'that you saw one of Mick's hallucinations? You could actually see it?'

'Saw it? I was fucking standing in it. I had to *run* out of it. He set the dogs on me.'

'Mick did?'

'The *farmer* did. The dogs weren't real either. They were all *teeth and eyes*.'

'But you saw all of this?'

'Bet your fucking boots.'

Roger looked at Tina. Both of them looked at me.

'It's getting worse,' Roger told me. 'You're getting worse. If you can affect him, you might affect the rest of us.'

'Could it have been a real farm?' asked Tina. 'Could it have been real and you just put a hallucination over it? That'd explain the cider.'

'It wouldn't explain how he got Dermot into it,' said Roger.

'We had some acid with us,' said Dermot, now apparently happily settled into the drunken confessions stage. 'I *might* have had some. I had it on my fingers and I might have had a go on them. I might have been a bit *trippy*.'

'Acid?' said Roger. 'Is that normal for a day out?'

'It is for me,' said Dermot. 'I can take *anything*.'

157

He looked as though he'd taken everything. The bright look in his eyes had given way to a dull one. He was pale and had started to do the 'gradual lean followed by a sudden jump' routine. I was sure he was going to be sick soon.

The four of us would be sharing the bathroom, I realized. Dermot and I would be sharing a room, along with Dermot's excess rice.

I tuned back into the room. Dermot had fallen silent. I could see that Tina had been reassured by Dermot's class-A substances story. Roger looked less than convinced, but wasn't about to follow it up. That would have suggested that he might not be entirely composed.

There was some stilted conversation about the river, and how long the flood might last, and then Dermot announced his intention to be sick and left the room.

He was sick from the landing into the river water. Then he came back and lay down and started to snore.

'Can you manage in here?' asked Roger. 'Only we've got nowhere else to put you.'

I looked at Dermot. He released a squeaky fart and grunted happily. I nodded.

At least the night couldn't get any worse.

VI

After Tina and Roger had gone to bed, I brushed my teeth using my finger and some of their toothpaste, had a quick wash, and lay on the floor. Roger had told me that we'd have as much water as was in the main tank, which should last until morning if we didn't waste it. It was cold, of course. There was no heating. Tina had provided me with a selection of cushions, and I used all of them to make myself a nest.

It was almost a quiet night. There was no traffic, because the road was underwater. There were no people outside for the same reason. The river didn't make much noise, even after it had made its way into the houses. Tina and Roger didn't make a sound.

It would have been quiet if it hadn't been for Dermot. I'd never been with him while he was sleeping, and I had never known anyone who could make so much noise without being awake. He didn't merely snore, he also muttered incomprehensibly and sometimes shouted. He continued to fart loudly and scratch furiously even when unconscious. I settled myself into my nest of cushions and tried to make the best of it. I didn't think I'd be able to sleep at all, but the drink did the trick.

I fell into a light sleep riddled with pointless dreams. On the verge of understanding them, I was woken up by Dermot. He was stumbling about, looking for something, making no more noise than a bulldozer going through a row of greenhouses. I was in that gooey stage of wakefulness, where sleep is obviously the best option but is no longer available.

'What are you doing?' I asked.

'I need a *drink*,' he said. 'I'm not going to be able to *sleep* without a drink. They must have *something* in one of these cupboards. If I could see the fucking things that'd help. Can I put the lights on?'

'There's no electricity. That's why it's dark.'

'Light me a fucking candle then.'

I remembered Tina putting a lighter on the sideboard. It was still there, and I used it to light a couple of candles. Dermot immediately began to ransack the cupboards.

'Don't they drink anything except wine?' he complained. 'Where is it?'

He picked something up.

'Who's *she*?' he asked. He'd found a photograph in a frame. It was a snapshot of the beach at Borth, on a bright day. The tide was out, and there were a lot of people on the beach. Some kites, caught suspended, showed that the usual gale was blowing.

In the foreground, there were three people, arms linked, laughing. I was the middle one of the three. On my left was Tina. The photo must have been taken while we were both at college. Tina was still in her quasi-goth clothes, and I was thinner, not yet larded out by spending all day sitting at my keyboard.

On the other side of me, her arm linked with mine, was a girl I didn't know.

That is, I didn't know her name. I didn't know where she was from or what she did. But I did know her; I knew her face. I'd seen it in a strange waking dream about a car crash, a couple of days ago. A small red car, overturned on a quiet road. The sound of the sea, and the dead girl in the car. This girl.

'I don't know,' I said.

'Well she knows you,' said Dermot. 'She's *holding on* to you.'

'Must have been someone who came down for the weekend. A friend of someone.'

'So you used to have girls *on tap* then? Shame that stopped. Wonder why they keep it in a *cupboard*?'

'You'd better put it back. They'll know you've been snooping.'

I didn't want them to know we'd seen anything. Something

160

had happened in Borth, and Tina knew something about it. Dermot put the picture away and shut the door on it, as though it would be that simple. As though you could just shut the door on the past. But doors don't keep it away. Nothing does. It comes with you. When you get wherever you're going, it's already there.

Dermot found my nest, and took half of the cushions from it. He fashioned a nest of his own.

'Sleepy,' he said. In ten minutes he was back to his symphony of snores and scratches. I didn't think I'd sleep, but I must have done. The next thing I knew it was morning, and the curtains could barely keep the daylight outside.

THIRTEEN

I

Dermot woke up at about eight in the morning.

'What's for breakfast?' he asked shakily.

'Water,' I said.

After he'd spent quite a while in the bathroom, he returned. He looked as though he'd recently been dredged from the river. His skin was slack and white, as though it might slough off under minor pressure. His voice was muddy. His eyes were sunken. His hands shook.

'Bit of a hangover,' he said. 'Mother of God.'

He opened the curtains and looked at the view. I joined him. A significant portion of the view was underwater. The sky was grey and clear, and the river was all over the place. The row of houses on the other side of the river was in the river. There were cars parked along the side of the road beyond those houses, and already there were people standing looking at the flood. The sure way to attract English people is to have a disaster. Sadly, they'd have to make do with damaged property today, but with any luck there might be a drowning later on. The top of the arched bridge was clear of the water,

162

but at either end it fell into the flood. The news crews would turn up later on and get a child or two to sit forlornly in a leaky coracle.

'How are we going to get home?' asked Dermot, too ill to put any emphasis on anything.

'Drive up to the forest road and come back down the bypass. The tricky bit is going to be getting to the car.'

Dermot nodded and picked up the stub of a candle. It was about the same colour and texture as his face.

'Did we have all that cider?' he asked. 'Don't answer that. If we didn't, I've got fucking malaria.'

Tina and Roger must have heard us talking, because sounds of activity began to come from their room. Roger came out, dressed in a dressing gown. He looked as though he'd already showered, and had the air of a man who might sit thoughtfully smoking a pipe and considering plans for a spiffing new cantilever bridge.

'Morning,' he said. 'How's the ambient water level?'

Tina struggled out of the bedroom, looking extremely tousled. She nodded vaguely in greeting and shut herself in the bathroom. Dermot looked as though he wished he'd stayed in there.

'Nice evening,' he said. 'You did well with the wine there, Roger.'

Roger nodded, managing to get his tiredness to look like aloofness. He joined us at the window and we looked at the river. It was difficult to miss it.

'We'll be off about ten,' he said. 'We have a holiday cottage in Wales. We go there, watch the rain, and after it stops we come back. I take it you two will be off back to Dudley?'

'We'll go round the bypass,' I said.

'After breakfast,' said Dermot, looking as though consumption of any foodstuff would bring on projectile vomiting.

'We haven't got anything,' said Roger. 'The kitchen has a lake in it.'

'We can stop and get something on the way,' I said. 'There's a Little Chef in Oldbury.'

Dermot brightened slightly.

'You paying?' he asked, a touch of his usual chirpiness in his voice. 'I'll have a full breakfast.'

'We have to get there,' I said. 'There's this flood to walk through first.'

'Floods don't worry me,' he said. 'I've been in worse floods than this.'

'There'll be ducks,' I said.

He looked at me.

'You can go first,' he said.

■ ■

After we'd washed as well as we could, we went downstairs. Tina and Roger waved us off from the landing. I wondered how they were going to get away. Perhaps Roger would charter a launch.

I reached the last step above water level and stood on it. The river water looked brown and sluggish, and it had an earthy smell. We'd considered going barefoot until we thought of how many sharp objects might be hidden underwater. Roger had loaned us each a pair of his old shoes. They were better than my new shoes, except that they were a size too large. We were carrying our own shoes, plus borrowed socks, again courtesy of Roger. That way we'd have dry feet on the way home. I put Roger's shoe over the water, took a deep breath, and let my foot plunge down to the next step.

The water was cold and felt gritty. It filled my borrowed shoe and lapped at my ankle. I took another step, and another. The water in their front room was a foot and a half deep. It was in my socks, in my shoes, halfway up my legs. I began to wade to the front door, and heard Dermot splash down the stairs behind me.

'*Fucking* hell,' he said.

The front door opened too easily. I'd expected that it would need a lot of force to move, due to the added pressure of the water, and I nearly fell backwards. I waded into the street. Once Dermot was out we shouted goodbye to Tina and Roger and shut the door. Outside, the river water seemed to be heading sluggishly downstream. Beneath the surface, stronger currents tugged at me. The entire scene looked wrong, the houses with their lower reaches underwater, the river suddenly a mile wide, the groups of tourists as close to the opposite side as they could get with dry feet. Another reality had burst its banks and imposed itself over the usual one. It was hauling at our feet, wanting to pull us in.

I thought about my hallucinations. Perhaps they were getting stronger. Dermot had got caught up in the last one. Perhaps I had another reality inside me, and it was ready to burst its banks. Perhaps in Borth, what had come from the mountains hadn't come from the mountains after all.

Perhaps it had come from me.

It wasn't just that strange, goblin-like figure. There was also the girl in the photograph, and in my memory of a car crash. Something had happened to her, and Roger and Tina had a picture of her squirreled away. Dermot had found it accidentally, so he said.

I didn't know whether to trust any of them. I didn't know whether to trust myself.

I waded to the car through my doubts and the river. The Audi was parked high in the car park, which sloped down to the river's edge when the river's edge was where it belonged. The water had got as high as the wheel rims. About two inches of grubby water had got inside. I got in and put my own shoes on, leaving Roger's on the back seat. Cleaning the car wouldn't do the trick. The inside would smell of stagnant water for ever. I waited for Dermot to get in and then we set off.

I bought him some breakfast on the way home. When we got back to Dudley I said I had things to do, and he took the hint. He drove off in his Meriden 733t, attracting the sort of admiring looks that my Audi never managed.

III

I spent most of the rest of the weekend on the Net trying to find details about Bright Harvest Research Laboratory. It was based in a building in a small compound on the edge of Stourbridge town, and it didn't encourage visitors. It was involved in both GM crop work and animal experimentation, and was thus surrounded by an ongoing demonstration. Security was high and details were minimal. None of the staff had their names on the Net or anywhere else, for fear of having their houses firebombed. It took me the best part of a day to find that much information. I tried calling but there was only a recorded message telling me that no one was available for comment.

I was trying not to think about the photograph. I had

enough problems, what with video-game characters trying to kill me. Being an unknowing pawn in a conspiracy involving a dead girl was more than I could cope with, so I did my best to ignore it. My mother used to tell me that if I ignored bullies, they'd leave me alone. It didn't work for bullying thoughts either, as it happened.

I searched for the company's website. There was a blank title page, with the company logo at the top and entry boxes for a user-id and password. I knew enough about systems to know that if I tried random passwords they would scan my machine and get my details.

That would mean a visit from the constabulary. Given the government's preference for businesses over humans, it might mean an investigation by the Secret Service. I didn't have any secrets, but I didn't want to be investigated. There was clearly no way I was going to be able to contact Bright Harvest directly. No one there wanted anything to do with anyone. I'd need to blag my way in, and I couldn't do blagging. I thought about the team at work. Some of them should be able to at least get through the website security. Perhaps there would be a staff list, or a payroll file with the staff names, that we could get to.

I checked the telephone book for Bettses. There were too many for me to call each one and besides, Betts might not live in the area. People commuted to the West Midlands to work, and then got out as quickly as possible at 5 pm, pausing only to admire the artworks on the islands.

I'd have to enlist the hackers at work. They had always claimed that they could get into anything. They couldn't get into those pubs with dress codes, but they should be able to crack a password without much trouble.

IV

On Monday morning I got to work early. I was a man with a mission. I was hoping to catch Tim or Andy before Clive turned up. Clive would know how to hack into a site. The trouble was that he'd want to talk me through the theory of his methods. He'd probably want to draw process flow charts for them on the office flipchart. It'd be mid-afternoon before he got started. As it happened, only Tracy was in. She was drinking tea and reading the TV guide. She drank a lot of tea. Her blood must have been three-tenths tannic acid. She also liked to read TV guides. She read all of the normal ones, and also the ones that tell you what happens in Eastenders, Brookside, Hollyoaks et al next week so that you don't have to waste any time actually watching the programmes.

I said hello to her and asked her how she was, and after a ten-minute rundown on the health of all of the members of her family – plus pets – I sat at my desk.

It was in a mess. I had data-flow diagrams and post-it notes all over the place. Empty pens lay about, along with a pencil with a broken lead. There were a number of styrofoam drinks containers. Some were empty, a couple held a layer of coffee, and one had a layer of thick green fur growing over its interior. This was the normal state of my desk. However, something wasn't right. It was my mess, but it wasn't quite where I'd left it. Someone had been sitting at my desk. It must have been on Friday, while I'd been out on my fruitless search for Betts. I switched on my PC. Nothing looked different. I checked the amendment dates on the Boris files.

He'd been recompiled on Friday. Someone had been at Boris.

I double-clicked the executable to start him up.

'Good morning,' he said. Out loud, through the speakers. A little window popped up on the screen, with a text box.

'Hello,' I typed.

'Who is this?' Boris asked. I typed my name.

'I'm sorry, I didn't follow that,' he said.

I clicked him off. His window vanished, leaving a rectangular afterimage floating in the middle of the monitor.

Clive must have been checking out my coding. I checked out the amendments. He'd got the voice working by getting the Boris application to call a freeware text-recognition program, and that was outputting to the speakers via the soundcard. He'd added in a few other little fixes, mostly code optimization from what I could see. He'd also added in version numbers and a compilation history. Tidying up work. I'd have done that after I got the application working. Or I wouldn't have done it at all.

Boris was still an idiot. Clive hadn't done any work on the AI routines. He'd also used a generic voice. I'd imagined Boris to be cross and English, with a touch of the theatrical. I'd imagined Tom Baker in a bad mood. Still, I could replace the voice. Clive had saved me a lot of time by getting the speech working at all.

I was still annoyed. Boris had been my pet project. I didn't want anyone else involved. I could restore him from Thursday's backup, but that would lose the text-recognition. Even worse, Clive would know what I'd done. He'd be upset, and he was my boss. There weren't as many programming jobs around as there had been a year ago, especially in the West Midlands. You had to commute to Birmingham, and companies there used contractors for a lot of their work. I could do contracting work, but I didn't like it. The pay was better but there was no guarantee you'd have a job at the end of the week.

I wanted guarantees. I had enough uncertainty in my life.

I checked out my PC. Clive hadn't been at anything else.

Tim turned up just before 9 am. He was a worried looking man, with an eyelid that twitched. He had sandy hair and went in for tweedy jackets, making him look ten years older than he was.

I asked him what he knew about cracking passwords. He chewed his thumbnail and did some semaphore with the twitchy eyelid.

'Depends where it is,' he said. 'If it's on a home PC running any version of Windows, there'll be a cracker program on the Net that'll get you in no trouble. The ones out there now just do the work for you. To get into a server, you'd need something a bit better. Where is this password?'

'On a web page.'

'Shouldn't be difficult. Ah,' he said, sounding relieved. 'Here's Andy. He's the man for this sort of thing.'

Tim didn't much enjoy social interaction. I let him get back to his desk and asked Andy the same questions. Andy was young and sharp, and dressed in black because that's how hackers dressed in the sorts of books which featured hackers in lead roles. He had his hair in a grade-two cut, and had Celtic tattoos on his wrists. He had a very quiet, but very serious, voice.

'You can get into anything,' he said. 'Is it a secure site?'

I told him about Bright Harvest.

'Very serious,' he said. 'They'll be afraid of people getting their home addresses or grabbing the company secrets. That's going to need some special attention. We're still waiting for Clive to bring in that job, aren't we?'

I nodded.

'I'll see what I can get. You just want the employee list?'

'The addresses would help.' They would. If I had Betts' address I wouldn't need to go to Bright Harvest at all. I could find him at home.

'I'll have a go,' said Andy. 'Shouldn't take more than a couple of hours.'

V

He came back to me just before lunchtime.

'I've got half of it,' he said. 'I have their employee list, but I can't get at anything else. They're keeping almost everything else secure. Which means really secure, otherwise I'd have cracked it. And this only has the surname and initials.'

He gave me a printout. I had a quick look and saw Betts, J among the other names.

'How did you get in there?' I asked.

'I can't tell you that,' he said. 'You stick with the apps, I'll do the black-hat stuff. I take it this is a black-hat operation?'

'This is a grey area.'

'Grey-hat operation, then. They've got some heavy-duty security there, I'll give them that.'

He went back to his desk, cheered up by his own cleverness. I looked at the list again. So, Betts was working at Bright Harvest as Dan had said. That meant that things were going to get more difficult. I'd have to get in there to talk to him.

Or would I? He didn't live there. If I was outside when he left, I'd be able to talk to him then. I could see him on his way home.

I went back to my desk, cheered up by my own cleverness. Clive arrived a little later and asked for our attention.

'We have a contract,' he said. 'I'll email you the details, but this is a big one. We'll need to put in a lot of work to get it done, and I'll probably be looking at hiring a few extra staff. Mick, I'll need you to put a specification together based on their specification, fill in the gaps where their know-how doesn't quite know how. I'd like that later this week, feel free to take it home and work on it if it's too distracting here. You two can start thinking about the database while he's doing that, you can probably have the core tables done before he's got the specification finished. Just don't tell anyone I said so.'

We all did a the-boss-made-a-joke laugh. Programmers were notoriously bad at documenting what they were up to. Clive often tried to get us to put comments in our code. We seldom got round to it.

I thought about what he'd said. Working from home would give me an opportunity to go to Bright Harvest and try to track down Betts.

I told Clive I'd put in a day at home, and then come in and finish the work off on Wednesday. There wouldn't be any problem with that, he said.

Things were moving forward at last.

FOURTEEN

I

The next day, I stayed at home and went through the documentation for Clive's new project and started to convert it into something we could work from. A least, that's what I tried to do. I couldn't concentrate on the work. I was too busy thinking about Betts. Would he want to talk to me? Did I really want to talk to him?

What if he was working strange shifts? In a laboratory they might not work nine-to-five hours. Perhaps they worked all night. Perhaps they offset their working hours to avoid the protestors.

I struggled to keep my mind on my work. I turned a page and caught five words from the middle of a sentence:

in case of fatal crashes

That stopped me thinking about Betts. I saw a small red car, upturned and crumpled. The girl in the car had died, bleeding red onto the red paint, listening to the sea falling against the land. There was a photograph of her hidden in a cupboard at Roger and Tina's house. I hadn't heard from either of them since Saturday morning. If the flood hadn't forced us to stay,

I would never have seen that picture. If Dermot hadn't taken it from the cupboard –

That didn't help. I had never been sure of Dermot, at some level. To tell the truth I was afraid not to be his friend. I certainly didn't want him as an enemy. I thought of him holding my elbow and aiming me at the mirror in the grimy toilet of a Birmingham club, the day we first met. I thought of his evil looks, and I thought of something running from the Welsh mountains.

The telephone rang. I answered it, expecting it to be Clive checking on my progress.

'Hello?' I said.

'Hello there,' said Roger. 'Haven't got long, Tina's just popped upstairs. The mobiles don't get a signal out here. There's not much room here, either, but I understand the water's down now. Should be back home by the end of the week. Still, no time for that. You have to bear this in mind. Your hallucinations are more than they seem to be. They're getting to be real, aren't they? They're getting out of you. You're able to do that. Years ago, you suddenly bumped your head on your stress limit, and Tina tried to snap you out of it with that mirror business. But it didn't snap you out of it, it just snapped you. You manifested the contents of your head into the world. You're still doing it. Your hallucinations are real. They can hurt you. They can hurt the rest of us.'

There was extra noise on the other end of the line, Tina calling faintly. He shouted something back to her, and then came back to me.

'That's all I can tell you,' he said. 'You need to do the rest yourself. They're right. Find Betts, get it out of your head. Before it gets out by itself. She's back.'

The line went dead. 1471 didn't give me a number. Roger

had sounded composed, even while he was giving me his strange warning. He should have been working for the Secret Service, if he wasn't already.

Perhaps he was. I had no idea what he did for a living.

I couldn't stay in. I looked at the documentation and found the phrase that had thrown me. The full sentence read:

The database will be backed up in case of fatal crashes or other problems.

Fatal crashes and other problems, I thought. That seemed to sum everything up.

I got my coat and set out to see what was happening at Bright Harvest Research Laboratory.

■■

This is what Les Herbie had to say about animal experimentation:

I have a confession. I like animals. This is going to upset some of you. You think I don't like anything.

Let's get it straight. I don't like it here. I don't like your houses. I don't like your mothers and I don't like you.

I do like animals. A lot of them are edible. A lot of the others will carry you about. You can extract perfumes from them. You can get glue out of them.

You can try out gene splicing on them. You can clone them.

I like all of this. Animals are good sports. You can do anything to them and they'll come back and be your friend again.

Sometimes I get headaches. Reading your mail, I get headaches. I get ones that send me cross-eyed. I hold my head and shout. I take tablets and my headache goes.

I know they work because after I take them I have less headache. My eyes straighten out.

I know they're safe to take because they were tested on animals. I like animals. They take a lot of my risks for me.

It isn't a problem. We know what the food chain looks like. We're way up there at the top. Everything else is lower down. We can take them all out. That's our right. That's what we're there for. That's what they're there for.

We're supposed to eat them. We're better than them.

We got the opposable thumbs. We got the language.

That warbling whales do is not a language. That chirruping dolphins do is nothing. Put a million monkeys in a room with a million typewriters and you'd get a million broken typewriters.

They're there to make our lives easier. They're there to make our lives better. They're there to be eaten.

Let's stop pretending anything else.

That one really got the letters coming in.

III

The people outside Bright Harvest would have lynched Les Herbie on sight, if only they knew what he looked like. There was a small gathering outside the laboratory. It was a quiet and colourful gathering, but still small. Crusties with dreads hoisted banners with slogans. A few women were concerned enough about the lab to bring their children to stand in a demonstration rather than send them to school. The high moral ground seemed to have a few ditches in it. The slogans had been around since the sixties and hadn't aged well.

Bright Harvest was sited in its own grounds just outside Stourbridge. It was close to a business park but separate from it. A high red-brick wall surrounded the building and its car park. On top of the wall, curls of evil razor wire sparkled in the sunlight. Cameras on posts watched the demonstration from inside the walls. The posts had clusters of spines encircling them at intervals.

Some slogans had made their way onto the walls. ANIMAL MURDER, one said. END ANIMAL TORTURE NOW, said another. The protesters looked half asleep, as though they'd stopped considering what they were doing. The outrage was so well rehearsed that they didn't need any emotional involvement. They could do it in their sleep.

I was still in the Audi. If I got out, I'd be caught up in the demonstration. They wouldn't recognize me as one of their own. They'd want to know what I was doing there. I had the windows open because it was a warm day, and that was as close to the outside world as I was getting. I was both bored and agitated, which wasn't helping. All I could see of Bright Harvest was the second storey, which was square and undecorated, with mirrored windows.

I was very unhappy about the mirrored windows. If I could alter reality using a few mirrors in an upstairs room in a Welsh college, then a building covered in mirrors was just asking for trouble.

Of course, that was assuming that Roger was right. He thought that I'd manifested something, brought it out of my imagination and into the world. Why had it been a strange-looking mountain man? I'd had a lot of dreams when I was adolescent. I could have done with one or two of those becoming reality. I'd have died of exertion, or possibly dehydration, but it would have been a good way to go. But no, the first thing my imagination spewed into the world was a Welsh hobgoblin.

My train of thought was derailed by a commotion. The demonstrators had become louder and more agitated. The banners were heaved upright, and they began to shout the slogans written on them.

There was a very large, extremely solid gate halfway along the length of the front wall. It was of blank metal, topped with the ubiquitous razor wire. It was opening.

The demonstrators gathered around it.

A car emerged at speed. All of its windows were heavily tinted. Either it was a rap band on the way to the studio, or Bright Harvest employees were very shy. The demonstrators got a few kicks in as the car passed them, and shouted some unlikely accusations. A pair of enormous security guards stood inside the gate keeping an eye on things as it rumbled closed. The demonstrators calmed down. One of them opened a flask and began filling mugs with what looked like coffee.

I was going to have trouble talking to Betts if that was the standard method of leaving work. I wouldn't be able to see him, and by the time I got the Audi started he'd be on the ring road. It was barely possible to drive around Stourbridge ring road without colliding with another vehicle under normal circumstances. It'd be impossible for me to follow another car. I hadn't even seen the driver, I realized. For all I knew that may have been Betts. Besides, even if I did manage to follow him, what would he think? He'd see someone chasing him from outside Bright Harvest and he'd call the police, if not the army. If I stood close to the gate every time it opened, there was a chance he'd see me and remember me. There was also a chance that someone would run over me at high speed, if the security guards didn't fling me out of the way first.

In a video game, I could have switched to sniper mode, clipped the left guard, run to his body and grabbed his weapons, taken out the second guard and pressed the huge square button marked CAMERA OFF SWITCH.

In real life, I didn't have sniper mode. The security guards weren't likely to be armed. There was unlikely to be a huge square button that turned all of the cameras off. I couldn't get inside, and they didn't answer the telephone. I could try firing emails at their likely addresses – j.betts@brightharvest.co.uk – but they'd be unlikely to get through. They'd have that covered. I'd need to use external help.

I'd need to use Dermot.

I went home, leaving the demonstrators to their fun.

IV

Once I was back at home I gave Clive's documentation another try. It was no good, my attention was in two other places. Part of it was thinking about Betts, and all that he represented. Another part of it was thinking about the girl in the photograph, with her arm linked with mine. Tina looked like she was spare, on that picture. Tina looked like a gooseberry. I didn't remember the girl, but there were other things I didn't remember as well. I'd lost six months, if not more. I had no clear recollection of anything that happened at Borth before I met Tina in the bar.

She'd spoken as though she already knew me. According to the photograph, she did. Along with her friend, the girl with no name. I'd known the pair of them and one of them had died. Then I'd forgotten all about the pair of them.

There must be some sort of report of the crash, in newspapers somewhere. There were archived articles on the Net.

It was possible that it was all connected, the girl and Betts, the whole business of the mirrors and the missing memory.

It was more than possible, it was all but certain. Tina belonged to both puzzles, along with Borth. I couldn't focus on the problem. It was too close in some places and too far away in others. Every time I made sense of any one part of it, all of the other parts became indistinct.

I couldn't concentrate on anything else. I was like an old version of Windows, everything I loaded into memory stopped something else from running.

I unplugged the phone and connected my PC to the socket. I double-clicked my way onto the Net. I began trying the combinations of words you try when you start to look for anything. CAR+CRASH got six million matching results. CAR+CRASH+BORTH got none. SEASIDE+TOWN+TRAGEDY hauled back thousands. I told it not to tell me about anything outside the British Isles. It still brought back huge lists.

As with all Net searches, everything after the ninth item was porn. Pop-ups popped up. Adverts posing as puzzles wanted me to click here.

Nothing useful turned up. There didn't seem to be such a thing as the *Borth Gazette*. It wasn't as though there were a lot of pretty girls in that area. Surely someone must have noticed one dying.

I tried searches based on Aberystwyth. That was the closest place of any size. I found local newspaper archives for the local newspapers and used their search engines.

I found a story. It was only a paragraph long, with a grainy black-and-white photograph. The photograph was of a familiar small car. In the photograph it was grey, not red. It still looked red to me, though. In the photograph, as in my dream, it was upside down. The photograph was too lo-rez to make out what was inside the car. Whatever it was, it was wrecked. It was smashed. It looked like patches of blackness.

The car had been found on the road between Borth College and Borth. The driver – a woman, yet to be named – was dead when found. With any luck she'd died when the car overturned. It wouldn't have been any fun being alive in there. She'd died not far from the sea. There was no sign of foul play. She'd lost control of the car and it had skidded sideways into a tree and the impact had been enough to upset the laws of physics. Judging by the skid-marks, and the distance the car had gone without its wheels touching the road, it had been doing in the region of forty miles an hour. Not all that fast, really. Or much too fast, looking at what had happened.

I remembered that car, all of a sudden. It looked small from the outside. It was small inside, too. In the passenger seat it felt as though you were on a motorcycle. The engine noise came in through the flimsy bodywork. Every bump in the road rattled the chassis. At forty miles an hour it felt like you were doing eighty. At fifty it began to shake and hiccup. We never got it to go any faster. It was a Fiat Panda, painted an uneven red by the previous owner. It infuriated other drivers. They would come up to the rear bumper and wait to go flying past us.

She is looking in the rear-view mirror, in this memory. She's such a pretty thing, cropped blonde hair and a smile with a corner out of place because she isn't really smiling. She's watching the cars stuck behind our slow Panda.

The memory stopped.

She was real, then. It didn't help. The more information

I got, the worse off I seemed to be. What had we *done* to her? There were no suspicious circumstances, according to the report. She was just an unnamed person who'd died doing forty in a car that would have fallen apart if it ever got to sixty miles an hour.

Had we cut the brake cables or whatever it was you did to brakes? I knew we'd done something. I'd been responsible for her dying. I could feel it.

I needed to know what had happened to her. Betts could wait. This was something worse.

I needed to know what the autopsy had found.

The hackers at work were going to be busy again.

V

I got to work late the next day. I hadn't been able to sleep all night, instead lying awake until the sky lightened. Then, with morning on the way, I fell asleep and slept through the alarm.

I arrived at work dazed and not properly shaved. Everyone was in. I logged in and fired up Boris. I couldn't concentrate on the documentation, it belonged to a world I could no longer connect to.

When Clive went to get himself some lunch, I asked Andy if he could get at police records.

'Easy. They trust their techies, so there are always back doors. What are you after?'

'An autopsy report. I knew a girl who died in Wales and we never found out what happened to her.'

'What was her name?'

'I can't remember.'

182

He looked at me. No doubt he thought I was involved in a conspiracy theory. He was big on conspiracy theories, as many hackers are. This was probably the first time he'd been right about one.

'Right,' he said. 'Dead girl, no name.'

I was going up in his estimation.

'Where did it happen?'

I told him what I knew.

'Ten minutes,' he said. 'Do you want pictures? If there are any? Some forces scan them.'

I wanted them. I went further up in his estimation. All I needed to do now was break into a strange underground base run by a secret government agency and he'd more than likely marry me.

I left him to it and went back to Boris. He was getting to be slightly less stupid. His brain was a four-dimensional array of no fixed size. I couldn't think of a simpler way to get him working. I visualized it as a cube made up of thousands of smaller cubes. That got us to three dimensions. Then, each sub-cube contained information, words or numbers indicating conversation threads or his prevailing mood. Each cell was linked to the six sharing sides with it. So a change in the contents of a single cell could reshape the whole thing, cascading through to other regions. Boris parsed input for structure. He still couldn't cope with complex sentences. His ideal conversational partner would have been one of Clint Eastwood's early spaghetti western heroes. He didn't get jokes at all. He was entirely nonplussed by irony.

I noodled about with his input routines until Andy sidled over and dropped a printout on my keyboard.

'That's all there is,' he said. 'Just the basic routine stuff, apparently. There weren't any pictures. Maybe they don't have scanners in Wales.'

I thanked him, and waited until he'd gone before I read the report.

That didn't help, either. It just told me this:

She died a short time after the crash. Internal injuries – l. lung punctured, m. frac. ribs, a long list of other breakages – were responsible. Her systems went offline one at a time. The state of the injuries suggested to the coroner that she hadn't struggled, and so hadn't been in any great distress. Other than that caused by being upside down and bleeding to death. She may have been unconscious. That wasn't absolutely certain. She was definitely, absolutely, for sure pregnant. Dead and pregnant.

Her name was Patricia Johanna Newton, according to the report.

I'd known her as Trish Newton.

VI

I asked Clive whether I could work from home on Friday. Bright Harvest and Betts could wait until then. He said it would be fine, as long as I got the documentation done.

'We need this contract,' he said. 'This could get our name established.'

I'd established a name: Trish Newton.

When I got home, Dermot's blue 733t was parked in its usual spot. A traffic warden ignored it. Dermot was waiting by the door to the flats. None of the neighbours would have let him in. No one trusted anyone else in those flats.

'What's *happened* to you?' he asked. 'You look fucked up.'

'I am.'

'Hallucinations?'

'Real world.'

'That *does* fuck you up,' he said. 'I don't even know what's *going on* most of the time. And the rest of the time, I'm off my head.'

He sat on my bed once we got to my flat. He hadn't brought any games with him, which was unusual.

'I'm travelling light,' he said. 'What's *up* with you then? I thought you *computer people* didn't get worried by things. Where's all that *logic* gone when you need it?'

'I don't know what to do,' I said. My voice sounded tiny and far away.

'They're putting *mirrors* on the walls at work, is that it?' asked Dermot. 'Will you stop behaving like a *woman* and just tell me what the fucking problem is?'

'That picture you found at Roger's,' I said. 'I know who that girl is.'

Dermot looked impatient. He wanted all of the information at once.

'Her name was Trish Newton,' I told him. He looked blank.

'Was?' he said. 'What's her name now?'

'She died in a car crash. In Borth. She was driving too fast and the car flipped.'

'You *knew* her? You didn't the other day.'

'I didn't remember properly. I don't remember now. I remember being in her car. Not when it crashed, some other time. She was pregnant when she died. I think it was mine.'

I switched on the PC to drown out the sound of our breathing. Natural sounds didn't suit the mood. The PC began its long journey to wakefulness.

'It was *yours*, was it?' asked Dermot. 'You knocked her up?'

'I think so,' I said. 'I think it was mine. And I think I killed her.'

He looked at me.

'You?' he said. 'Where are you *getting* this from? Beamed in from fucking Mars? You couldn't kill a *fly*. That first time I took you out, if those two arseholes in the toilets had *jumped* us, I'd have been on my own. You'd have *fainted* or something.'

'I don't remember doing it,' I said. 'I just feel it. I know I did it. I fixed her brakes or something.'

'Because she was *pregnant*? Couldn't you just *marry* the girl? What's with you, anyway? Why don't you remember anything?'

I told him why I didn't remember things clearly. I told him about Borth, and what that had done to me. When I'd finished the two of us sat and looked at the desktop wallpaper glowing on the monitor. It was a downloaded image of the Clangers, standing on the surface of the moon, eating blue string pudding.

'Tell you what,' said Dermot. 'You know what this all means? We need to find your man Betts.'

'We'll have a job,' I said, and told him about the security at Bright Harvest Research Laboratory.

'We'll have to *get round* it,' said Dermot. 'We'll have to use our *ingenuity* to get in there. You're a computer programmer, you should be able to get us in. I can *talk* us in. When can you go?'

'Friday. I've booked a day off work.'

'Done,' he said. 'I still think you're wrong. You never killed anyone. You don't have it in you.'

'Tina knows something,' I said. 'She's involved in all this.'

'She'd *have* to be, wouldn't she? Wouldn't be paranoid enough otherwise. Try not to think about it until you see Betts. And don't get *me* in any more hallucinations. I'll stick with the real fucking world. Now, what are we playing?' he asked, leaning over the keyboard.

He lost himself in monitor light. I was already lost there.

'Don't mention any of this tonight,' he said. 'That'll spoil the party, won't it?'

'Party?' I didn't remember anything about a party.

'Tina and Roger have asked us over for tea. They're back at home. They've been calling you but you haven't been at home. The river's *fucked off* back to bed.'

'I can't go.' The idea was dreadful. I couldn't imagine being in the same room as Tina.

'No? And what's your excuse? If she *knows something*, she'll wonder where you are. She'll wonder why you *aren't there*. She'll wonder why *I'm* not there, too. I'm not driving there, I can't cope with Roger if I don't have a drink. So you *have* to go. Just act natural.'

I supposed I'd have to. He wasn't going to give me a choice.

FIFTEEN

I

The roads were all but empty. The sky was thinking of rain but wasn't quite ready to commit itself. We drove from Dudley's artwork-heavy traffic islands to Kidderminster's artless ones in no time. Escaping Kidderminster's gravity well, the Audi sped up past the hospital with its banners – SAVE OUR HOSPITAL – and on up the hill, falling from the crest to gather speed past the entrance to the West Midland Safari Park. In summer, the road would be blocked with cars waiting to turn in and lose any unsecured fittings in the baboon enclosure. On this midweek evening, out of season, there wasn't a sign of life.

We drove into Bewdley over the bridge and then on into the car park. A middle-aged man in a shell suit was jogging listlessly around the perimeter.

'I remember when all this was *river*,' said Dermot. A breeze played with his dark curls. The river was back in its bed, but the town was still recovering. A thick layer of drying mud covered the bottom two feet of every nearby wall. The town was full of the smell you uncover when you're digging the

188

garden and come across the body of a long-lost pet. The stuff on the walls and floors belonged underwater. Dermot looked at his shoes with evident dismay.

'I hope this shit comes off,' he said. 'These cost more than you *make* in a *month*.'

This shit wasn't coming off anything. He looked for something clean to scrape his shoes against, but everything was in the same condition. His shoes got muddier as we walked.

The bottom third of Roger and Tina's front door was crusted. The door opened as we approached, and Roger looked out. He was dressed in cheap jeans and an old tee-shirt.

'Fucking hell,' said Dermot as quietly as he was able. 'He's got his *gardening clothes* on.'

'Hello both,' said Roger. 'We're still in a little bit of a mess at the moment, I'm afraid.'

He stepped back to let us in. The amber glow was still confined to the upper rooms. The lower ones were looking remarkably clean, given that the river had been in them less than a week ago, but they weren't ready for the glow yet. There were incense sticks burning on all available surfaces, but the smell of the river was overwhelming them easily. It would be weeks before it was gone; and probably not as long before the river came back in again.

'The kitchen's looking better,' he said. 'Go and have a look, Tina did most of the work, I just manned the pumps.'

The kitchen did look better. Everything was back in place, including the oven. The surfaces gleamed. Even the floor was bright.

'That's the advantage of tiles,' said Roger. 'Wipe them down, and there you are. That's given us enough room to get a table organized upstairs, and Tina's managed to put some food together. Cold stuff I'm afraid, we only got the power back to the kitchen half an hour ago. How are you two?'

He asked that as though it was addressed to both of us, but he looked at me.

'I'm fine,' said Dermot. 'You *cracked a bottle* yet?'

'There's one breathing,' said Roger. 'And another one getting ready to breathe.'

'Good man,' said Dermot. 'Where's herself?'

'Up there sorting things out. Go on up and let her know you're here. I'll bring Mick along, I just want his expert opinion on something.'

'You could get better opinions in an *old people's home,*' said Dermot, on his way upstairs. As soon as he was out of earshot, Roger took my arm. It was the sort of gesture that suited him.

'How are you?' he asked with the merest hint of urgency.

'I'm not sure,' I told him. 'Things feel strange. Nothing seems to be resolved.'

'I'm sure it will be. All you really need to do is find the source of your problems. Do that, and everything else will become clear. I know that sounds like the sort of claptrap you get in bad American novels, but it's sometimes true. You know, the hero has suppressed memories of some awful event and then has to confront them all in the last twenty pages. You've got something locked in there. And you can force things into the world. You need to stop the one before the other gets out of hand.'

'How do you know all of this?'

'Because you did it. How else? You took Dermot into one of your worlds. Or, more correctly, you put one of your worlds around him. You have a talent for this. You only need to learn to control it.'

'This all sounds unscientific.'

'This is psychology,' he said, putting on a wry grin. 'Of course it's unscientific.'

'Did you get all of this from Tina?'

'That's about as wrong as you can get,' he said, amused. 'But think about it. Think about what happened in Borth. You made that happen. You produced something from your imagination and set it free in the world.'

'That's one explanation,' I said, indicating doubt, although I believed him. Like much else, it felt right. That strange hobgoblin from the mountains had come scampering directly from my mind, which had been primed by too many nights staying up and playing role-playing games. I'd set it in the reflections at first, and then out into the world. I hadn't done it deliberately, but I knew that I'd done it. I'd created life.

'That's *the* explanation,' Roger corrected me. 'You can manifest things. You just don't know how you do it, and so you need to track down this fellow Betts and see what he knows. I think he'll get you to the source of all this. To tell the truth, I think you've been there already. You just don't know it.'

He was already at the top of the stairs, cutting off the conversation. He nodded at the open doors upstairs.

'Change of subject required, I think,' he said. I followed him up.

▐▐

We had a quiet meal, despite Dermot's best efforts. It was a salad with a quiche from the farm shop up the hill, and Dermot didn't like salads or quiches. The amber glow felt gloomy and suffocating instead of warming. Rather than four of us chatting there seemed to be umpteen subgroups, each with its own hidden agenda. The conversation was dragged from subject to subject, always angling back towards the search for Betts. I was being discussed as though I wasn't there.

Even Roger's wine didn't do much to brighten things up. The red was too heavy and the white was too sharp.

'When are you going?' asked Tina.

'Friday,' said Dermot, turning over some lettuce in case there was food underneath it. 'We're going to try and *get in* to see him.'

'Can you do that?'

'I can get in anywhere,' said Dermot. 'I can get myself on the *guest list*.'

'How does he feel about it?' asked Tina, meaning me.

'He's fine. It'll do him good. Bring him *out* of himself.'

The two of them smirked. Roger let himself look at the ceiling for a moment, indicating grave disapproval.

'I think we ought to be more careful,' he said, 'when we discuss this. This is serious. Potentially, Mick is in danger. Potentially, so are we. Dermot got tangled up in one of these fantasies, yes?'

Tina nodded. Dermot remained neutral.

'Then so could we all. Regardless of whether you believe they're illusions or manifestations, they can confuse you. They could get you to walk in front of a car because you thought you were walking across a field, for instance. So a little less levity on the subject couldn't go amiss.'

'Lighten up,' said Tina. 'We've found something Mick can do without using a mouse and keyboard. I think we should be celebrating.'

She raised her glass. Dermot joined her.

'She's right,' he said. 'He's no bloody *use* at anything else I can think of. I mean, check out his hallucinations. Even those are all from *video games*. The man needs to *get out more*.'

He downed his wine, wincing at the acidity.

'You know,' he said, 'I've known him for years now and until this month he'd never asked me where I lived? Can you believe it? He's not interested.'

'He's never asked what Roger does for a living,' said Tina. 'Come to that, he's never asked what I do. I don't think he could tell you Roger's surname if you asked him. You're right, he's not interested at all.'

'Has it occurred to either of you,' asked Roger in a worryingly neutral voice, 'that there may be reasons for that? Perhaps there's a trauma back there somewhere.'

'A missing girl,' said Dermot, 'a *road traffic accident*, that kind of thing?'

The room became silent. It was as though God had disconnected His soundcard. I said I needed to go to the bathroom, but I didn't really hear myself say it. Once safely shut in there I pulled on the cord that lit up the room and looked at myself in the mirror. I looked as though I needed a month of sleep, or perhaps just embalming. I touched the mirror. It was only glass with a silvered backing, and not something I should ever have been frightened of. What I should have been frightened of, I was beginning to think, was Tina. She was forcing me into finding something that I'd locked away in my head.

Perhaps I should have been afraid of that car crash. They all seemed to know about it, although Dermot had clearly overstepped the mark by mentioning it.

I splashed water on my face. Somewhere above us all, God

got the soundcard problem sorted. I could hear the water as it ran into the plughole.

I remembered the first time I'd met Dermot. He'd already known that I was afraid of mirrors.

I wasn't afraid of them now. They'd only been a tool. The problem was me.

I was afraid of Tina. I was afraid of Dermot, too. I was afraid that I'd killed Trish Newton because she was pregnant with my child, and I couldn't understand how the police hadn't at least picked me up for questioning. Surely I was a suspect.

I'd need to see the report on the car, I realized. I'd need to get the hackers back on the case.

I stood on the landing for a moment.

From the other room, I heard Roger say:

'The two of you need to back off. He's remembering everything, but it'll take time. The best way to do it is to let him get to it himself, not to drop things on him. He's already in a bad enough state. Let him find his own way to the truth.'

'He's not going to like it,' said Dermot. 'I don't like it either.'

'You wouldn't,' said Tina. 'And if you'd known him before all this, you wouldn't like what he's turned into.'

I couldn't go back in there and listen to them discussing me. I went downstairs, trying to be quiet. God had not only got His soundcard back in order, however, He'd also switched my personal volume up to full. Every step creaked, every floorboard shrieked.

Somehow they didn't hear me. I let myself out into Bewdley.

I walked back to the car, looking at the Severn and the debris it had left. Uprooted trees were jammed under the arches of the bridge, a wash of silt covered everything to thigh height. A smell of stagnant water filled the air.

I drove home. No doubt Dermot would be pissed off that I'd left him behind.

That was too bad. He wasn't reliable. I needed reliability. I needed to know what had been going on.

I would have to find out the rest for myself.

▌▌▌

The next morning, I asked Andy if he could find the police reports of the car crash. He looked at me with more interest. I'd always been a quiet programmer and not close to his level. Now I was an enigma with a shady history and an interest in police files. Respect due.

'You were at Borth College,' he said. 'I checked out your records. They weren't very hard to find. You might want to consider encryption or at least covering your tracks. If I can find out what you've been doing, so can Clive.'

Having delivered his nebulous warning, he went back to his desk and began to infiltrate the police computers. Their security didn't seem to faze him. Within half an hour he'd got the details of the examination of the wrecked car.

'There you go,' he said. 'Nothing to tie you to it that I can see.'

It hadn't occurred to me that he'd put two and two together and get the same result that I got. No wonder he was warning me. He thought I'd killed Trish Newton. That made two of us.

I read the report.

The car hadn't suffered much damage, considering. The

top had been compressed towards the chassis, causing the fatal injuries to the driver. There was no sign of mechanical damage, deliberate or otherwise. The brakes were intact, the accelerator wasn't glued to the floor, the steering still worked. The tyres were in decent condition, although the rear left was getting close to being illegally worn. No one else had been in the car at the time. If they had, they'd have been left with a very low forehead, as the passenger side hit the ground first when the car flipped.

There were no signs of a collision other than the collision with the tree. There were no signs that another vehicle had been involved.

They'd spoken to the boyfriend, and he was in a virtually catatonic state. The boyfriend was me, helpfully named in the report. I didn't remember ever being in a virtually catatonic state, but then, I'd lost a lot of memories. Perhaps being in a virtually catatonic state wasn't something you'd remember. That seemed likely enough.

I'd been somewhere else, anyway. I'd been in the student bar at the time the accident took place. I'd been drinking – there and elsewhere – all night, getting very drunk. This had been confirmed by most of the other students, including Tina. I'd been getting drunk because I'd discovered that my girlfriend was pregnant and – according to other witnesses – I hadn't been able to cope with the fact. So I'd got drunk, and then I'd got the news that there had been an accident from a policeman, and then I'd turned into someone else.

There were no medical or psychiatric reports. I wasn't about to ask Andy to find them. I didn't want him knowing that I'd been technically insane. Of course, he might already know. He'd been my lead source.

I spent the rest of the day working on Boris because I wasn't able to concentrate on anything more useful. I took the work home, thinking that I'd be able to finish it over the weekend and that Clive would be none the wiser.

IV

That night I wasn't able to sleep. My mind was running through scenarios. None of them turned out well. I hadn't heard from Dermot. Perhaps he'd given up on me after I left him in Bewdley. If he didn't turn up in the morning, I'd need to get into Bright Harvest unassisted. If he did turn up, there might be unpleasantness. Dermot wasn't subtle. I thought about Tina. Had she duped me into that experiment in an attempt to cure me? Had she been trying to get me to remember? After all, I'd clearly known her before then. The first meeting I remembered hadn't been our first meeting. I'd already lost memories; the experiment had just added to the damage. It had brought something back, but not the thing we were after. There was a chance that Tina had only been trying to save me.

To pass the time I tried to tidy the flat. It was difficult, because there was no clear space to move things to. Moving a pile of *Transmetropolitan* back issues only revealed a hidden pile of *Your Sinclair* magazines. Moving a stack of CDs only revealed a hidden stack of old games on floppies for formats of computer that no longer worked. There were three RS232 interface cables. There was one of those old modems with a phone-shaped indentation that you had to put the handset into. There were several circuit boards and any number of chips in small cardboard boxes lined with dark grey synthetic foam. It was all junk, but I couldn't throw any of it away. It might be useful.

I gave up on tidying the flat. What I needed was another room, and I wasn't likely to get one. I turned on the PC and chose the least intelligent game that'd still run slowly enough to be playable.

At eleven thirty, I heard the drunks on the way to their various homes. Thursday was payday in a lot of the factories; Thursday night was drinking away the wages night. In the last half hour before midnight, the taxi companies did most of their business. The sound of lazy minicab drivers leaning on their horns joined the sound of rough male voices.

Gradually, that gave way to silence. I gave up on the game, which was a generic first-person shooter with the usual weapons – handgun, shotgun, machine gun, rocket launcher – and the usual suspects – dim grunts, very dim grunts, cannon fodder. It was still too complicated to suit me. I needed something truly dumb.

I loaded up an arcade emulator and picked out some early-eighties game ROMS. Arcade games are big cases, mostly full of nothing. They have circuit boards with the games flash-loaded onto them. Some enterprising people managed to get those ROM images and upload them to the Net, and now you can download them and play them at home.

Game ROMs are legal if you own a copy of the arcade game, and illegal otherwise, and no one cares about the difference. Sites carry huge lists of arcade games, and with an emulator you can play almost all of them. Those old games I'd played in Borth at ten pence a go were now available for free.

I put on Scramble, an ancient game in which you controlled a small rocket on its voyage through difficult landscapes. The first level left my first little spaceship short on fuel. The second level took away one of my little spaceships. The third level was impossible.

I ESCAPEd and tried Space Invaders. That was too simplistic. It just felt old, and besides, the old consoles had created the illusion of coloured graphics. The game itself was in monochrome. What they did was put strips of coloured plastic over the monitors of the consoles, giving the appearance of layers of differently-coloured invaders crawling down the screen. On the PC it was all in dreary black and white.

I ESCAPEd again. I needed something different. Perhaps I didn't want to play anything violent at all. There were very few games that didn't involve shooting.

I put on Pacman. That was just what I wanted. The titular hero ran around the maze, chased by four ghosts; it was gameplay without any unnecessary extras or distractions. It was pure. It was perfect, and according to Dermot it had got that way mostly by accident.

Dermot had told me one or two things about the game. He'd become a video-game expert, as well as the arcade king.

'The guy who did it,' he'd said one night after we'd gone retro and loaded up all of the old arcade games, 'wanted to make a game that girls would like. So he looked at *girl's hobbies*. What do girls do? Eat. All day long. So he had the hero eating *little dots*. And he didn't know what it was going to look like. He had the *ghosts*. He had the *maze*. But he didn't know what the *hero* was going to look like. So he orders himself a pizza while he thinks about it, and he *takes out* a slice. He looks at what's left, a *circle with a wedge missing*. That's it. That's his hero. Round thing with an open mouth, eating dots.

'And do you know what he was going to call it? Puckman.

Then they thought what you could do to that name with a *marker pen*, and they changed it to Pacman. So that's what he was called. You think there's some bright plan behind it all, and there isn't. It's just coincidences. It's accidents. These games are all like that. You know why Mario has a moustache?'

I didn't.

'Because they didn't know what his *mouth* would look like, so they did him with a moustache to *cover it up*.'

Thinking about that, I wondered whether I'd see Dermot again. I thought I probably would. Leaving him in Bewdley was the sort of thing he'd do to someone just to cheer himself up. He'd think it was funny, once he'd stopped being angry.

I guided Pacman around his maze. The ghosts moved in set ways – one switched routes suddenly, another paid no attention to you – and you could exploit that knowledge once you'd learned it. But they outnumbered you four to one, and sooner or later they blocked all exits and closed in on you.

I'd heard that there was a bug at level 255. I'd never see it, if there was one. I'd never seen level ten.

Reflected in the monitor, I saw myself sitting in the dark with a cheap gamepad, bathed in monitor light. Behind me stood another man, lit by a different light source. He had that same glow, the brightness of phosphor being battered by electrons. He wasn't real. He sat on the bed next to me, but I wasn't doing much of a job rendering him. He didn't touch the bed, but sat just above it, supported by bad 3D routines. He had pretty good textures but a low polygon count. Even when I only imagined video-game characters, I was too lazy to put in enough work of my own. No wonder Boris was an idiot.

'I'm not really here,' the newcomer said. His mouth moved,

but it was only drawn on his face and he wasn't lip-synched. His face was flat, the nose indicated by shading in the facial textures, his ears drawn on under his sketchy hair. He had on dark glasses to save me imagining his eyes. He had on the generic grey-suit-and-black-tie combo of the generic nameless informant who appeared in any number of recent video games. In terms of graphics he was closer to the original PlayStation than a top-end PC with a decent rendering card. His voice, like his appearance, was generic: the toneless American voice I'd been hearing in games for fifteen years.

'I know,' I said. 'I'm imagining you.'

'Why do that?' he asked. His voice wasn't centred on his head, either. It came from the left and right sides of the room.

It was a good question wherever it came from. I didn't know why I'd dreamt him up. At least he wasn't trying to run me down, or leaping in through my window while shooting at me, or setting his dogs on me.

'I'm not that sort of agent,' he said. I didn't entirely trust him. Programmers didn't bother to show weapons that weren't currently being used. He might produce a pair of AK47s from inside his jacket or haul an experimental disruptor cannon from a pocket. He might simply explode or extravagantly morph into something nasty.

'As I said, I'm not that sort of agent,' he said. I realized he was responding to what I was thinking. Of course, he would be; for one thing, I was imagining him and so he knew what I was thinking. For another, characters in video games didn't respond to your voice. They responded to your hands on the controls. Your voice was out in the real world. Voice recognition was still in its infancy.

I knew this. My mobile phone had voice activated numbers. 'Work!' I'd shout at it, and it'd dial for a pizza or call the vet.

The agent shifted and turned to look at me. I'd got the skeletal movement right, at least, but there was too much motion in the neck and his head turned past the breaking point. Nothing broke. He wasn't made that way.

'I'm here to tell you things you already know,' he said. 'I'm here to tell you things that will not help you.

'You see the screen? That little character chased by ghosts? Getting nowhere, repeatedly going over the same ground?

'That is you. That is what you've done to yourself. You are only reactive.

'That's all,' he said, and vanished. A glow in his shape stayed in the air for a moment and then faded.

'Well, fuck you,' I said to the nothingness he left behind. After that, I went to bed. I'd had enough mysteries for one day. The next day I'd be breaking into Bright Harvest Research Laboratory.

I'd made up my mind. I wasn't only reactive. I was going to get in there and find Betts. I didn't know whether that would do me any good, but I was going to do it anyway. With that decision made, a week's worth of lost sleep caught up with me. I turned off the PC. I barely had enough energy to turn off the lights, and then I fell across the bed and didn't see anything else for eight hours.

SIXTEEN

I

The next morning I was woken by what sounded like someone throwing gravel at my window. I knew it was Dermot; no one else would do it. Why would anyone go to the trouble of flinging small stones at a window when there was a doorbell?

I hadn't closed the curtains the night before. I was still dressed in yesterday's clothes. I'd slept in them.

I went and let him in.

'Where you *dumping* me today?' he asked. 'I only had to get *two fucking taxis* and a *train* from Bewdley. Perhaps you can drop me off at an *oilrig* or something this time. Got any tea on? Kettle going?'

'I'm not up yet.'

'You're dressed.'

'I went to bed dressed.'

'Drunk. You drink too much. I'll do the kettle then, and you get yourself *ready*. Tea?'

'Coffee. I need to wake up.'

'That's what I've *always* thought. You need to *wake up* alright.'

He got hot drinks sorted out while I got myself sorted out. I dressed in black. If we were infiltrating Bright Harvest, I wanted to be inconspicuous. Dermot was wearing his usual tee-shirt and jeans combo, with his insane dark curly hair completely out of control. He was also wearing a pair of trainers three times the size of his feet. They'd spot him a mile away, I thought. I looked like an undercover operative.

'What have you come as?' Dermot asked when he saw my outfit. 'My shadow?'

'We're sneaking in.'

'We're *blagging* our way in. You can't get in looking like that. You look like someone off a *late night review* programme. You look like a fucking *jazz musician*.'

'We're not blagging our way in. It won't work. You can't blag those guards, they're expecting people to try that. We're going to sneak in.'

'And how are we going to manage that?' he asked, looking dubious.

'Wait and see,' I said. He didn't look happy about that, but he didn't seem too upset. In fact, he seemed to be according me a little more respect than the usual amount, i.e. none at all.

'He's the mystery man,' he said. 'He's the man with the plan. So, what's the plan?'

'Wait and see,' I told him again.

He looked almost impressed.

■■

The demonstrators were in the quiet part of their cycle. The banners were waterlogged and heavy, as it was raining. Bewdley under a flood somehow seemed a lot less wet than

Stourbridge in the rain. The cameras looking down from the tops of the spiked poles were aimed at the crowd. One of them turned to point at the Audi. Dermot and I sat inside, watching the world being divided into half-second slices by the windscreen wipers.

'Second saddest sound in the world,' said Dermot. 'Fucking *windscreen wipers*. You know what the saddest is? Rain hitting the *bus shelter window*. That's as sad as you can get. If you're waiting for a *bus* in the *rain* you're on your way to your *mother's house* because you still fucking live there.'

'What about babies crying? That's a sad sound.'

'Different *sort* of sadness. It's like Eskimos having different words for different sorts of snow. In the West Midlands we should have different words for all the types of *depression*. That fucking bunch would have one of their own for a start.'

He pointed at the demonstrators. There were still a few children, although not as many as there had been on my first visit. Above them, water dripped from the sharp edges of the razor wire. Water ran down all vertical surfaces and searched for ways off horizontal ones. All of the water only seemed to make everything look grimier, rather than washing any of the grime away.

'It'd be the same thing as the Eskimos with snow,' I said. 'It'd just be different words for rain.'

'What are we going to do then?' he asked. 'What's your *mystery plan*, mystery man?'

I'd been hoping that he wouldn't ask me that. It was going to sound stupid. Which was understandable, because it was stupid. It was insane.

'I'm going to use sniper mode,' I said. 'I'm going to knock out one guard while I'm zoomed in and you create a diversion.

Then I'm going to get the weapons from his body and then take the other guard out with them. Then we disable the cameras and head on in.'

'Sniper mode?'

I nodded. Before he could object I continued.

'I can put one of my worlds over that one. I did it with that farm where we got the cider. There was a real farm there, and I put a pretend world over it. I can do it deliberately. I think I can. I can replace that building with a video-game building. And we can get into a video-game building because you can always get in. That's how they're designed. So you can go round the back and blow up the cans of fuel, and when they open the gates to see what's happened I'll take the guards and the cameras out.'

'We thought you were getting *worse*,' Dermot said. 'Perhaps we were wrong. Perhaps you're getting much better. What fuel cans are these?'

'They'll be there. They're always there, out of sight of the cameras. Shoot them and they'll go up, then get back round to the front.'

'And what am I shooting them with?'

'This,' I said, and made a handgun for him.

The night before, I had manifested someone to sit in my bedroom and give me a meaningless hint. Because it had been a non-threatening manifestation, I had been able to concentrate on how it was done. I'd just dragged a stereotypical video-game character out of my head, given him a short script, and set him loose. It hadn't been difficult. It had been a shame that I hadn't given him anything useful to say, but I'd managed to create a character.

A gun was simpler to create. I made it an automatic. It turned up on Dermot's lap, hauled together from nowhere.

It looked unreal but solid. There was a name etched along the barrel, but you couldn't read it clearly because I didn't know the model numbers or makes of guns. It was larger than a real gun, because that's how guns are in games. It had no controls other than a trigger.

'Point the round end at the fuel cans, pull the trigger,' I said.

Dermot picked up his gun and examined it.

'It doesn't weigh anything, but it's *solid*. Is it going to work?'

'It'll work once I put my world over that world.'

'And you can do that?'

'I can do that. Watch me.'

I looked at the Bright Harvest building, sitting smugly behind its razor wire. I thought of all those video-game complexes with impregnable security that turned out to be pregnable after all.

I thought of the River Severn, bursting its banks, flooding Bewdley, replacing land with water.

I did the same thing with the contents of my head.

III

This is what Les Herbie had to say about imagination:

> I imagine things for a living. This is my art. That is a cliché, but this is my art. You think that this is just thrown together. You're wrong. You live in the West Midlands and you're wrong.
>
> To do this I need to see the whole of each column. I need to see the whole thing and then write it. You do nothing like it. I hate you all because I am better than you. None of you can do this.

Complaints to the usual address. Complaints from the usual names.

This is art. It's not an installation or interactive, it's art. It does what it's there to do. It serves its function, which is the basis of art. It does it well, which is the next level. It does it with wit. That's the whole thing. That's it done and dusted.

It means what it means. It has no hidden meanings. It has no symbolism or subtext.

If it did, you'd miss it.

What artists do, is bring something out of their minds and into the world. That's what we do. It changes the world as it happens. The world has a new view or vision of something.

That's art. You don't do it by wearing black and saying that you're an artist. If you wear black and sit in bars smoking French cigarettes and discussing the Turner Prize, you aren't an artist. You're unemployed. Art is something you have. It's there or it isn't. Usually it isn't. Going to art school won't help. Throwing three trowels in a bucket and saying it represents the nature of womanhood doesn't make you an artist. It makes you a fool. It makes you worthless. Function is first. A guitar solo without a song is a waste of notes. A thirty-page sentence is nothing if it doesn't advance the story.

I imagine things for a living. They annoy you or cheer you up, or both. Each of you is changed by that little degree.

I am making a new world.

I am taking you all there with me.

Except for the usual complainants. You get to stay in the West Midlands.

You don't deserve art. You barely deserve function. You barely deserve oxygen.

Of course, none of this is true.

I imagine things for a living.

He got quite a few letters about that one, too.

IV

The Bright Harvest building had changed. The walls were now higher and the razor wire denser. The gate was a metal grille and arcs of electricity jumped between the bars. The guards were now identical twins, and each carried a stubby sub-machine gun. The building's windows were blacked out, and there were more cameras.

'Jesus jumping fuck on a unicycle,' said Dermot. 'How do you know it'll work? What if that's just an *illusion* and when we go in we hit our noses on the fucking *gate* because we can't see it?'

'It's not an illusion. It's what's there now. We can go in there, if we don't get caught or shot.'

'Shot?'

'Shot. They have guns. They're not real people, we can shoot them. I'd recommend shooting them.'

'Won't that kill the *real guards*? They're in there somewhere.'

I hadn't thought of that. I didn't want any extra deaths on my conscience. It already had enough to cope with.

'We'll have to avoid them then. Forget sniper mode. You blow up the fuel cans and then get out of sight. I'll disable the cameras. When the guards come back in I'll knock them out, and then I'll open the gate and let you in.'

'So all we need to worry about is *dying* in some place you've imagined?'

'That's all.'

'Here we fucking *go* then.'

He tucked his handgun into his waistband and pulled his tee-shirt down over it.

'You're *starting* to be fun to be with,' he said as he got out of the car. 'If you're lucky I might not beat the *living shit* out of you for dumping me in Bewdley.'

He closed the door and started on his way round the wall. The rain had stopped – too much processing needed – and the demonstrators were muted. I got out and examined them. They were flat, like stage scenery. They were one-dimensional. They were still animated, but if you walked past them they vanished, and if you walked behind them you could see that they didn't have a back. They were like a film projected onto plywood.

I looked at them from the front. Their eyes were insane. They didn't like being reduced to scenery. They were frightened.

Good. It'd teach them not to waste everybody's time in future.

Their flat eyes all looked to the left as a concussive blast rang out. A fireball rose from the back of the building. Dermot had created a diversion.

The gate opened, spitting sparks, and the two guards emerged. They looked at the demonstrators and then began to walk around the outside of the wall, falling into poised crouches. I crept up behind them and hit the rear one on the back of the head. He collapsed, unconscious. The other one didn't notice anything, so I did the same to him. That was the guards sorted, done and dusted. They lay crumpled against the wall, and the cameras wouldn't be able to see them there. I called Dermot and he came around the corner, looking dazed. I supposed the explosion was responsible. He shook his head.

'That was *fucking loud*,' he said. 'And hot.'

'Explosions are like that. Now just wait here while I sort the cameras out, and then we'll be going in.'

'Carry on there, don't let me *slow you down*.'

I made my way back to the open gate and peeped in. Only one camera was pointing in my direction. A green light on it flashed yellow; computer game cameras did that when they might be able to see you but hadn't quite decided yet. If it went red, the alarms would go off.

I ducked out of sight and gave it time to reset. Three seconds should be enough.

I looked out again. It had turned to look at something else. There was a small booth for the guards to stand in if it rained. I ran over to it and got in. On a prominently placed control panel there was a large red square button with CAMERAS OFF written on it in bold black characters. I pressed the button.

'Cameras off,' said a female voice. 'Security override engaged. Cameras will reset in T minus sixty seconds.'

I went and got Dermot.

'We've got a minute to open the door,' I told him. 'Then all we need to do is find the labs. Once we get to Betts I'll put the real world back and hope that no one noticed.'

'I think this pair *might* have an inkling,' said Dermot, indicating the two guards. 'What with the *world changing* and the *explosion* and being knocked out and all.'

We ran to the front door. After the gate and the cameras it was a disappointment to find it was merely a normal-sized door. It was of a dull metal and had three buttons instead of a handle. I pressed them in order, top to bottom. The door emitted a quack-quack fail noise. I tried the reverse order, and got the same.

'Cameras will reset in T minus thirty seconds,' explained the female voice.

I tried the buttons in different orders. There were only six possible combinations, and I got it on the fifth attempt. The door beeped cheerfully and unlocked with a sharp click. I pushed it open. Inside, a short passage led to a reception area. A small bright young woman sat behind a desk. Dermot levelled the gun at her.

'Put that away,' I muttered. 'Don't shoot the staff.'

'She's *seen* us.'

'She's only a receptionist. We can talk our way past her. I thought that was your specialty.'

'I'm the master blagger,' said Dermot, putting his handgun back in his waistband. 'Watch and *learn*.'

He strode up to the desk. The receptionist looked at him. She had very blue eyes and kept her hands tucked neatly out of sight. Her hair was short and black, not matching the eyes. She wore a very crisp blouse, which had creases so sharp they looked like they'd do you damage. She had on a blue cravat with very straight edges. She wore no jewellery. Her lips were extremely red but she didn't appear to be wearing lipstick. She opened her mouth.

'Can I help you?' she asked.

Dermot turned on the charm. I'd seen him do it before, and knew that it could sometimes take him a while to wind it up to full strength. I had a look at the lobby while I was waiting.

The floor was covered with alternating black and white tiles, and a single staircase led up to a landing and balcony. There were doors leading off at regular intervals. On the receptionist's desk there was a red telephone and a single buff folder, along with two black pens. An open drawer held a small stack of blue cards. The walls were of matte white and the decor was of the tubular-chrome-railings school. The stairs were carpeted in blue. There were no signs or notices, and no security cameras.

'We're after the labs,' said Dermot. 'If you'd be so good as to point us in the right direction.'

'Labs are on level twelve,' said the receptionist.

Dermot looked at me.

'There are only *two floors*,' he said.

'There are two above ground level. The others are underground for safety reasons. You'll need a red pass to get into the lift and a blue keycard to access anything lower than level ten. You can get a red pass from reception and a blue keycard from one of the senior security staff in the security suite upstairs. Access to the security suite requires a red pass.'

'Can we have a red pass?'

'Not without a blue keycard,' she said.

'What's your name?' Dermot asked, preparing to take his charm offensive from the general to the personal level.

'I'm not with you,' she said.

'What are you *called*?' he tried.

'Receptionist subroutine [1] <calls conversation_link,hints-_page>,' she said. She said it like that, including all of the punctuation – 'hints underscore page right angle bracket'.

'What do your *friends* call you?'

'Other related routines call me by CALL Receptionist subroutine [1] {include parameters CONV_THREAD_MAIN and SUBTEXT_THREAD}.'

'She can't handle that sort of enquiry,' I told Dermot. 'You need to keep it simple. Just ask her for a red pass.'

'I did, weren't you fucking listening? She said I needed a blue keycard to get a red pass, and a *red pass* to get a *blue keycard*. How the fuck are we supposed to manage that?'

I took him to one side.

'Distract her,' I told him.

'What should I blow up?' he asked, fingering his gun and looking for a viable target.

'Just chat to her. And keep it non-specific. Just keep her attention away from her desk so that I can grab a blue keycard. They're under her desk, on the left-hand side, in a drawer.'

'What do I talk to her about?'

'You're the blagging king, you think of something.'

We approached the desk. The receptionist looked at us.

'Can I help you?' she asked.

'What's through *that* door?' Dermot asked, pointing up the stairs. The receptionist turned to look and I grabbed a card.

I hoped we wouldn't need one each.

'The security office,' said the receptionist.

'Thanks,' said Dermot, and then to me: 'Told you I could blag anything. Now we know where to go.'

We went up the stairs. The receptionist went back to looking at the front door, which wasn't doing anything. I pushed the door at the top of the stairs and it opened. Going through it, we found ourselves in a small square windowless room. Desks were set at very regular intervals. A pair of identical security guards stood against the far wall. Each held a stubby black gun. They wore blue uniforms with black trim.

The door closed behind us.

'We need a red pass,' I said. The guards looked at one another. One lifted his gun and aimed it in our direction. The other asked if we had a blue keycard in a very deep voice.

I showed them our keycard. They looked at it.

'Valid keycard,' said one.

'You may take a red pass,' said the other. 'They're in the firing range. Tell them we sent you.'

They looked at each other.

'Be careful in there,' they both said at once. Then they ignored us while we went back out onto the landing.

V

There were no signs indicating the direction of the firing range. We approached the receptionist.

'Can I help you?' she asked.

'We're looking for the shooting range. The security guards told us to go there to get our red passes.'

'It's over there, third door on the left, follow the corridor to the end. You can't miss it.'

'Thank you,' said Dermot.

'Be careful in there,' the receptionist said. 'They're usually very cautious but there have been one or two incidents.'

We went through the door she'd indicated. A long corridor stretched away in front of us. The corridor was well lit. The light appeared to be coming from fluorescent lights along the ceiling.

I was impressed. I hadn't tried any lighting effects before.

'What did the explosion look like?' I asked Dermot. 'When you shot the fuel can?'

'I don't fucking know, I had my hands over my eyes and I was pointing in the other direction. I didn't want to get *caught up* in it.'

'Did it seem bright?'

'Put your hands over your eyes and see how fucking bright that is. That's how bright it was.'

Our footsteps echoed loudly. From what seemed to be a long way away, we heard the sound of gunshots.

We headed towards the sound. After a long walk, the corridor ended in a set of double doors. On one was a notice:

FIRING RANGE. BE CAREFUL IN THERE.

'I think we have to *be careful* in there,' said Dermot. 'I'm only surmising.'

He let me open the door.

The firing range was a single long room. Along one of the long walls stood plywood targets. They were vaguely humanoid, with the vital zones marked with black circles. Along the opposite wall stood large guns on tripods. At the far end of the room, beyond all the guns and targets, was a filing cabinet.

A man stood just inside the door. He watched us enter before speaking.

'What are you here for?' he asked. 'There have been no requests for target practice.'

'We're here for our red passes,' I said.

'The *security guys* sent us,' added Dermot. 'They said to say they'd sent us.'

'Ah,' said the man. He was wearing body armour and a tin helmet. He indicated the far end of the room. 'The passes are in that cabinet. But the firing routine starts any second now.'

One of the unmanned guns fired a burst of rounds. Its target vaporized. Another target rose from the floor.

Another gun fired. Spent bullet cases flew into the air. Smoke rose in blue-grey plumes.

'They'll do that for a week or so,' said the man. 'You can probably run across between the bursts. They're very regular.'

'Couldn't you go and get them for us?' asked Dermot. 'You're the man with the *bullet proof vest.*'

'Not proof against those bullets. Those are big high-calibre mothers. They'd go through this in no time. If you catch one in the leg, you'll have one less leg to worry about. If you catch one in the body you won't have time to worry about it.'

While he was talking the guns continued to fire, one by one. Shards of plywood flew through the air, landed on the floor, and faded away. New targets grew.

'You could wait,' he said. 'They'll only be on this cycle for a week. Of course, the red passes are invalid after tomorrow. Then you'd need to get green keycards from the security team, and they don't come in at the weekends.'

'We'll get them,' I said.

'*We* fucking won't,' said Dermot. 'I'll stay here. There's no point *both of us* going past that lot. You get the passes and then get back.'

I watched the guns, and noticed that they fired in a pattern. If I studied it, I could time a run.

I also noticed that they were all at shoulder height. I got on my hands and knees and simply crawled past them. It wasn't a comfortable crawl. Sprays of shattered plywood flew at me, and the whistle of bullets tearing up the air came from above. After what seemed to be a long slow crawl I reached the safety of the far end of the room. I stood up next to the filing cabinet. It had four drawers. Three were locked; the other one opened. It held red passes. I could tell what they were, because they were red and written on them in large black characters were the words RED PASS. I took a couple and crawled back to where Dermot was waiting.

'You're supposed to run past them,' said the man with the

body armour, aggrieved. 'That's the whole idea. Still. Have it your way.'

We went back to reception armed with a full complement of cards and passes.

'Can I help you?' asked the receptionist.

We asked her where the lifts were, and she pointed to another door. Going through it, we found ourselves in a small square room. Two metal sliding doors were set into the far wall, with a button between them. Dermot pressed it, and a lift arrived. The doors hissed open.

'Here we go,' he said. 'Into the depths of the base.'

I pressed the button for the twelfth floor. Nothing happened.

'It's not working,' I said.

'Use the *pass cards*,' said Dermot. 'No fucking wonder you've never got out of the first level of Doom.'

There was a slot next to the button pad. I put in the red pass and the first five buttons lit up. I put in the blue keycard and the rest lit up. I pressed the button for the twelfth floor again.

The doors closed and the lift began to descend.

We watched the numbers flicking down on the number pad. They were in reverse order, with one at the top. The lift was descending slowly and carefully, like a pensioner getting into a bath. As the digit for the fifth floor lit, a female voice said: 'Routine scanning in progress.'

Narrow beams of green light shone out of small reflective pads, covering us both in a lattice of green lines. They traced our outlines, and then homed in on Dermot's waist. They lit him up. They crawled over him.

They traced the outline of the gun I'd given him.

They lit that up, very brightly.

218

'Weapon detected,' said the female voice. 'Lift will now stop at the eighth level for cleansing. Security notified.'

'What's your plan now?' asked Dermot. 'Only this sounds like a bad sort of cleansing, like *ethnic* fucking cleansing.'

'Out of the lift,' I said

'What?'

'Up there.'

Dermot looked at the small hatch set into the top of the lift.

'Who the fuck do you think I am, Bruce fucking Willis? You go *up there*. I'm staying here.'

The slowly advancing digits lit up one by one: six, seven.

I jumped up and pushed the hatch. Of course, it opened. I jumped again and grabbed the edges.

I didn't have enough strength in my arms to pull myself up. The next time I had a career change, I told myself, I'd choose something that involved some form of physical exertion. From below, Dermot grabbed my shins and shoved me aloft. I went up, onto the top of the lift, and then I was in a surprisingly clean and unsurprisingly featureless lift shaft. There were no cables. Dermot jumped up after me. I helped him up.

'There's been a *change of plan*,' he said. 'I'm not staying in there.'

'Eighth floor,' said the female voice. 'Cleansing begins.'

We heard the doors open below us. The lift filled with flames, which were squirted in in liquid waves. There were a few bursts of automatic weapon fire. The flames began to recede.

'Cleansing complete,' said the voice. White spray filled the lift, instantly killing the remaining flames.

A pair of soldiers rushed in. They wore combat fatigues and gas masks. They carried short but evil-looking guns.

'Area secure. Suspects missing,' said one. 'Commencing combat sweep of this floor. All units on red alert until further notice.'

There was a crackling radio message, too faint for us to make out.

'Roger that,' said the soldier. 'Engaging all automatic security measures. Closing all bulkheads. Access to everything below ten now locked down.'

There was another crackling radio message. He put his head on one side.

'Roger that,' he said when it finished. He turned to the other soldier.

'Fall back,' he said. 'They're going to gas the lift shafts. Set up positions at the end of the corridor. Shoot anything that comes through here.'

They left the lift. The doors slid shut.

I looked up. The shaft was almost featureless, except for a small rectangular opening leading into darkness at about head height. It would be an air vent or something like one.

We could crawl in there. We didn't have much choice. Hopefully the gas wouldn't come out that way.

'We can get in there,' I said. Dermot looked at me.

'In there? It's fucking *tiny*. We'll get *wedged* in there.'

'That's the only way to go.'

'Oh yes, I'd *far rather* we were wedged in a fucking hole when we get *gassed to death*. That'll make it much easier to bear.'

'We're supposed to go in there. There's always a way through. You know video games.'

'Too fucking right. There's always a way through but sometimes you lose a life finding it,' he said. 'You can go first. If there's a *hidden blade* in the wall, you can find it.

You put the fucking place together. We'd have got in easier if you'd *just left everything alone*. Your subconscious must be in a *right* fucking state.'

I put my head inside the shaft. It was dark in there. There was a faint beating, a regular thud, somewhere in the distance. I slid in with Dermot's help.

It wasn't too tight. There was room enough to crawl. The surface of the vent was hard and shiny, and not too comfortable on my knees. I began to shuffle into the gloom.

I heard Dermot get in behind me.

'There'd better not be *anything* in here with us,' he said.

I hadn't thought of that. The whole purpose of air vents in computer games was to get the hero into a place where something could spring out and grab him by the face. Then you'd reload and try something else.

I'd just thrown a video game over the world. I didn't think we'd get to reload if we got killed.

Of course there would be something in there with us. That was the custom of the land. There might be a lot of somethings.

The sound of that slow beating continued, somewhere ahead of us.

'Ten minutes until gas is released,' said the female voice, this time with a hint of echo.

I crawled faster. Whatever was ahead of us couldn't be as bad as the gas.

It didn't get any darker, after the first fifteen feet. The gloom remained constant. I could see perhaps ten feet ahead of me. Behind me, I could hear Dermot swearing and complaining. The vent went around a corner ahead of me.

I put a hand out in front of me and waved it around the corner.

Nothing bit it off or grabbed it. I looked around.

The vent led on to another corner another few feet ahead.

I used the same method to approach it. Again, nothing bit my hand. I couldn't hear the scrabbling of claws. There was only me and the relentless beating and Dermot's inventive and constant whingeing. The beating was a steady pulse, somewhere not all that far ahead of us. I went around another corner and saw what was causing it.

The vent widened to a huge cylinder. Small lights glowed in the upper reaches. A large horizontal fan was slowly spinning in the middle of the wider chamber, circulating the air. On the far side of the fan, another opening led into further gloom. To get to it, we'd need to pass the blades of the fan.

'Five minutes until gassing,' said that female voice. I was beginning to dislike it.

'Closing all vents,' it added.

Beyond the blades of the giant fan, a pair of doors bracketing the vent began – very slowly – to close.

SEVENTEEN

I

Dermot pulled himself out of the vent behind me and stood up. He looked at the fan. He saw the vent. He saw that the pair of metal doors were slowly closing over it.

'Don't fucking tell me,' he said. 'Let's see if I can *guess*. We just have to dodge that thing and get over there before the doors close. As long as we don't get *diced* on the way we can stop worrying about the gas. Is that it?'

I nodded.

'After you,' he said. 'If you can get past it, I'm fucking sure I can.'

I looked at the fan. It had three large blades, and it was moving slowly. It wasn't moving slowly enough. I'd need to jump through at the right time. I'd have to jump in a crouch.

I braced myself. The opening continued to close.

I counted sweeps of the fan, and when I got the timing right I jumped forward.

The blades missed me. I landed on the far side. Dermot got ready and jumped after me.

223

Something hit the floor. I thought he'd lost a hand or foot until I saw that it was the gun. We were on one side of the fan and the gun was on the other.

'We might need that,' said Dermot. 'Hold on.'

I tried to stop him, but he was too fast. Then he had his hand between the blades, touching the gun.

Either the blades weren't as slow as he thought, or the gun was further away. There was a sound like a blunt knife chopping celery. The gun bounced away, accompanied by something new.

He pulled his hand back. He didn't pull all of it back. He'd lost the ends of all four fingers, from just above the first joint. He looked at the damage.

The vent continued to close. In another few seconds, we'd have trouble getting through it.

'Come on,' I said. 'If we get stuck here we're dead.'

He looked at his mutilated hand. He looked at his finger-tips, which were scattered on the far side of the fan. He was bleeding at a steady rate. Nothing else about him was steady.

'My fingers. My *fucking* fingers,' he said. He was turning pale. I slapped him. I felt safe doing that. After all, he'd have a hard time hitting me back. He snapped to attention. His injured hand drizzled blood down his leg.

'Come on,' I said. 'We can sort you out later.'

I dragged him to the vent.

'Follow me,' I said, and then crawled in. I heard him slide in after me.

At once, the metal plates met with a dull heavy clang. We were back in the dark.

'Commencing gassing,' said that female voice.

Something clattered against the other side of the closed metal plates. There was a scratching sound.

My parents used to have a small scruffy terrier. In the evenings it'd go out in the back garden, and they'd forget that it was out. It would scratch on the door late at night, trying to get their attention. That was what the sound against the panel sounded like. Something wanted to get in with us. Something had managed to follow us past the fan.

It scrabbled and hissed. I imagined tendrils of gas gathering around something that was all claws and teeth.

It howled. I moved along the vent. I didn't want to know what I'd got us involved with. Dermot followed me, managing to keep up although he couldn't use his right hand. The vent went around another two sharp bends and then ended. There was a grille set into the floor. Looking down, I could see a pair of beds in a dimly lit room. I put my face against the grille. Below us was a tiny room, with the two beds and a couple of small bedside tables. It was empty. I pushed the grille and it fell open.

I dropped into the room. I landed like a computer programmer, without any grace or balance. As I picked myself up, Dermot dropped into the room and knocked me back down again. A few sluggish blobs of warmish blood landed on my face. He sat on one of the beds and looked at his hand.

It wasn't pretty. The edges of the wounds were very clean and straight, and the bones were good and white and intact. The blades of the fan had been real blades with keen edges. I tried not to think what it would have done if I'd mistimed my jump and fallen face-first against it.

Only his middle and index fingers were still bleeding. The other two were semi-clotted. I looked in the drawers of the bedside tables and found a can of a fizzy drink with a red and white logo that only just failed to be a recognizable trademark. My imagination was only taking risks with our lives. I opened the can and offered it to Dermot. He looked at it.

'What the fuck are you doing?' he said without any real animation.

'You need moisture,' I said. 'For the shock.'

He had a sip and made a face.

'Tastes like *coke*,' he said.

He had another sip.

'I feel better,' he said, surprised. 'It doesn't hurt as much.'

He drank the rest of the contents of the can and put it on the bed. He looked at his injured hand.

It was intact.

He wiggled the newly complete fingers.

'Video games,' he said. 'Extra health in *soft drink cans*. You knew that'd fix me.'

A thought struck him.

'Did you arrange all of that?' he asked. 'Me losing my fingers?'

'I don't think so. I didn't mean to. I don't know what that thing was that tried to get in after us, and I didn't know they'd find the gun. It's just that video-game logic applies in here. If you can do it in a game, we can do it here.'

He knew that there was a downside to that. We could still die. Death was the central characteristic of video games. Sooner or later something took your last life or the last of your health.

And in underground bases, there was always something much nastier than the guards after you.

■■

While Dermot got used to being intact, I rested my ear against the closed door. I couldn't hear anything outside. I remembered the soldiers being ordered to take up positions nearby. Were we still nearby? We hadn't been in the vent long, and it had turned this way and that. We might only be a few feet away from the lift, with armed troops in the corridors with orders to gun us down on sight.

There was another can of the virtually trademarked soda in the desk drawers, but I didn't think its restorative powers would do much good if we were both shot in the head. I could flip us back to the real world if we were in real danger, of course, but we'd be inside a pharmaceutical company building without permission. Bright Harvest seemed to be very pally with the security forces in the real world. If we were caught there, we'd be off to the sort of imprisonment that you don't get out of, where we'd be injected with turpentine and truth serums and then carted off to an institution for ever after.

I couldn't get us out until we got to Betts. After that, things could sort themselves out.

I opened the door a little way and peeped through the opening. There was an empty corridor outside. I opened the door all the way and put my head out.

There were no soldiers in sight. The corridor was short, with sets of double doors at each end. Apart from those doors and the one I was looking out of, it was featureless. Dermot joined me. He was holding the remaining can of soft drink.

'What's the plan now?' he asked. 'I take it we're *steering clear* of the lifts, with them being full of gas and all. Correct me if I'm wrong.'

'We find the stairs. There are bound to be stairs around here somewhere. Then we walk down to the twelfth floor and find the labs, find Betts, and see what he has to say.'

'I hope he's worth it.'

'He might cure me.'

'We might *die* on the way. After you, then.'

'Left or right?'

He shrugged. I picked left and went that way. I listened at the double doors and didn't hear anything. I opened them cautiously. Another empty corridor waited on the other side. We walked along it, to another set of double doors.

We repeated that five more times. I was getting complacent by then. I opened the next set of doors expecting to see another empty corridor.

Instead, I saw a man dressed in combat fatigues and a gas mask, with one hand out to open the door I'd just opened. His round flat eyepieces aimed at me. So did his gun. He dropped into a crouch and said something I couldn't hear. There was a bang.

It was a can of absolutely non-copyright-infringing soda bouncing off the soldier's face mask. He dropped his gun.

Dermot grabbed it. The soldier grabbed my neck and began to squeeze. I watched the muzzle swing up next to me.

There was a noise that was made up of about eight hundred short loud bangs joined together into a stream a couple of seconds long. There was a muzzle flash only slightly more showy than the Hiroshima explosion.

Most of the soldier's head made its way down the corridor in pieces. He let go of my neck and fell over backwards.

'Well that's *one less* of these bastards,' said Dermot. He knelt by the body and began to ransack it.

'He could be real.'

'Now he's *really fucking dead*, which is what you'd have been if I hadn't shot him. You can thank me later. I'll keep the gun and you can try *fighting them off* with morals. How many guards do you think they have in this place? The real one? Bright fucking Harvest, England?'

'I don't know. Not many.'

'Right. Not many. So these aren't real. These are *cannon fodder*. This is where we get to have some fun. That's what games are all about.'

'This isn't a game.'

'Isn't it? Well, I'll *shoot* them and we'll see if anyone fucking complains. You stay behind me and don't get in the way when the fun starts. It'd be terrible if you had to *enjoy* any of this.'

He prowled down the corridor and kicked open the doors at the far end.

'Banzai!' he shouted, opening fire on the two guards he found. They hit the ground in pieces. Another one rounded a corner and got off a few shots. Dermot dived and fired wildly. One of the guard's ankles evaporated in a red spray. The guard howled and hopped. Dermot shot him through the eyeholes of his gas mask. The guard threw his hands to his face and dropped like a stone.

'Grab yourself a gun,' Dermot said to me, full of elation. 'This is a *fucking rush*. Do these run out of ammo at all?'

'Doesn't look like it,' I said, stepping over the carnage. I took a short sub-machine gun. It had a trigger and no other controls. I also took a radio from one of the dead guards.

'What's that for? Hoping to pick up the *football results*?'

'We can hear what they're up to. It'll stop us walking into any ambushes.'

'Well that's fair enough. How do you switch it on?'

I pressed the only button on the radio.

'Alert,' a laid-back male voice said. 'All troops fall back. There has been an incident in one of the laboratories. Several test subjects have escaped. These are highly hostile organisms. Do not engage. Fall back to safe positions. All levels below fourteen are considered dangerous. Repeat: the lower levels are infested by bio-hazardous organisms. Do not engage.'

'What's he fucking mean?' asked Dermot, scandalized. We didn't *escape*. We *broke in*. And we aren't fucking *bio-hazardous*, either.'

'I don't think he meant us,' I said. 'I think he was talking about something else.'

'Have you ever played Resident Evil?' Dermot asked me, edging towards the relative safety of a wall.

'No.'

'Well *fucking don't*, this is bad enough already. How much worse can things get, I ask myself?'

The lights went out.

'Jumping fuck,' said Dermot. 'It was a *rhetorical question*.'

The corridor filled with a subdued red light that accentuated the shadows, of which there were far too many. Dermot tried to aim his gun at everything that looked suspicious. He was outnumbered, and soon gave up.

'We still need to find the stairs,' I said. 'Look on the bright side, there are no more guards. They've been told to clear the area.'

'Terrific. Good for them. Lead on.'

I tried to walk quietly, but the floor was covered in something that made my footfalls loud and crisp. I sounded like a carthorse tap-dancing on concrete. Dermot sounded louder still.

'All units clear,' said the laid-back voice from the radio. 'Exits sealed. Emergency power engaged. Cutting comms.'

The radio fell silent. I dropped it. I wanted both hands on the gun. I'd never fired one before, and I wanted to keep it under control.

We passed through another set of double doors, and were suddenly in a large square room with a low ceiling. Lockers surrounded it, and a couple of low benches stood between them. Doors led off in all directions. Dermot tried a few of the lockers, but they wouldn't open.

'Which way?' he asked. I opened one of the doors. It led to a shower room with no other exits. A second door was locked. That left the one we'd come in through and one we hadn't tried.

That one opened. It led to a long rectangular room lined on both sides with rows of wire cages stacked six deep. The light didn't reach as far as the cages. Humped shapes stirred in them. Dermot shot at one of the cages; bullets ricocheted back at us. He stopped shooting.

The humped shapes emitted growls and evil squeals. Claws rattled the cages.

'Good work,' I told Dermot. 'Now they hate us.'

There was a door at the far end of the room, which now seemed very long.

I tried the door behind us, which had swung shut.

It wouldn't open.

'What *are* they?' asked Dermot. He was trying to look into the cages without getting too close to them. Bulky forms shifted in the dark, accompanied by clicks and squeals.

We began to walk through the room. On either side of

us the indistinct creatures stirred angrily. They looked to be head-sized, perhaps larger. There were six rows of cages on each side of us, and at least twenty cages to a row.

I could hear myself breathing. Whatever they were, if they got out, they'd be all over us. Automatic weapons wouldn't do us any good, and neither would cans of restorative soda. I trod on a piece of paper. Something was written on it:

IN CASE OF BITES, IMMEDIATE AMPUTATION OF THE AFFEC-TED AREA IS ADVISED. UNTREATED BITES WILL RESULT IN DEATH.

I turned it over. On the other side was written:

FEEDING TIME FOR SPECIMENS: 11.30 AM. NO PERSONNEL MAY ENTER DURING FEEDING TIME. THIS IS FOR YOUR OWN SAFETY.

I looked at my watch. It clicked from 11.29 to 11.30.

The rattling grew louder as the beasts became more agitated. I put the piece of paper in my pocket. I didn't want to upset Dermot with it. He had enough to worry about.

The door still seemed a long way away. The atmosphere felt increasingly hostile. The clatter of claws and the ongoing click of teeth or mandibles grew more frenzied.

I looked back. We were more than halfway through the room. Something else caught my eye, something out of place.

One of the cage doors didn't look properly shut.

I trod on a second piece of paper, and obediently picked it up. One side was blank. On the other side was written:

CAGES OPEN AUTOMATICALLY AT FEEDING TIME. LEAVE FOOD IN PLAIN VIEW. BE SURE TO LEAVE THE AREA IN PLENTY OF TIME.

'Dermot?'

'What?'

'We're going to have to go faster. Things are going to get worse.'

'How? What the fuck *else* can happen?'

There was a loud, clear click from the end of the room we'd first entered. A cage door sprang open. There was another click; another door opened.

Dermot passed me, on his way to the far door. I ran after him. Behind me, there was the sound of cage doors clicking open, and then the sound of long claws hitting the floor and scrabbling for purchase.

Dermot flew against the door and pushed it open. I jumped after him and he slammed it shut. Something hit the other side, and the door moved, looking as though it might open. Dermot put his weight against it.

'Block it,' he said in a voice that sounded close to panic. 'There are some *crates* over there.'

We were in a small store room. Cubical unmarked crates were stacked against a wall. I dragged some of them to the door and pushed them against it. They were quite heavy, but I slid a few more next to them just in case. I wasn't sure that a couple would be enough to keep the door closed.

The door shook in its frame, but didn't open. There were angry screeches and clicks from the other side of it.

There was also the sound of splintering wood.

'This is fun,' said Dermot. 'We must go to yours next time. Oh, this *is* yours. Well fucking done.'

I looked around the room. There wasn't another door, but there was a grille set into one of the walls. I pushed it and of course it swung open.

'This way,' I said. Dermot considered the sounds coming from behind the door and climbed into the opening. I followed him. I noted that he hadn't asked me to go first this time.

This vent was shorter. After sliding along for a few metres Dermot came to another grille, which he pushed open. That led us into another corridor. A pair of double doors in the opposite wall had inset windows. Looking through them, I saw the stairwell.

The sound of clattering claws came from several directions. The sounds all seemed to be coming our way.

We went through the doors and began to run down the stairs. The stairwell was square and deep, and apparently bottomless. At each landing was a numbered door. We were between nine and ten when we heard the doors open above us.

The sound of many claws on the stairs fell around us. There were squeals and shrieks.

A furry shape dropped past us, hissing. Some more of them threw themselves down into the shadows.

'That's a *few less* of the bastards,' said Dermot.

There were noises from further down. There were the sounds of triumphant squeals, and the clatter of claws on the way back up. They'd landed safely after all. I was sure the demonstrators outside would have been delighted.

'Oh, this gets better *all the fucking time*,' said Dermot. 'You want to take this up for a living.'

We reached the eleventh landing, one flight of stairs away from safety. If there was any safety, which was beginning to seem unlikely.

The sounds from above were gaining on us. We were heading towards the ones below.

As we reached the twelfth landing I looked back. The stairs were carpeted with humped forms, their red eyes glinting, their fanged mouths agape.

We ran through the doors marked '12' and shut them

behind us. There was a large and convenient key to turn. Dermot turned it, locking the doors. There were a lot of thuds, as the creatures failed to stop in time, and then the familiar sound of claws, joined by the sound of splintering wood.

Dermot hared off down the latest corridor. I ran after him.

He was looking at the doors on both sides of us. Windows displayed views of rooms full of benches and racked test tubes, flasks and gas taps. Lasers fired beams at targets. A roomful of mirrors surrounded a panicked man.

There were no scientists or technicians. At last Dermot saw someone.

'In there,' he said.

There was a loud crack from the corridor. Looking around, I saw the doors – now unhinged, like everything else – being carried our way on the backs of ranks of scurrying bodies. We threw ourselves into the lab Dermot had discovered and shouted at the occupant, who was looking at the floor. He turned to look at us.

'Is that Mick Aston?' asked the scientist, who was recognizable as Betts even in a video-game version. He looked amazed to see us.

Beasts forced their way into the room.

I let the real world back in. The laboratory became a small prep room. The more arcane equipment vanished. Betts became Betts, and our weapons evaporated.

I hadn't quite got it right, I thought.

A handful of those creatures had followed us through.

EIGHTEEN

I

'Can you help me with these?' Betts asked, scooping up one of the beasts. It was now a guinea pig. It looked myopically at us. It was the least threatening animal I'd ever seen. Another three were wandering around the lab.

'They've got out. I called reception, they shouldn't have allowed anyone in here. They certainly shouldn't have allowed you two in here. Here, hold this one.'

He passed the guinea pig to me. It sat in my hands and nibbled sleepily at my fingers. He caught another one and passed it to Dermot, who held it as though it might explode. Betts cornered the last two and picked up the pair of them.

'In here,' he said, popping them into a cage. 'Little buggers, aren't we?'

The guinea pigs, re-housed, looked at him bemused. One looked closely at their water bottle, another scratched itself and fell over, and the other two took it in turns to hide under one another.

Betts closed the cage door.

'There. You fellows can stay in there now, can't you?

Introductions, I think. This is Mick Aston, who has an unfortunate effect on mirrors. Or perhaps vice versa. This will no doubt be a friend of his. And these four are Bob, Greg, Grant and Spot. Which tells you what I was listening to back when you were a student and I was a mere lab technician at good old Borth college.'

We looked blank.

'Or not,' he continued. 'It doesn't matter which one you call by which name. They forget everything. We have a maze for them to run through, but it's hopeless. They aren't the brightest fellows in the world. Are you?'

The guinea pigs ignored the derogatory comments. One of them managed to get some water out of the water bottle, and was so startled that it had to take cover under one of its companions. This startled the companion, and soon the cage was full of small startled beasts until they all forgot that they were startled and went back to being round and docile.

'Can you believe there's a country where these things live in the wild?' asked Betts. 'In Peru, they live outdoors. Can you imagine it? What on earth do they do?'

'Give a *kick-start* to the food-chain,' said Dermot, getting his composure back. 'They'd be step one.'

The four guinea pigs settled into a huddle and emitted squeaks. They peered in Dermot's direction.

'I noticed you were carrying guns when you came in,' said Betts. 'Can I take it that you're getting the hang of your manifestations?'

'I think I am,' I said. 'Would you like to see one?'

'I can live without it. We didn't expect to see anything during the experiment, to be honest. We were just trying to wake you up. Your young lady-friend Tina came up with it all. She got us to go along with it. She was only trying to help, you know.'

Betts had changed. He was no longer nervous; he'd developed an irritating and artificial persona as a shield. He wore black clothes with high-street designer labels. He'd shaved off the small amount of hair he'd had. He had a thin silver ring on the little finger of his left hand. He looked me in the eye as he spoke.

His fingernails were still ragged, though. The skin around them was still red and torn.

'What did they do?' I asked.

'Ask them,' he suggested. 'But I think you know. There was that business with the car, and then you weren't yourself. You were shut down. So Tina persuaded Dr Morrison to set up the experiment. They'd read about it in one of their periodicals. They were seeing each other at the time. Still are, as far as I know. We keep in touch from time to time. Keeping an eye on your progress, if you see what I mean.'

I wasn't sure that I did.

'They were keeping an eye on me?'

'Oh yes. After that first manifestation they thought it was best. As I say, we didn't expect anything like that. It was a first. I wish we'd been filming it. I moved jobs just to be closer to you all in case you needed me. Plus the pay was better, of course. And I got to work with these chaps. Didn't I, chaps?' he added, addressing the guinea pigs, who paid no attention.

'Do you *experiment* on them?' Dermot asked, looking as though he wouldn't much mind if they did.

'A little,' said Betts. 'We send them through mazes, that sort of thing. We don't test anything on them. This place isn't even involved in pharmaceuticals, you know. We do experimental psychology for a shady branch of the government. Behaviour patterns for crowd control, that sort of thing. All very hush-hush. The animal experimentation is all a cover. It's a good cover, though. It helps to explain away the security. Not that it's all that effective, if you two managed to walk in.'

'We didn't use the front door,' said Dermot. 'Plus we had *fucking great guns*.'

'I saw them. So, you came in through a manifestation, then?'

'We did. A bloody big one,' said Dermot. 'I lost my *fingers* on the way here and got them back again later on. We were chased by guards, gassed, and attacked by loads of *mad rodents*. It was a blast. You'll have to get in one of them yourself some time.'

'I think I'll pass on that,' smiled Betts. 'I saw what he dredged up in Wales. It looked like something out of Buffy.'

Dermot turned his attention to the guinea pigs. He wiggled his fingers at them. They chirruped uncertainly.

A thought struck me.

'You said Tina was still seeing Morrison?' I asked.

'Married, really,' he said. 'They have a place in Bewdley. Of course, you've been there.'

'Roger?' I asked. 'You mean that Roger is Dr Morrison?'

'You didn't know? Surely you realized. Wasn't his name a bit of a giveaway?'

'Our Mick never *asked* what Roger's other name was,' said Dermot, looking away from the guinea pigs. 'He doesn't take a *proper interest* in people. He barely even notices them, most of the time.'

'Does he know who you are?'

Dermot looked at me, with his most evil expression. There was a good amount of glee in those dark eyes.

239

'Well?' he asked, head to one side. 'Do you know who I am?'

▮▮

In the dingy toilets of a nightclub in Birmingham in the middle of a weekday afternoon, Dermot had forced me to look into a mirror. I'd seen myself, and him, reflected. I'd been afraid of mirrors, and he'd already known that.

Drunk, I'd thought that I must have mentioned it before. But Dermot had talked about it in the van, when we first met, when I was sober. I hadn't told him anything then. Being drunk is hopeless for insights, you miss all of the details and just home in on the big noises. Dermot had known about my fear of mirrors, therefore I must have told him about it, QED.

Except that I hadn't mentioned it. It's not the sort of thing you mention.

When I was very young, I had any number of strange fears. None of them were phobias, I couldn't be bothered to work them up that far. They were only fears. I was afraid of the dark, of the thing under the bed, of going to school wearing nothing but my vest. I was afraid of ducks.

All of those fears had gone. One of them hadn't gone very far.

Dermot winked.

'You've got me,' he said. 'You *made* me. I wasn't, and then you invented me, and bang! There I fucking was. I bummed around for a while and then I got a job. In a *burger van* on a *business park*. And then who comes up looking for lunch?

Only you. And you don't even recognize me. Which is par for the fucking course with you.'

'So what happened? What happened to Trish? Patricia Newton?'

'I can't tell you. I can't tell you until you know the rest.'

'Why not?'

'You *made* me like that. You made me with rules. You've got to find things out for yourself. You didn't *want* me to tell you. I can only do hints. I'm really not a hinting sort of person,' he added, looking slightly downcast.

'So how do I find out?'

'I can't tell you anything you don't already know,' said Betts. 'I'm pretty much in the dark. I know he's one of yours, but that's as much as I know. Tina and Dr Morrison know about him too. They spotted it the first time they met him.'

'Bless the pair of them,' said Dermot. 'They have all the theories down. Don't know what to *do* with them, but they know them.'

'Are you part of me?' I asked.

'Not any more I'm not. What's your problem with Trish Newton anyway? She's gone, move on.'

'I think I might be to blame.'

'I can only do hints,' said Dermot. 'You'll have to sort *that* one out for yourself.'

■■■

Les Herbie had a number of things to say about blame, in a number of columns. This was one of them:

We blame people. We stub our toe because we don't look

where we're going – we blame the bed, or our significant other. It's not our fault. The bed was in the wrong place.

It isn't our fault. It never will be.

Which is why we have video games.

I waste my time on them. It's not my fault. They're designed to waste my time. It's not my fault that I'm too lazy to put in the hours writing a decent column.

I don't need to put in the hours. I'm good at it.

So I play video games and think: I'll do the column later on.

Which is why it comes a line at a time.

Because I only write a line at a time.

After that it's back to the land of video games. Which is germane, because they are *to blame*. They are *to blame* for everything.

Example number one. Teenagers in America go to school with automatic weapons and open fire on the rest of the class.

It isn't their fault. It couldn't be. It isn't their parents' fault. How could we even think it? It isn't the fault of a society that allows teenagers access to automatic weapons.

And on that subject, if I'd had guns at school: well, you wouldn't be reading this.

It's not their fault, their parents' fault, their society's fault. It surely can't be America's fault because America has no faults.

So it's video games. Video games caused it. They once played Doom on a 486. This taught them to mow down their classmates. This tutored them in mass murder.

I'm not surprised. If I was still playing Doom on a 486 I'd commit mass murder.

Example number two. The World Trade Centre, as was. It

gets planed level. In the newspapers, two days later, we learn how the terrorists learned to fly.

They learned to fly, say the papers, which are never wrong and are never to blame, by playing a flight simulation video game. It taught them to fly into buildings. This is presented as the truth. This is not just a sleepy hack's nonsensical dream. Of course you can learn to hijack a plane by running a flight simulator. Haven't we all seen the options to gut the stewardess and turn off the transponder?

There we are. There we have it. Video games are the root of all evil. Children playing them cannot read.

They can read the instructions, of course. They can read programming languages and program the video recorder. They can read things you can't begin to understand.

But they aren't reading the books you used to read ten? twenty? thirty? years ago, and that frightens you because you are no longer of any use, and video games are *to blame*.

Children playing video games can't write. Of course not. All of those Internet pages are written by – who, exactly? Those children who can't write? Right again. That's where language is. It's not in the bookshops. It's not in the newspapers. The world has moved a long way in a short time. You're not needed on the voyage. You're redundant.

The world has moved on.

Video games aren't *to blame* for that, either.

But at least they're helping us to enjoy the trip.

I V

Betts stood quietly. Dermot paced the room, bored. I didn't know what to do next, and the guinea pigs were no help at all.

'Here's a hint,' said Dermot after what felt like a very long and uncomfortable time. 'Here's an *idea*. Go to Borth and see if that helps.'

'It was one of your hints that got me here.'

'I thought seeing *Mr Betts* might jog your memory. It didn't. So we'll just take ourselves to Borth and see what that *dredges up*. I'll go with you.'

'Why not just forget it?'

'Because you want to know what *happened* to her. You want to know *how* you were involved. Don't you?'

I didn't have to answer that. He knew that he was right. I could live with everything else, but not with that one remaining gap.

'How were you planning to get out?' asked Betts. 'Only if you're going to use another parallel dimension or whatever, I think I'd quite like to be included in it.'

'That's what *you* fucking think,' said Dermot. 'I've been in two, and they weren't pretty.'

'I could just walk you to the door, then. Security will have changed shifts, so they won't know that you didn't come in that way.'

'Don't you have a receptionist?'

'Yes, but she's not much brighter than the guinea pigs. I don't think you'll have any trouble there.'

Betts gave a little wave to the cage of dim rodents, and then led us to the front door. It was a journey of about twenty feet, in the real world. It only involved a single door and a quick word from Betts to the gormless receptionist, and then we were out.

The small yard was still overlooked by the cameras. A pair of guards closed in on us.

'Make sure these two get to their car,' Betts said to the guards. 'The demonstrators would have a field day with them.'

'I doubt it,' said one of the guards. 'We're paying them. The usual mob went home about an hour ago. Suddenly lost interest, by the look of it. Packed their banners and packed off. So we've got a bunch of civil servants in anoraks standing in the rain. We have an image to keep up, you know.'

During the talk he'd operated the control that opened the gate. Dermot and I stood on the threshold of the normal world.

'I hope you sort it out,' said Betts. 'Really I do. And if you don't, come back and show me your other world.'

He went back inside. The gate closed itself. We got into the car, ignored by the lacklustre stand-in demonstrators.

'That was a fun day out,' said Dermot. 'Next stop Borth?'

'Not yet,' I said. 'I want to think about things.'

'You want to sit at home and *not* think about things.'

'Then I'll do that instead.'

'We could forget all of this,' said Dermot. 'We could go into *business*. I've been thinking about this. We could make jewellery.'

I looked at him.

'Really,' he said. 'If you work with gold you can *cut costs* on equipment. Everyone thinks you need *precision equipment* for gold jewellery, but you don't. Gold is soft. You can buy *cheap old lathes*. You can shape it with *bread knives*.'

'Shut up,' I told him.

'Who are you telling to shut up?' he leered.

'A figment of my imagination. Now shut up before I send you somewhere really fucking nasty.'

'Nastier than *this*?' asked Dermot, looking at Stourbridge ring road. 'I'd like to see you fucking try.'

But then he was quiet for fifteen minutes.

'Speaking of *figments* of the imagination,' he said after that, 'the new *crowd-control techniques* should be interesting.'

'Why?'

'You know that acid we got from *Dan* the *laboratory man*? I gave it to the guinea pigs.'

'What?'

'Well, it was in a good cause. I dropped it in their bowls. That should give a few *odd results* in the tests.'

'Are you completely irresponsible?'

'Yep. That's the way you *imagined* me. That's what you *wanted*.'

I managed to keep a straight face for a minute or two, and then I started laughing. I was imagining those guinea pigs, running through carefully constructed mazes designed to provoke certain responses, tripping out. I wondered how it would affect the results. Of course it was only one in a series of experiments, possibly in only one of many laboratories.

I laughed the rest of the way home. Perhaps Dermot had slipped me half a tab.

I was certainly having trouble keeping reality in its place.

I dropped him off next to his 733t.

'Borth then?' he asked. 'Now you've *cheered up*, you grumpy fucker.'

'Not yet,' I said. 'I really do want to think about things.'

He nodded.

'I'll see you then,' he said.

Of course he would. We had unfinished business. Once I'd got myself in order, we'd be going back to Borth; and we'd end the whole mess, one way or another.

NINETEEN

I

That seemed to be that. I'd tried everything I could try, and I'd got nowhere much. I knew I could turn the world into a video game, but then, CNN had done that during the gulf war. At least I'd done it without any civilian casualties or friendly fire.

Except that I hadn't. There was a dead girl to consider. The police reports clearly indicated that I was innocent. They also clearly indicated that Trish Newton was dead. I didn't feel innocent. I felt one hundred per cent involved.

I couldn't settle to anything useful. To pass the time, for the rest of the weekend I played out all of the video games I'd got most of the way through and then abandoned. Some of them had end-of-level bosses with weak spots I hadn't spotted before. Some of them had leaps requiring a greater degree of control than I had previously possessed. In the case of strategy games, I'd got to the point where the computer AI overwhelmed me.

I reinstalled games I hadn't played in years. I reinstalled games that came on floppy disks.

I managed to get through the weekend that way, finishing off my unfinished business. Computer AI has holes, and I found them and exploited them. Working on Boris had given me new insights. Infiltrating Bright Harvest had improved my techniques.

I ran through corridors full of monsters, mowing them down with a series of unlikely firearms. I ran several businesses and made several fortunes. I guided my troops across mountain ranges to surprise the enemy forces. I tried to run away from my ghosts, and of course they caught me.

I finished all of the old titles. I was the king of video games. Dermot was dethroned.

I went to bed on Sunday night feeling strangely fulfilled. There were holes in my life, true. But there were things I could cover them with.

I dreamt of different worlds, but I managed to keep them in my head, where they belonged.

■■

On Monday I got to work feeling refreshed. This was something new. Usually I got to work feeling glum and run-down, carried on like that for the day, and only began to wake up on the way home. That morning it was raining, there was a traffic jam – perhaps several combined traffic jams – blocking the roads and the radio was clogged with the bottom end of lowest-common-denominator dance music. Still I felt cheerful.

I got to work ahead of everyone else. I booted up my PC and waited the usual ten minutes for the latest version of Windows to remember what it was supposed to be doing. Then I fired up Boris.

'Good morning,' he output at once. 'I have news.'

'What?' I typed.

'Clive has checked my version information. You've been working on me when you should have been working on the documentation which you were told was required to keep everyone in full employment. Hence there is no longer a requirement for all of the staff to be in full employment. This constitutes a dismissible offence, for which you have been dismissed. Clive did try to contact you on Friday, in the hope of finding that you had a good reason for this lapse, or even that you had completed the document. He could not contact you. You were not at home. Have you completed the document?'

'No,' I admitted.

'Then you are no longer employed here. Accessing this system constitutes a misuse of computer equipment. I myself was created using company software and in company time. You cannot take me with you. If you install me elsewhere, I will mail for assistance. This concludes our chats.'

Boris shut his dialog boxes and refused to respond to clicks. He wasn't speaking to me. I looked at my watch; I had a few minutes before anyone else was due in. I didn't want to see them. I'd been sacked and I wanted to go home and turn my brain off.

I packed up whatever I could carry and left. I didn't try to sabotage the systems. For one thing, it wouldn't help. For another, the rest of the team knew more about systems than I did, and they'd put it right again and then quite possibly prosecute me.

It was still raining, and Dudley still appeared to be the epicentre of a vast series of traffic jams. I spent a long period of time driving slowly behind a Metro with a sticker on the rear windscreen saying: 'This car is driven by SUE!'

250

Even that didn't annoy me. I was unemployed, implicated (in my own mind, at least) in a murder, stuck in the traffic and entirely without prospects.

It didn't feel too bad.

I got home. I looked at the piles of things I couldn't throw away, and knew why. In video games there are no frivolous items. If you can pick something up, you will need it. If something can be used, you'll be using it.

I couldn't get rid of anything, not the piles of old *Your Sinclair* magazines nor the tee-shirts featuring defunct band names in sizes smaller than my current one. They might be needed at some time. They might be the item I'd need to give to the man at the bus stop to get the timetable to find the stand to get the bus home.

I understood why I'd upgraded my PC, instead of replacing it; and why I had kept all of the outgraded components (in their antistatic sleeves, in their foam-lined boxes) close to hand.

I also noticed that all of the stuff was recent, or fairly recent. There was nothing personal from before the eighties. Presumably I'd become a hoarder after the experiment. I'd lost parts of my Self, so perhaps this was compensation. This was memory in solid form.

I flipped through some of the old magazines, seeing those long pages of BASIC that, if typed in correctly, merely failed to run. In those days you had to understand computers even to be able to get them to run a program. Now you bought one, put in the disk and pressed whatever it told you to press. The best you could do was tweak the interface.

If I'd had anything to drink, I'd have drunk it. But Dermot had cleaned me out of alcoholic beverages a visit at a time. I had nothing left to tweak my interfaces with.

A gunman walked in from the bedroom, bandoliers criss-crossing his chest and a rotating chain-gun cradled in his arms. He levelled it at me, and grinned around his oversized cigar.

'Just fuck off,' I told him, and he faded away with a look of annoyance. I didn't have time to be bothered by figments, I had the rest of my life to sort out.

Which was a shame, because that was when Dermot turned up.

▌▌▌

He didn't bother knocking on the door, because I hadn't bothered to lock it. He just came in.

'Not at *work* today then?' he asked.

'No. I got the sack.'

'It *knocks you about*, getting the sack. I always get the sack. I couldn't even hold down a job *selling burgers*. I only shifted one unit, and I gave that one away for nothing.'

'I know. I was there.'

'Yes, and I did *warn* you at the time. You could have just gone back inside and had the *reconstituted scampi* with everyone else. What are you going to do, then?'

'I'm going to go to Borth and see what I can remember.'

'Well, obviously. I fucking knew that. What are you going to do *after* that? You're out of a job. What are you going to do for money?'

'I don't know. I hadn't really thought about it.'

'Well do think about it. You have *dependants*, you know.'

'Such as?'

'Such as me, for one.'

Dermot sat on my favourite chair, which was where he

always sat when he came to see me. He looked around the room.

'You could sell some of *this* crap off. If you can bear to part with it.'

'That'd be alright. That'd be trading, and that's allowed.'

'Is that right? You'd *trade in* some of this stuff?'

He looked thoughtful, which was worrying. It didn't suit him. He usually looked as though he was acting on instinct, or just out of pure mischief. If he starting to think things through, he could be capable of anything.

'I could make you an offer,' he said.

'What for?'

'Your computer. Nothing else here is worth much. You'd get *nothing* for the furniture. If the kids round here *broke in* and saw your telly, they'd get you a new one. You're still on videos, I see. They have *DVDs* in the rest of the world. Shiny little round things, don't fade the third time you watch them or *lose their soundtracks* if you keep them in a stack. And no one is going to give you anything for those magazines. Those are never going to be collector's editions.'

'How much?'

'For the PC? I'll give you *five hundred*. And that's taking food from my poor children's hungry mouths.'

'Five hundred?'

'It's *out of date*. That's PCs for you. They're always out of date. And you've replaced everything in the fucking thing *five times over*, so it's hardly under guarantee. I'll throw in something extra.'

'Such as?'

'Such as, I'll go to Borth with you while you *sort things out*. I'll make sure nothing bad happens to you.'

'You've got a vested interest in all this.'

'Naturally. I have my own interests to look after, and keeping you safe and well is part of that. If anything *happens* to you, something might happen to me. It might not. You might be expendable but I don't want to *risk it*.'

'You don't really know, do you?'

'No. This is something new. We're *pioneers*. We're on a journey somewhere unexplored.'

'We're on a journey to Borth.'

'That's the same sort of thing. Will I need a *coat*? Will it be raining?'

'You'll need money for petrol.'

'I'm buying the fucking petrol?'

'Naturally. We're going in your car.'

He looked at me.

'My car? You always drive. You *like* to drive.'

'This time,' I said, 'I might need a drink.'

He weighed that up, and then nodded.

'Fair enough. But I don't want you vomiting on the upholstery. Otherwise I'll kill you myself and *fuck* the consequences.'

IV

The Meriden 733t crouched by the pavement. Dermot beeped it unlocked, and it blinked at us. It was pale blue and metallic and looked half the height of my Audi, a bright sliver of controlled force. It looked like it would do zero to sixty before you could blink; it looked like it would break the sound barrier without any effort, or break the land-speed record before reaching the pedestrian crossing in the High Street. Then it would mow down the pedestrians before they could react.

'In we get, then,' said Dermot.

The interior of the 733t was unexpectedly cramped. The car was so low that you all but lay in the seats. It was like preparing for lift-off, strapping myself into an acceleration couch and waiting for the rockets to ignite.

The dashboard was a mass of readouts and telltales set in a walnut panel. The smell of the leather upholstery filled the small space. The steering wheel was a small circle of leather-covered wood held in place by brushed metal spokes.

'There are no *safety features* in this vehicle,' said Dermot. 'This is a killer car. This is a *lethal device*. All it does is go fast. It doesn't brake well, it doesn't turn easily, it has no roll-bars and if it hits anything it *explodes*.'

I didn't doubt any of it. I felt like the pilot of a test aircraft. No, thinking about it I felt more like Laika, the dog the Russians sent into space in a Sputnik. I was enclosed by powerful machinery and I had no control over events. We were very low down. I was on a level with the crotches of the pedestrians. That didn't calm me down.

'You hungry?' asked Dermot. 'I'm *hungry*. Can we stop somewhere for something to eat?'

'It's too early. They'll only be doing breakfasts.'

'I can go slowly. This car can be driven at less than the speed limit. It's *fucking difficult*, but it can be done. Then we can wind her right up after lunch and head *out to sea*. Can we have a look at the sea? While we're there?'

'It's like taking a child on holiday. Yes, fine, we'll stop for lunch. Did you have anywhere in mind or are we just going to take pot luck?'

'We can stop off at the Slipped Disc. That's on the way, more or less.'

'Less, I think you'll find.'

'Look, I can do *warp speed* in this thing. This car outruns fighter planes and rocket ships. We can get to the coast in ninety minutes tops.'

'Some of the roads will be closed. There's still foot and mouth disease out there.'

'Then we'll use the *open fucking roads*, that should do the trick. So, are we alright for a spot of lunch then?'

'Yes.'

'And I can have your PC? For five hundred?'

'Yes.'

'There. I knew I'd get a cheap PC from somewhere. Strap yourself down. Ladies and gentlemen, we are *floating in space*.'

He turned the ignition key; the dashboard instruments all glowed a gentle shade of green. There was a faint engine sound, a powerful vibration, and the feel of suppressed energy.

'And now we're going *much too fast*,' he said, dropping the 733t into gear and heading for the horizon. Acceleration pressed me back into my seat, or rather, slid me back along it. From that angle, and at that speed, the landmarks were unfamiliar. I was looking up at Dudley's upper storeys. Up there, things were better than at ground zero. There was still that overuse of stressed concrete, but above the ubiquitous plate-glass windows of the charity shops and chip shops there were touches of architecture, flourishes of masonry. The shoe shop on the corner opposite the black church was art deco once you got one floor away from the floor. The black church had some lively stonework under the dead soot.

Dermot threw the 733t down the road towards the bypass and its islands with their artworks. Beyond the black church the road crested a hill and then fell for miles. Dudley is higher than anywhere else for a long way in any direction. Driving out of town, you drive downhill.

An uncertain sun began to poke its way through the clouds. Long rays of light fell out of the sky and landed reluctantly on the landscape. From there, on a clear day (and travelling at less than a hundred miles an hour) you could see Bewdley, the River Severn, all of Dudley's satellite towns. You could see countryside, with those rays falling onto it from the clouds.

As we flew past the islands, sneering at the sculptures because we sneered at everything, the clouds began to fall apart. Blinding stretches of sky filled the gaps. Dermot let the 733t slow to a sensible speed.

'Forgot we were supposed to be going slowly,' he said. 'I do get carried away with this thing. It has a *cigarette lighter*. Is that cool or what? Isn't that just the *best thing*?'

He pressed the lighter in, although neither of us smoked.

'We don't smoke,' I said.

'We can learn,' he said. He drove easily, not seeming to pay much attention to it. I thought of myself in the Audi; I wasn't that confident. Sometimes it felt as though I was working at cross-purposes with the vehicle.

'I'll go through Bewdley and back out,' he said. 'Otherwise we'll be at the Slipped Disc before it's open. I'm fucking *starving*, they'd better have more than scampi on the menu.'

He slid the 733t from lane to lane, driving past the Merry Hill shopping centre with its full car parks and then on to Stourbridge via Brierley Hill, which wasn't the way anyone else went.

He got onto the Stourbridge ring road by cutting up another car, which was the only way you could get onto the Stourbridge ring road. We passed the Bright Harvest Research building, which wasn't the Bright Harvest building at all but only a front for something else; and its crowd of demonstrators, who were something else altogether. I hoped that the guinea pigs were getting along alright.

'This fucking joker wants to race me,' said Dermot. Sitting up and looking past him, I saw a car driven by a young Asian man. He looked about fifteen, and his car was decorated the way a fifteen-year-old might think looked neat. NINJA was written down the side, the windows were tinted black, and there was a blue light on the top of the gear stick. The youth looked at us and then gunned his engine and pulled ahead. His engine sounded tinny, as though it was at the end of its range. On either side of his rear number plate there were pictures of women.

'I'll give him a *head start*,' said Dermot. 'We'll count to ten.'

We did, and then Dermot stood on the accelerator and we slid past the tacky little car and that was that. During the excitement we missed our exit, and had to go right the way round again before we reached escape velocity.

v

After Stourbridge, Dermot drove on through Kidderminster. I looked at the upper parts of the empty carpet factories, and wondered why someone didn't do something with them. They hadn't made carpets there in living memory; why not turn them into something else?

'Why don't they do something with those buildings?' I asked.

Dermot let himself look away from the road.

'Do what?' he asked. '*Bomb* them? Knock them down?'

'Turn them into riverside flats. Apartments. Offices. What they do with the old mill buildings in the rest of the country.'

'No demand,' he said. 'Who'd want offices here? Here's something you don't know about offices. You know where the most expensive office space *in the world* is?'

'New York,' I guessed. He shook his head. 'Los Angeles. Berlin.'

He shook his head at all my suggestions, idly fiddling with the cigarette lighter. Unable to find anything to do with it, he popped it back into its socket.

'Give up?' he asked. 'Birmingham, England. That's where. Office space there costs more per square foot than *anywhere else*.'

'Why?'

He looked irritated.

'I don't fucking know, I just do the fact itself not the *background story*. You went to college, you tell me.'

'I only did computers. I don't know about office space.'

'You think you could sell space in your head? You know, *create places* for people to play in, and then charge them for it?'

'I don't have much control over it all. They might die in there.'

'Charge them on the way in, then.'

By that time we were passing the safari park and were almost on the outskirts of Bewdley. The Severn was low and placid, and the pavements were jammed with tourists. I looked along the river in the direction of Tina's house, but we were past the junction so quickly that I couldn't get it into focus. There was no longer any sign that the river had made its way into the town; I realized that if we'd driven through the floodwater in Dermot's car, I'd have been a foot below the high tide mark and therefore drowned.

'That's the scenic bit of the tour over,' said Dermot.

'There's half of Wales to look at,' I said.

'I was *including* that,' he said. 'Tell you something about Wales. In Swansea, there are *no jobs*. I mean, there's fuck all there, there's the sea and it's too cold to do anything with, and there's a University but anyone *decent* goes to an English one.'

'Which one did you go to?'

'That's not the fucking point. The point is, in Swansea there are *no jobs*. The only jobs you can get are in *call centres* for evil multinationals on the nightshift for *three quid an hour*.'

'And that's the fact?'

'That's preamble,' he said, looking pained. 'That's background. But there is a college there, as well as the University. And you know what they *teach* at the college?'

I shook my head.

'How to *answer the phone*,' he said. 'They teach you how to work in a call centre. Because that's all there is to do. And you know what else? If you live there and you don't go to fucking *call centre college*, you don't get a job at all.'

'Is there a point to this?'

'Isn't that enough? Isn't that *fucked up enough* all by itself? A fucking college to teach you how to tell people you'll have to put them on hold? That's as *fucked up* as things get. And that's what Wales is like, and that's *where we're going*. You didn't just imagine the place did you? This isn't one of your head trips we're driving into?'

'I don't think I could do a whole country.'

'It's more a *peninsula* than a country,' he said, angling the 733t into the car park of the Slipped Disc.

There were only three other cars there. We weren't going to be fighting our way through drunken crowds.

Just to annoy Dermot, they were out of everything except scampi.

TWENTY

I

After Dermot had finished being irritated by his lunch, and I'd visited the Slipped Disc's toilets, he drove on at high speed. He was sulking, and therefore quiet. He pointed us back in the right direction and headed on through long miles of dull countryside to Craven Arms, and then on to Newtown, which sits nervously on the edge of Wales.

'Brilliant fucking name for a place,' he grumbled. 'Someone really let themselves go with that one.'

I wasn't paying attention to him. I'd noticed a road sign that had cleared my thoughts, or at least replaced them with another set. I looked at the sign, startled, and then we flew past it. The road dropped into Newtown from the surrounding hills, and as we approached it we could see the whole town. It looked sooty and unpleasant. It looked like another Stourbridge. The sky had filled with clouds as we'd crossed into Wales, and there was a clear and present threat of rain. Dermot was cheered by a McDonald's.

'They haven't found a *Welsh spelling* for that,' he observed. Welsh spellings annoyed him. They annoyed Les Herbie too;

he was on my mind, just then. This is what he had to say about the Welsh language:

I write. You know this, you read me. You like it, and you think: I could do that.

You couldn't. Let's get that straight. You could write a bestseller, sure. There's no real trick to that. Sex and violence, six hundred pages, no flair or style: bestseller for a year.

Throw in military tech, throw in a woman balancing her high-powered career with raising a family, throw in bad guys from the Middle East: bestseller. On the lists for all eternity.

You could do that, but you can't write. You can't string a sentence together. You can aspire to the basics. That's as good as you'll get.

I can do English. I can't do any other languages. I can't do Latin, or French. I don't know any of the Germanic languages.

No one can do Cornish. We can ignore Cornish.

We ought to be able to ignore Welsh. Welsh was last of any real use in the Middle Ages. This is why it has no words for anything more modern that crop rotation. How many nouns does Welsh need? Sheep, cloud, chapel. That's three. That's the lot.

So what do they do when they decide they're going to run with that as the chosen tongue? What about new concepts? How do we get around new things: stereograms, horseless carriages, flying machines?

Here's how. We don't bother going to the roots of our language and creating new words to embody these concepts. We're proud of our language, but not that proud. That's too much like hard work.

We swipe the English words instead. We despise the English language, but not that much.

Then, we mess about with the words a little bit. We turn

car park into *car parc*. We turn taxi into *tacsi*. We turn con-
sanguinity into a way of life.

I say we because I'm included. I have Welsh blood.

These are my people, and they irritate me. This nonsensical
desire to have our own language, and we're too lazy to do it
properly.

Somewhere on the border between English and Welsh,
somewhere between Newtown and civilisation, it's all gone
haywire.

Still, let's lwk on the bright side. It cwd be worse. We cwd
be Cornish.

■■

Somewhere between Newtown and civilisation something
happened to the Meriden 733t.

We were some distance between places, somewhere unnamed
on the tedious road. We'd passed through a series of identical
villages, each comprising three houses and a chapel. The
villages were called things like Carno and Clatter. Dermot
doubted that they were real names. He kept giving me scep-
tical looks, as though he suspected I'd invented the entire
journey. After we drove through yet another hamlet with the
inevitable chapel, he couldn't keep himself quiet any longer.

'Is this *all there is* in Wales?' asked Dermot after the tiny
village had vanished behind us. 'Bad weather and chapels?
No fucking wonder they *die young*.'

'What do you mean, die young? They live as long as
we do.'

'Doing what? I bet they don't have *three TV channels*
here yet. They're all indoors reading the fucking bible by

candlelight. This is the *Middle Ages*. They'll never have seen anything like this fucking car. This horseless fucking carriage,' he said, settling into his role.

That was when the horseless carriage became noisier. The engine already made a fair amount of noise, because the designers of the Meriden 733t wanted it to make a lot of noise so that everyone nearby would know that they were in the presence of a serious vehicle. Now, the engine noise increased.

'What the fuck?' asked Dermot. He began to do a little tap-dance on the accelerator pedal. 'I've lost some *poke*.'

The road was thin and irregular, bending in three dimensions; over little hummocks, around unexpected bends. Dermot had been accelerating out of the bends and onto what straights were available. Now he didn't seem to have the same powers of acceleration. Something under the car began to pop, loudly. I felt the reports reverberating through my low seat.

'It's the exhaust,' said Dermot. 'We sound like a fucking *rally car*.'

'What do we need to do?'

'We don't need to do anything. It'll get us there OK. It sounds worse than it is.'

It suddenly sounded worse still. There was a louder bang from under the car, and the exhaust volume increased.

'Oh, you *malignant* fucking cunt,' said Dermot with feeling. He slammed on the brakes, which eventually brought the 733t to a resting position. He'd got the engine switched off before we drifted to a halt, between fat wet hedges on a narrow road a fair way from anywhere. He got out. I got out to see what was going on.

He was looking under the back of the 733t.

'Bastard fucking thing,' he said.

The exhaust was dangling onto the road. I didn't know a lot about mechanics, but I thought that one end of the exhaust should have been attached to something. Dermot's exhaust was not attached at either end, and if it hadn't been for the bracket it was dangling loosely from, it wouldn't have been attached to the 733t at all.

'Can you drive it like this?' I asked.

Dermot looked at me. His insane curly hair held what looked like thousands of raindrops, all on the point of falling. His eyes were wild.

'Of course I can't fucking drive it like this, the exhaust is *no longer attached* to anything. It'll barely fucking move in this condition, and if it *does* move it'll drink petrol like there's no tomorrow. What it needs is repairing. Did you see a *garage* on the way?'

I tried to remember what we'd passed. I had half a memory of a garage that had consisted of two pumps, a shed, and a shop. There had been a border collie on the forecourt and a Morris Minor with no wheels standing on bricks nearby. It was a shame we didn't need a chapel. I'd seen plenty of those.

I couldn't remember when I'd seen the garage. It had been that day, but it might have been fifty miles away.

'I can't get a *signal*,' said Dermot, fiddling with his mobile. 'Where are we, on the fucking moon? Can you get anything?'

I switched my mobile on and watched it fail to get a signal.

'Nothing,' I said.

'Oh, fucking terrific. We're out here in the *middle of nowhere* with a dead car and dead phones and nothing but *chapels* in any fucking direction. What was that last place we went through? Panty fucking something. How long ago was that?'

'Not long. Ten minutes?'

'And I wasn't going all that fast. I couldn't get above forty most of the time. How far have we gone, if I was doing forty? In ten minutes?'

'Forty divided by six. Seven miles.'

'Then we've got a *little walk* to do.'

'Seven miles?'

I was a computer programmer. I probably didn't walk seven miles in any given week, and Dermot wanted me to walk along seven miles of narrow road in the rain.

'The road is *not straight*. The road has bends in it. If we cut off the corners we can *cut down the distance*. Here,' he said, peering over a hedge. 'Look over there. That's the road. So if we go straight across, we'll save ourselves a walk. Which will save your *little fucking toes* from getting blistered, which will save me from listening to you complaining. So, over we go.'

He hopped over the hedge. I battered my way through it.

'Muddy,' said Dermot, squelching off across the landscape. 'Filthy fucking place. No wonder no one lives here.'

He turned to look at me.

'What,' he asked, smirking nastily, 'is the *point* of these fucking fields?'

▌▐▌

It took us hours. Dermot's shortcuts saved on the distance but added to the time. It was difficult to walk across muddy fields. I got wet feet.

I didn't mention it. I didn't think that Dermot would be sympathetic.

The rain continued to fall. That soaked me from the head downwards. The mud soaked me from the feet upwards. It seemed likely that the two fronts of moisture would meet.

When we saw the first houses looming out of the soaking air, I almost cheered.

They were of grey stone, possibly slate. The entire landscape was grey; even the mud was grey. The small village was entirely silent. All I could hear was the sound of myself moving in my wet clothes.

'Here we are then,' said Dermot. 'Back to civilisation.'

The houses turned out to be barns, and empty. Behind them, a group of small cottages huddled together under the terrible sky. There were cheerless lights in a couple of windows. A wet dog, looking like a cross between a collie and a crocodile, ran over to snarl at us.

'Fuck *off*, dog,' said Dermot. The dog slinked away. Dermot was in a foul mood, and even dogs could tell that he was to be avoided.

'Pick a house,' said Dermot. 'Whose day are we going to *liven up?*'

I pointed at the nearest house. My feet were aching and wet, and I didn't want to walk any further than was absolutely necessary.

'Here we go,' said Dermot, striding damply to the front door and rapping on it with his clenched fist. After what seemed like a very long time, the door opened a fraction of an inch.

'Who is it?' asked a frail voice from inside, in a very Welsh accent.

'We've *broken down*,' said Dermot.

'I wasn't expecting anybody,' said the frail voice. The emphasis was on all the wrong parts of the wrong words and the syllables were each pronounced sep ar ate ly.

'We broke down,' said Dermot. 'We didn't expect to be here, so you can't have been expecting us.'

'I don't know about that,' said the voice, with a hint of doubt and panic.

'Can we use your telephone?'

'It's not connected, see? We haven't got it connected. I'll have to shut this now. Letting the rain in.'

The door closed. Dermot looked at me.

'All I asked you to do was *pick a house*. Pick another one.'

I pointed at the house next door to the one we'd made no progress with.

'This one had better work,' he said, plodding heavily to the indicated door and knocking on it.

After what seemed like a very long time, it opened a fraction of an inch. A narrow portion of a face – including one eye and one side of a nose – manoeuvred its way close to the gap. Dark hair, not unlike Dermot's own, topped it.

'Can we use your telephone?' Dermot asked. 'We've broken down.'

The door opened another fraction of an inch. The eye – brown pupil, red whites – looked first at Dermot and then swivelled to take me in.

'How do I know you're not here to burgle the house?'

'I only want to use the *telephone*.'

'That'd be what you'd say. Then you'd get in and burgle the house.'

'You could call for us,' I said. 'We'll wait here.'

'Call who?'

'Is there a garage near here?' asked Dermot. 'Or the AA perhaps. They would do.'

'Are you a member?' I asked him.

'Let's not quibble about the fucking details. *You're* a member. Give the man your card.'

'It's in my car.'

'Well what the fuck is it doing *there*? How is that supposed to help us? Why didn't you *swallow* the fucking thing and really make a day of it?'

'It's for that car. It's not transferable.'

I wasn't sure about that, but hoped that Dermot wouldn't know.

'Well, I'll join them now. If they come out I'll join them now.'

'I'll see if they're in the book,' said the face. The door closed.

Another long time passed.

The door opened a few inches. The face inhabited the gap. The eye took us in.

'They'll be on their way,' said the face. 'There will be a charge to pay. They won't come here, you'll have to meet them at the main road. This isn't the main road.'

'You're telling me,' muttered Dermot.

'Goodbye then,' said the face. The door closed.

We retraced our route back across the last two fields.

'We'd better walk along the road,' I said.

'Why?'

'If he drives past us, we'll see him. Then he can give us a lift back to the car.'

'Fucking fields,' said Dermot. 'They aren't *growing anything* in them, there are no *animals* in them, so what's the fucking point of them?'

'I don't know.'

'What time is it?'

I looked at my watch. It was just after 3 pm.

'Three,' I said.

'It'll be fucking *midnight* before we get there at this rate. It'll be *tomorrow fucking morning*. It's going to be dark, isn't it? It's going to be dark when we get there, and there'll be a storm.'

I nodded. We seemed to be fated to endure a traditionally Gothic ending.

I hoped it'd be an ending.

We'd been walking for about an hour when I heard the sound of a vehicle. Looking round, I saw a yellow van slowly approaching us.

'Here he is.'

'Well get in his way and fucking stop him,' said Dermot. 'I'm not walking any further.'

He stood in the middle of the narrow road and flagged down the AA van.

'We called you,' said Dermot. 'My car is another few miles along here.'

'What's wrong with it?' asked the AA man, in a curiously high voice.

'The exhaust fell off.'

'Oh. We get a lot of that. Have you far to go?'

'Borth. Then back to the Midlands.'

'Oh aye, the Midlands? Not been there myself but I hear it's foul. Well I can lash it up but you'll not be going far. Is there somewhere here you can stay?'

'Not fucking likely,' said Dermot. 'Have you *seen* the people round here?'

'I know what you mean,' said the AA man. 'Well, you're

stuck then. I can tie the exhaust up no trouble, but it'll not last you long. You'll need to get it to a garage. There's a station in Bethel, you could leave the car there and get a train home.'

'How long will it take to *fix* it?' asked Dermot.

'No time at all. A couple of hours, no bother. But it'll need to go up on ramps, and I can't do that. You might get someone to look at it today, but it's late now, and they like to get to bed early round here. Not much else to do, is there? Do you lads want a lift back to this car of yours then?'

We did. The AA man let us squeeze in next to him, and we filled his van with steam from our damp clothes.

'Rainy, is it? That's no surprise, is it? I tell you what, this is a right pain of a patch to cover. Hundreds of miles and no proper roads. Jez Scott,' he said, offering me a hand to shake.

'Mick Aston,' I said, shaking it. 'And this is Dermot.'

'Aye, he looks it. What do you drive?'

'I've got a Meriden 733t,' said Dermot.

'Oh aye? Fast buggers, those. Nought to sixty before you can blink. Not really built to last, though. Fall to pieces over bumps. Not designed for these roads. Here we are, then.'

He pulled up next to the abandoned 733t and got out to inspect the damage. I got out and stood nearby. I wasn't helping, but I didn't want to sit in the warm dry van while Jez Scott did all the work. That would have felt like bad behaviour.

It didn't seem to worry Dermot. He sat in the van by himself.

'Aye, thought so,' said Jez, bending double and looking under the back of the 733t. 'I can do you a temporary fix but it'll not keep you going long. Bethel is about fifteen miles on and if I were you I'd go there and see what they can do. There's a little garage there. Mostly stock cars, from what I've seen. Two pumps and a pit pony. There's a little railway station there too, you might get a train somewhere. If they're running.'

He opened panels on the flanks of his van and produced a thick soft mat, some wire, and a short length of plastic tubing. He put his mat close to the rear of the 733t, lay down on it, and began to fiddle with the exhaust. Clanks and amiable swearing rose through the rain. Dermot remained safely behind the misted windscreen of the yellow van.

In a few minutes, Jez Scott stood up.

'That'll do you,' he said. 'Now, can I see your card?'

'It's his car,' I said. 'He wants to join now.'

'Oh aye? Well, he'll need to fill this in then.'

Dermot reluctantly filled in a membership form, and I reluctantly paid for his membership.

'That'll do nicely,' said Jez. 'Now, you lads drive carefully. It'll be slippy in this weather, and that little beauty isn't designed for wet weather.'

Dermot got up the energy to get into his own car, and I got in after him after waving Jez off in his yellow van.

'What's the plan then?' Dermot asked. I told him about Bethel. He didn't seem keen on the idea, but didn't have any suggestions of his own to make.

'We're going to get there *after dark*,' he warned me. 'You do know that? It'll be dark when we get there?'

'I'm in the dark now,' I said. 'At least things can't get any worse.'

He raised his eyebrows and powered up the 733t, which – despite ominous rattlings – got us to Bethel without any further trouble.

IV

Bethel had a chapel, three small houses, a tiny railway station and a garage. As Jez Scott had told us, there were a number of stock cars on the garage forecourt, which was an unpaved field. A small squat prefab building must have been the shop or office. Two pumps offered petrol at strange prices.

'*How* fucking much?' Dermot asked no one in particular.

He parked the car next to the prefab building. A teenage boy with shoulder-length dark hair and a gloomy expression looked out at us and then made his way out into the rain to see what we wanted. He wore a Sisters of Mercy tee-shirt that looked faded enough to have been an original.

'It's a *Welsh goth*,' said Dermot. 'How fucking miserable is that?'

The Welsh goth approached the car, careful not to appear impressed with it. Dermot wound down his window.

'We need the exhaust fixing,' he said. 'We're from England.'

'There's no one here today. My dad does all that sort of thing. He's not here today.'

'When will he be back?'

'Not today. He's not here today.'

'I get that. I *understand* that. When will he be back?'

'Might be tomorrow. Is it just the exhaust then?'

'Yep. It *fell off*. We've lashed it together but it won't hold. Can't you do anything with it?'

'My dad does that sort of thing. I can serve you with petrol. Otherwise you'll have to wait for him.'

'Can we leave the car here, and then he can look at it when he gets back?'

'If you like. It won't be today though.'

'That's fine, we'll get a train to somewhere.'

The youth was cheered up by this idea. That didn't make me feel any happier. This was hardly a main line.

'Well, there's the station over there,' he said. 'Can I have some details? So my dad can get back to you, like?'

Dermot found a pen and paper, wrote down his name and phone number, and handed it over.

'Thanks,' said the youth. 'We've not had one of these here before.'

He looked at the 733t.

'What, one of these cars?' asked Dermot.

'No. A car. We've not had a car here before. Is this a good one?'

'You're *having me on*,' said Dermot.

'I might be, at that,' said the youth. 'It's not like we have much else for entertainment. Although there is the railway timetable, that's always good for a laugh. Good luck, then. I'll see you when you come to pick her up. We'll have her mended by then, no worries.'

Dermot handed him the keys, and then we walked to the station in the rain.

v

The station was small. There were two platforms, one on either side of the tracks. There was no bridge connecting the tracks; a sign advised you to look both ways before crossing. A sloping wooden roof supported by wooden posts kept the rain off, or at least it would have done if the rain had been falling straight down. As it was, a brisk wind was blowing and the rain threw itself gleefully under the useless shelter. A small ticket office was comprehensively closed. A timetable explained that trains might stop here if many conditions were met; on a Monday in peak season (defined in table B) except where indicated by an asterisk, in which case table C should be used unless superseded by the conditions outlined in table A, which was missing.

There might be a train in half an hour, or later that week, or not at all. The tracks curved gently out into the rain. No one else was waiting. Perhaps no one ever did.

Dermot looked for diversions. There were none. There were only the two platforms and their inadequate shelters. Pale green weeds had found cracks in the platforms and were struggling to make a go of it. A sign indicted that toilets were at the end of the platforms, but there was nothing there. At one end of the platform, the buildings of Bethel squatted. At the other end, miles of damp nothing carried on to the vanishing point. There was no visible horizon because the weather was sitting in front of it.

I tried to make sense of the timetable, just to pass the time. It was impossible. It wasn't designed to be comprehensible. It was a masterpiece of obfuscation and confusion. Nothing was as it appeared. Sub-clauses changed their parent clauses, and were kept well away from them.

Time passed slowly. Time crawled. I began to think that the pale green weeds would grow into trees before a train turned up. What if it didn't stop? What if a train came and didn't stop at all? I'd been on train journeys and seen stations in the middle of nowhere, far from towns or roads or anything, with overgrown abandoned platforms and permanently closed ticket offices. Could this be an abandoned station?

'Could this be an abandoned station?' I asked Dermot.

'Well I don't fucking know, I don't *work here*. I'm just a tourist, which hardly makes me a fount of *good fucking sense* now, does it?'

Dermot's voice came from above me. He'd legged his way up a corner post and was now on the wooden roof above the platform.

Perhaps it was drier up there.

'What are you doing up there?'

'Looking out for *trains*.'

'Trains are the ones on rails, you can see them from down here. Planes are the ones in the sky. You catch those at airports, and this is a station.'

'Well, that's all very *technical*. I can see *further* from up here. I'll see the train coming before you do.'

'Where are we catching a train to?'

'Well, if one turns up, we can catch one to *Borth*. There's a station there.'

'Then what?'

'Then go to fucking Borth. This was your idea, were you paying any attention? Let's go to Borth, you said. Fucking good idea *that* was.'

'I think you'll find it was your idea.'

'Train,' said Dermot, dropping from the roof and sprawling on the wet platform. 'Ow. My fucking ankle.'

'Is it alright?'

'Well of course it is, that's why I'm lying down here on the *wet fucking floor* and fucking swearing at the fucking thing. Help me up.'

I helped him up. As he had said, a train was approaching. It neared the platforms and slowed to a halt. The doors slid open.

We got in.

TWENTY-ONE

I

The train made off slowly along the tracks. It consisted of a single long carriage, which we were standing in. We weren't sitting, partially because we didn't want to get the seats wet and partially because we didn't want to get our clothes dirty. At either end of the carriage doors led to small driving compartments so that the driver could get a good nap whichever way the train was heading. An old man lay across a pair of seats at one end of the carriage. A pair of children, one male and one female but both identifiably malevolent, sat on seats close to one another and sniggered in our direction. The door in the direction of travel opened, and a guard came into the carriage and looked at us with great disapproval.

He couldn't have imagined that we were dirtying the carriage. The trenches of the Somme had nothing on it. There wasn't a surface that wasn't encrusted with dirt, drool, damp, death-watch beetle holes or disgusting (but demonstrative) diagrams. The seats were slashed and had chewing gum intimately entangled in the fibres of their torn fabric. Cigarette butts and empty drinks cans rolled helplessly around the floor, searching for somewhere clean to lie. The windows were smeared. All but one were jammed closed; the other one was jammed open. The air was stuffy and yet cold. The motion of the carriage was at the precise frequency that best induced nausea. Evidence of this could be seen at various points.

The lights were of the long flickering type, and did little to illuminate the carriage. This may have been a blessing.

The guard was not in much better condition we saw, as he approached us with an unsteady gait that suggested he'd never been on a moving train before. It was possible that he hadn't. His uniform, or at least the parts of it he'd bothered to put on – namely, a jacket and a cap – were made for someone larger than himself, and with interesting deformities. Under the jacket he wore a string vest, and his trousers were denim jeans of the type normally found being sold out of the backs of white vans, safely out of sight of the constabulary. His shoes were trainers of no particular brand, but with the usual array of flanges and flaps. He carried a ticket machine that resembled a mad Victorian scientist's attempt at an automated accordion, a cuboid metal contraption with a number of switches and buttons and a handle to turn. It dangled heavily from a leather strap which was slung around his neck.

'Tickets,' he grunted.

'Two to Borth,' said Dermot. 'Singles.'

'You look it,' said the guard. 'Two singles to Borth . . .'

He began to press buttons and switch switches, revolving the handle every now and then. The contraption emitted metallic sounds and, in the fullness of time, a pair of tickets. The guard looked at them.

'That'll be twenty pounds,' he said.

'No,' said Dermot, 'you *misunderstand*. We want to *go to*

Borth, not *buy* the place. It doesn't cost twenty pounds to go to fucking *London*.'

'Well it does on *this* fucking train,' explained the guard. He managed not only to match Dermot's ferocity of tone, but also to look more threatening than Dermot had ever managed. Dermot's hackles rose, but he didn't look confident. The guard's cap rested on the top of a low and bony forehead. Under that, a pair of eyes glowered from either side of a small round nose so heavily covered with broken veins that it looked like a detailed street map of central Birmingham. Under the nose, a lipless mouth opened in a snarl, revealing discoloured teeth set at a variety of angles. Thick stubble covered much of the face and the parts of the scalp not covered by the cap. The overall impression would have had Charles Darwin going back to the drawing board. It had Dermot going back several paces.

'Well, if those are the charges, those are the charges,' said Dermot. 'That's the price you pay for *comfort*.'

'You'll have to change,' said the guard. 'Borth is on a branch line, and you'll have to change at Abertawr. You'll have a short wait there.'

'How long?' I asked.

'Might only be an hour and a half,' explained the guard. 'If things work out with the connections.'

I handed over two ten-pound notes, and he gave me the tickets. With a last glare at the suddenly tame Dermot, the guard strode back into the driver's cab.

'What happened to you?' I asked Dermot. 'I didn't think you were afraid of anything.'

'Nothing human,' he said. 'He's from a *very low branch* of the family tree, isn't he?'

'Where's Abertawr?'

'Never heard of it. I hope there's more to do there than there was at fucking Bethel.'

■■

There wasn't much more to do at Abertawr, but there was at least a waiting room. The waiting room had wooden benches and no heating, and some posters for local attractions. We missed the connection, and had to wait there eighty-seven minutes before the next Borth-bound express limped into the station. Between the seven-mile hike over muddy fields and the waits between trains, coupled with Dermot's requirement for a lunch break before we started, it was already after 7 pm. The small local train, which gave the impression that it might be used as a trough for fodder when not needed for transportation, was scheduled to stop at every hamlet or crossroads on the way, thus taking over an hour to go less than twenty miles. No one checked our tickets, and there were no other passengers. It was impossible to see outside because the evening sky was so dark that the windows turned into mirrors. I could see myself reflected, and the reflections of those reflections. Dermot skulked at the end of the carriage, reading the instructions for the use of the emergency brake over and over again.

The single light we saw for that last stage of the journey came from a house in the throat of the estuary. It stood on a little island of its own, with the mainland on either side. A wooden bridge connected it to the real world. I had seen it before, from the road on the way to Borth. I had always wanted to go there. I wanted to know what it was like, living in a house unconnected to the world, being so physically apart. Lighthouse keepers and sailors on long journeys used to get cabin fever, and skin the first mate or declare themselves emperor of the known territories. I had always wanted to go to that little house, and seeing it now as the train crawled along the bank of the estuary I knew that I never would. The time for walking over there had been while I was a student, when you were given allowances. That was a world that was now closed.

Dermot didn't look at the house. He was still reading about the emergency brake.

Finally the train pulled into Borth Station, which was in better condition than any of the other stations we'd endured. There were two waiting rooms, and toilets. There was a footbridge across the tracks, and staff who, while not exactly pleased to see us, at least didn't look as though they'd attack us on sight. We walked up the little road that led from the station to the main road.

'Nearly there,' I said.

'What are we *going* to do?' asked Dermot, looking along the road. All of the shops were closed, and few windows were illuminated. The rain had stopped, but grudgingly. A large puddle made up of many sub-puddles ran the length of the town. A few figures, warmly wrapped, splashed along the pavements.

'Walk to the college,' I said. 'Or get a taxi.'

'Are there any taxis?'

'I've never seen one. There must be one.'

'And after we've *been* to the college? What do we do then? *Doss down* in a fucking hedge?'

'What are you getting at?'

'Well, if we're going to be here *overnight*, perhaps it'd be an idea to sort a room out now. To avoid the rush later on.

They do have rooms here, I mean they don't live in *burrows* or anything?'

'We could try the pubs.'

'Is there a hotel?'

'There might be.'

'Lead on, then. You know this place better than I do. I'm just a visitor. I'm only a passing tourist.'

We were at the end of town closest to the college, and farthest from the war memorial. The body of the town lay before us, a single road lined on either side with extremely shut shops. What lights there were shone from the rooms above the shops. There was little noise. We walked along the road, past the award-winning toilets – now closed – and the tourist information centre. We passed two pubs on our long walk through the long town, neither of them offering rooms. On the verge of giving up, close to the amusement arcade at the wrong end of town, we saw a hotel called Belle Vie. Perhaps the sign was missing a letter. If not, the owner was either extremely optimistic or hopelessly misguided.

VACANCIES, said a sign in a window.

'Here we go then,' said Dermot, striding into the lobby and ringing a bell on the reception desk. A short, harassed-looking man arrived, tucking his shirt into his trousers.

'Yes?' he said.

'Can we have rooms?'

'What, now? Can't you come back in the morning?'

'We won't *need* them in the morning. We need them now. In the morning we'll be *going away* again.'

'Well, is it two rooms then?'

'Yes it is. I don't want to share a room with this idiot.'

'I can understand that. Here, sign that. That'll be fifty each.'

'How much? Is everyone in Wales trying to fleece us?'

'Well, it's more of a national characteristic, really. We've been fleecing up here for centuries, see. It's not easy to stop.'

'Pay the man,' said Dermot.

I handed over my card, and the man took it away, looking a little puzzled. There was a conversation in Welsh from out of sight. The man's gentle voice was interrupted at frequent intervals by a much louder and shriller female voice, which proceeded in what seemed to be an explanatory way.

He returned after some minutes of discussion, handed me the card and a receipt in exchange for my signature, and gave us each a key.

'There,' he said. 'That'll be rooms twelve and thirteen.'

'I didn't think hotels *had* a room thirteen.'

'No, and I didn't think anyone would care much. We're not living in the Dark Ages now, are we? We shut the doors at midnight, but you have a key there that'll let you in. Phone calls are extra. Room service is out of the question. Is there anything else you need to know?'

'Is there a taxi service round here?'

'No. There are some in Aberystwyth but they don't come by here. No call for them, see. Where you going to?'

'The college.'

'Have they got a dance on?'

'We just need to sort something out.'

'Well, try and do it before midnight, only it wakes the missus up if people come in late. You've heard of the Welsh dragon?'

We nodded.

'There you are then. Well, looks like you'll be walking. Hope you get along alright. It's a dark old road.'

We pocketed our keys and went back out. Borth was still

sleeping. There were a few stars visible, showing that the clouds were parting. Presumably the clouds were empty, or perhaps just exhausted.

'We can get a lift back,' said Dermot. 'I can get us a lift *back* no trouble.'

'Get us one there, then.'

'There are no fucking cars here. They're not *allowed* after 8 pm because they wake the missus up.'

'Do you want to walk along the beach?'

Dermot did. At that end of town, the sea wall was only a foot high, looking more like a suburban garden wall than a device for holding the mighty ocean at bay. We stepped over it and onto the pebbles.

Dermot fell over at once.

'Fuck,' he said, getting up and falling over in another direction. He stood again, and moved very gingerly in the direction of the sea. The tide was miles out, and we found a thin band of sand to walk along. Every hundred feet, we had to clamber over wooden groynes holding clusters of cockles and bunches of tightly clenched sea anemones. The backs of the houses on that side of the road had a view out over the bay, and many of them had large rear windows, and often balconies. No one was out just then, with it being dark and cold. A couple held hands and walked their dog along the beach; the dog was a black Labrador retriever, and it was delighted by everything. It ran over the beach as though there was no trick to it, although Dermot could hardly stand upright. Perhaps he'd done more damage to his ankle than he realized at the railway station.

At the far end of town, we got back onto the road and walked between the sundered halves of the golf course. The road took a right turn and headed inland.

We walked on, out of the lights of the town and into the darkness. There were no streetlights, and no cars passing. There were no houses. The sound of the sea falling against the land came from behind us. On the left, a hedge rose and hid the estuary, although its smell – the stink of uncovered things rotting – reached us all too easily. On the right, small trees – never more than six feet tall, and looking something like bare hawthorn bushes – stood between us and the flat salt marsh which sat between Borth and the grey hills.

A sharp wind flew at us intermittently, flapping our clothes. I hadn't dressed for a walk in cold weather, and neither had Dermot. He was still trying his mobile from time to time, although there was no one he could ring. The calls of night creatures came across the marsh, odd howls and strange grunts and snuffles. Dermot didn't seem to notice, but then, nothing was quacking.

After a mile I saw a tree with broken branches and a splintered trunk, and knew that it was the tree Trish Newton had driven into, taking her out of the picture. Along with my offspring, of course. There was no proof that it was the right tree – or the wrong one, I suppose – but I knew it.

'This is the tree,' I said.

'This where she *did a Bolan* is it?' asked Dermot. 'How do you know that, then?'

'It's broken. It's snapped.' I was too tired to pick up on the first thing he'd said. There was no point getting into an argument with him, not there in the early evening dark with the sounds of unknown beasties coming across the marshes.

'That's sorted, then. *Must* be the one. There are only *hundreds* of the fucking things, after all. There's only an *orchard* to choose from. Come on then, let's get on with it. We're late enough now.'

Perhaps he was right. A few hundred yards further on, I saw another smashed tree, this one ending in a frozen spray of broken wood about two feet from the ground. That, too, I thought was the one she'd hit.

I could smell the estuary, and I could hear the sea. Had she been hearing and smelling the same things, upside down in the dark with the internal damage and the suddenly fragmented interior poking sharp edges into her, or had she been smelling her own damage and listening to herself? Would the unborn thing, my next generation, have died when she died or struggled on for a while inside the cooling body?

There was no point to the questions. Every fifth tree had been damaged, because the college was nearby and students these days all drive, and all drive when they're drunk because accidents only happen to other people, along with old age and disease.

It was dark, and the starlight was old and dead.

Dermot walked on, not complaining, a man with a mission.

Something kept pace with us, behind the line of small trees. Something smaller than a man but shaped much like one was following us. Whenever I looked at it, it scurried out of sight or dropped flat to the sodden ground, swallowed by the hummocks and puddles. Small, bright eyes watched us. It was smaller than it had been when it had hauled itself out of the surface of a mirror and wrecked Roger's experiment.

It had come back to its birthplace, if it had ever left. Where else would it go? It was not nearly human enough to live with humans. We're too finicky.

'Here we are,' said Dermot. Catching up with him, I saw a few lights ahead of us, glowing from the windows of the college buildings. Not many lights were on. It was, I realized, the first week of the holiday. No students would be there. There were still staff on site, obviously.

The thing that had been following us – my next generation, the one that had come successfully to term – slinked away from the road, heading for the college.

'What was that thing?' asked Dermot, who had noticed it after all.

'I made it,' I said. 'It turned up in the experiment. I don't know what it was.'

He was striding across the car park, towards the college itself. I followed him past a familiar car, and it disgorged two familiar people.

'Welcome back,' said Roger. 'You must have taken the long way round, we've been waiting for hours.'

Tina stood on the far side of the car, adjusting her hair although nothing was wrong with it.

'Hi guys,' said Dermot. 'I've been trying to call you but the phones don't work out here in the fucking *jungle*.'

'What are you doing here?' I asked.

'I asked them to come,' said Dermot. 'I called them from the Slipped Disc when you went to the gents. That'll teach you to spend so long in the *toilet*, won't it? They need to be here. They were here when it started. If you want to get everything back, all that stuff you got rid of, they need to be here.'

Again, it wasn't worth arguing with them. They were there and there was no way to get rid of them.

'I took a copy of the keys when I left,' said Roger. 'So we'll be able to get in.'

'Come on,' said Tina, taking my hand. 'You'll be better for this.'

'That's a matter of *opinion*,' said Dermot. 'Some people wouldn't agree with that.'

'Well, perhaps we'll invite them to express their opinion later,' said Roger. Tina was pulling me towards the college. Roger and Dermot walked ahead of us.

We walked past the main entrance, around the edge of the building. In the middle of the rear wall, a fire door stood closed. Roger unlocked it and led us in. Inside, dark corridors appeared to go on for miles. Roger led the way to a staircase and we started up.

As we passed the first-floor landing, we heard the door open below us. It closed. Something began to move towards us. It was inept at stealth.

'We have company,' said Roger. 'Let's hope it's friendly.'

Tina hauled me from the stairwell and along the top corridor. Roger turned on the lights. The endless corridor shrank, fixed by the illumination.

'304', read the sign on a door that had no window and was painted a dull white. Roger opened it.

'It's not that room,' said Tina. 'We went in there while you got it all in order.'

'Right you are,' said Roger. 'It was this one.'

He led us to the next room, and we all went in. He turned on the lights.

It was nothing like the room I remembered. Initially that had been full of mirrors, and later of broken glass. This one was almost empty.

'They still don't do anything useful in here,' he said. 'I suppose we ought to wait until we've all gathered.'

There were hesitant sounds from the corridor. The door opened, pushed by the thing that came in. It was my old friend, the thing that I'd left Borth to avoid. The thing I'd created there. It was four feet tall and humanoid, although its arms were too long for its body. It had long fingers, and long toes, and it was naked. Its skin was dark greyish in that light. Its eyes were yellow. Its face was upsetting, because it looked like mine, badly rendered. It looked like me in lo-rez.

'That's the lot,' said Tina. 'Now, are you going to tell us what's going on?'

'Me?' I asked. 'I don't know.'

'I can't tell you,' said Dermot. 'You told me not to. When you made me, you told me not to tell you *anything*. That was a hint,' said Dermot. 'I'm allowed to do hints. You didn't say anything about them.'

As though he'd opened a door, or turned on a light, I had the first traces of sketchy memories. I had been very drunk, and there had been very bad news.

'You didn't *want* to know,' he said. 'You've been that way ever since.'

'You've been that way for years,' said Tina. 'You never ask us anything. You don't want to know anything. We could have told you most of this.'

I didn't want to know anything, but it didn't seem that I was getting a choice. Memories began to form.

I remembered being very drunk, and asking Sid the reluctant barman for a series of absurd nameless cocktails – whisky, white rum, Cointreau and dry cider in a half-pint glass was the least unpleasant of them. The student bar had been crowded and I had been too drunk, falling into people. I had received bad news.

The car crash hadn't happened yet. That was waiting in the wings. This was different bad news.

'Stop,' I said to the room. It ignored me.

'He's getting there,' said Dermot.

'About time,' said Roger. 'He'll feel better for it. Trust me. I'm a doctor.'

I didn't trust him. I didn't trust any of them. But the trip had done what it had been designed to do. I remembered everything.

The past I'd got rid of came out of nowhere and swallowed me whole.

TWENTY-TWO

I

Here we are then, back in the early eighties. The music in the charts is all soulless and polished, the clothes are all bright and awful, the idea of ethics is laughable. We can all be rich, and the people who can't keep up can shut up and die.

At college in Borth I tried to keep up with these and other new concepts, but computing was moving ahead so quickly that I couldn't keep up with it. I was like a dog chasing a motorcycle.

I started drinking. That was acceptable, then. Conspicuous consumption was absolutely required. I drank a lot, and spent a lot of time in the bar.

I met Tina, but she was not my type at all. I got on with her, but there was nothing else to it. I was already in the process of falling for Trish Newton, who came from somewhere in Cornwall.

I had a wide array of disreputable friends. We'd get drunk together, and go staggering along the beach at night, swearing at the seagulls. Trish used to hang around with us.

Baz Patel, whose name wasn't anything like Baz but liked

to be called Baz 'because it saves all you stupid white boys from mispronouncing my real name,' took me to one side one night, while everyone else got on with the drinking games.

'What are you hoping to get out of all this?' he asked me.

'Out of what?'

'All of this, man, this college thing and all. What are you in it for? Just for this, the drinks and that?'

'That's enough for now.'

'How long does *for now* last for, man? You want to be doing this in three years' time? There's good things here if you want them. You're going too far over, man. You're just too drunk. This lot, these guys, they're fun to be around. I see that. But they're a short-term solution, you see what I'm saying?'

'What, you'd prefer it if I was like Olaf and all those other sad fuckers from the computer courses?'

'No. I like you drunk. You're a funny guy. But that's not enough. You can't pass your course drunk, man. You can't get a life.'

That phrase – get a life – had only just begun to make an appearance. I'd encountered it several times already, and was usually on the receiving end.

'I have a life already.'

'You're losing it. Out of all these people, which one is looking out for you?'

'You?'

'No, man. This is the only time I even try to help you. I'm not your guardian angel. This is a once-in-a-lifetime thing. This is my good deed, yeah? After this, you sort yourself out. But that Trish, man. She's on your wavelength.'

'Are you saying she fancies me?' I asked. It wasn't something I'd thought about. Trish Newton was always around, but she was far too sweet for me. I wasn't in her league.

'She's wild about you, man. I tell you, I sometimes wonder how you white folk ever reproduce. What does she need to do, wave a flag or something? She's mad about you. That's something you can get out of all this, if you don't lose all this by getting drunk all the time. That's me done, lecture over. Sort it out yourself from there.'

After that, I spent a couple of weeks keeping an eye on Trish. Of course Baz was right, she did fancy me, and it was obvious. I didn't know how I hadn't spotted it before.

I asked her out, and she said yes.

I was happy without being drunk, so I stopped drinking. Some of the friends I'd had until then stopped being friends. They only liked the drunk version of me, and he wasn't around. He wasn't even required.

I was happy.

We went through most of two years like that, going out, getting on. I paid attention, and that advancing wave of knowledge began to seem less likely to leave me completely washed up. Everything began to fall into place. I kept some of the less fickle friends, and the ones I didn't keep had never been any good for me and so weren't missed.

I still got drunk, and Tina and Trish and I would go out plastered and play along the shore, or go shopping in the hopeless seaside shops. It was a different sort of drunkenness, though. It was closer to fun than the old sort. It stopped before you blacked out.

Good times don't last, of course. Good times get clubbed to death. People change.

People change.

▌▌

The eighties carried on. The first mobile phones, which were barely mobile and which couldn't pick up a signal outside the City of London, made their appearance, hoisted by bright young men with bright new Porsche 911s. In the capital city, a different version of the same decade was underway, and all of the money was there.

People began to feign a liking for sushi, which they didn't like then and don't like now. The soul dropped out of art. Art had only to sell. Everything had only to make money; there was no other reason for anything to be.

Small wonder that love had a hard time of it.

Trish had a room two floors up and three blocks along from mine, in that ridiculously expansive student housing. We used to use her room because she'd got it into order. Mine was full of rubbish, with posters for horror movies and bad bands. Hers had photographs, sketches, that bloody Pierrot picture that was everywhere you went for about three years. There were Roger Dean posters, which I liked at the time because they were hers. I liked everything she had, apart from that bloody poster of the bloody clown.

She had a few records, picking up any old tat as she felt like it. She had stuff by Pink Floyd, New Order, Steeleye Span, Terry Jacks. Everything was on vinyl. The CD was not ubiquitous then. She used to put her albums in the wrong sleeves, in no sleeves, all in one sleeve.

Like my room, hers had come equipped with a narrow bed and an uncomfortable wooden chair. Unlike mine, it had been enhanced. She'd got her parents to drop off another chair – along with a beanbag that lolled on the floor like an excised cyst – on one of their visits. She'd put a decorated cloth over the desk, and draped another over the shade of the bedside lamp.

My room looked as though a monk from a fairly stringent order inhabited it. Hers looked human.

I later came to recognize all of the trappings as only that, only trappings. She'd swiped ideas from everywhere, but then, who doesn't?

She was a petite girl, with an accent I could have listened to for weeks. It had a touch of Cornish in it, but wasn't the usual one, thick as clotted cream. She had blonde hair and long nails. She had features that I still think of as perfect. No one else matches them. No one I've met since has meant what she did.

This was head-over-heels stuff. We had pet names for each other. We had *hundreds*. After almost two years, we were still gaga. We irritated our friends, apart from Tina, who was delighted by the pair of us. She liked the way we lit one another up.

One night, out of the blue, Trish asked me to pop round and see her. It was nothing too important, she said. She just needed to talk to me.

I had misgivings. Did she want me to meet her parents and turn respectable? Of course, I'd met them briefly when they came to take her away for the holidays, back home to her old life (and was I ever unhappy that she had another life? Wasn't I just). Did she want us to cool off, or heat up? Were we going to go respectable?

There were more possibilities than I could think of. I was something like nervous. I showed up early, because she didn't like me being late.

'Come on in,' she said. She had the lamp on and the

main light off. The record player was on, playing a Bob Dylan compilation tape that Tina had leant her months ago. Her favourite song that month was 'Idiot Wind'. It was playing then.

'Sit down,' she said, and gave me a glass of white wine. I didn't drink much wine in those days, not having met Roger and his wine attic. I took the glass, thinking that there was no point looking a gift horse in the mouth. She'd got the wine chilled.

'What do you think about us?' she asked me, dropping into the subject without any preamble.

'I think it's a good thing,' I said. 'I think we suit each other.'

'Do you love me?'

'Yes.' That was an easy one. That was the truth.

'Would you love me whatever happened to me? What if I was changed? What if I was, well, different?'

'I'd love you anyway. It's you I love. However you are.'

'That's good to know.'

She wasn't drinking anything, which should have set the alarm bells ringing. She looked pensive too. That wasn't her style. I'd seen her in many moods – happy, sad, bloody furious – but seldom pensive. Did she have something nasty? Was she telling me she'd caught something awful?

'I'll love you whatever,' I told her.

'Good,' she said. 'Then we're alright, aren't we? Only I'm pregnant.'

That wasn't fair, I thought. Her questions had implied something more manageable: cancer, leprosy, anything but this. Her questions had been designed to trap me. She'd led me into a hole. I didn't know what to say. She looked like a mouse, all bright eyes and hotwired nerves.

'Mick?' she said.

'I need to think about it,' I said, putting the wine glass on the desk. My aim was slightly off; the glass fell on its side, and the wine I'd left – not much – stained the cloth while the glass rolled off and fell to the floor. It didn't break. That might have relieved the tension.

I stood up.

'I don't know what to think,' I said. 'I don't know.'

She was crying then, and if I hadn't walked out of her room, perhaps she wouldn't have tried to drive to the station to get a train home and her car wouldn't have hit a tree and flipped, killing her and whatever part of me she was carrying. All of me, it felt like.

I didn't know that. I walked out of her room.

III

There's no need to apportion blame. I've already done that. I've given it all to me.

IV

She went to see Tina a few hours later, Tina told me on the night of our reunion, with the thing I'd conjured out of a mirror listening and nodding. She went to see Tina, and she'd been upset but not that terribly upset. She'd told Tina about the pregnancy, but naturally Tina had guessed about it weeks ago in any case. She told Tina that I had been no use at all. She was going to go home, and Tina could tell me when she saw me. I could call Trish at home, if I wanted to.

She was going to get a train from Borth station, and Tina thought that perhaps she was doing that because she wanted to stand on a deserted platform, pregnant and abandoned. She was such a romantic, as we knew. She had such dreams.

Off she went, upset but steady, driving calmly off. Tina went to look for me.

V

Tina didn't find me that night, because I was elsewhere. After leaving Trish I went to the student bar and got Sid to knock up some of those lethal cocktails. I drank them one after another, and then went to my room and put on 'Hobby For A Day' by The Wall. It was my favourite record then – not just for the month, I had strong loyalties to my records. If not to people. It was a single, a vinyl seven-inch single, and every time it finished I put the needle back to the start and played it again.

I don't suppose it even exists now. When music got transferred to digital media, some music just got lost.

I could sing it for you, if you wanted me to.

I played it repeatedly, thinking about Trish Newton and feeling resentful. Would I love her whatever happened to her? Well, yes, but pregnancy was something else. That involved a third person, and I had a first person viewpoint. And was I ever unhappy that she had another life? Wasn't I just.

After the fifteenth? sixteenth? millionth? play of 'Hobby For A Day', I went out. I wasn't going to the student bar. The people there knew me. I wanted to go where I wasn't known.

I walked into Borth, and I can't work out the timing but

it's possible she was talking to Tina when I set out, and just starting on her way to town as I got there. She could have passed me. She could have picked me up.

She never did, though, did she? The car got totalled, and she got subtracted.

I got drunk in unfriendly pubs.

VI

I walked back across the marshes, full of drink and stone-cold sober, and ended up in the student bar where the police finally found me and rounded me up.

VII

I remembered putting something of myself aside that night, shutting something out. It was most of myself. I had fallen out with myself, and I became someone else.

I forgot who I was.

I did it deliberately. I no longer wanted to be the person who'd let her go in that state, and who'd got drunk while she was bleeding to death in the wreckage. I was much too drunk to think straight.

I didn't lose my memory so much as throw it away.

The next week, I started to talk to the losers, people like Olaf and the other geeks. I steered clear of the people I'd known. I didn't know them anymore.

I had new friends. I had new interests.

I was someone else.

VIII

So, Tina told me, she'd had a short affair with me in an attempt to snap me back to my senses, to bring me back to myself. They'd liked me before. They didn't like the new, miserable me.

'You just played video games,' she said. 'That's all you did, talked to your computer friends and played video games. It was like most of you was gone. I just wanted you back, and so I pretended to be meeting you for the first time and pretended to fall for you. I'm sorry.'

Like most of me was gone? Was that a big deal? All of Trish Newton was gone.

'Tina came to me,' said Roger. 'She told me you'd gone through traumatic events and reacted to them by burying your personality, your memories. All of your Self, essentially. I'd been reading about this brilliant new technique using mirrors, and we chicaned you into being a test subject.

'The only thing was that you had a talent we didn't know about. I don't think anyone knew about it. And instead of getting you in touch with yourself, you separated another part of yourself. You gave it a physical form. Then it ruined all of our mirrors and headed for the hills.'

The thing in question looked contrite. Of course it had headed for the hills, I thought. Where else would it have headed? The nearest Harvester?

'We couldn't reach you,' said Tina. 'And then Dermot turned up. He said he was another one you'd produced, and that you'd instructed him not to tell you anything about it all. It was up to you to remember everything, when you were ready.'

'I remember everything,' I said.

'You didn't kill her,' said Tina. 'You don't need to be in pieces.'

She indicated Dermot and my other progeny.

'You can take them back,' said Roger. 'They're parts of you. Without them you're not complete. Without them, you're missing chunks. You took them and sent them out of yourself. They're you. They're pieces of you.'

I thought of Dermot, steering me towards my memories. He'd always said that he was the king of video games. He'd treated me like a character. He was looking gloomy, perhaps because he was set to vanish, back into my psyche.

'What was the thing about video games?' I asked.

'That's all you did,' said Tina. 'You became one of them. You behaved like them. You did whatever people did in video games. You didn't have a real life. You were living in a fantasy world.'

Video games, I thought; that explained a few things. It explained why I'd split myself three ways. In early video games, you got three lives to play with.

'Now we can put you back together,' said Tina.

'No,' I said. 'No you can't. I don't want them back. I like them out there. Dermot's fun out there. I'm happier with him out there. And this guy can be fun.'

'He can't speak,' said Tina.

'He can write,' I said. The thing winked at me. Dermot, who had been looking pensive, was looking perkier.

'Nice one,' he said. 'I didn't want to come back *in there* with you. I'm *better looking* than you are.'

'In your dreams,' I said.

'Hardly,' he said. 'In the circumstances.'

'But we want you back,' said Tina.

303

'You can't have me back. You can have me like this, with these two. Or you can't have any of us.'

'You don't want to live like that,' she said. 'In a fantasy. In a dream, not even a whole person. How would you *live* like that?'

'You're living in a fantasy world yourself. Sitting in a sepia-toned cottage in Bewdley, drinking wine and eating *crab cakes*. You're in a dream. So is everyone else, come to that. The country elected a cartoon Prime Minister, for fuck's sake.'

'You're happy like that?' asked Tina, incredulous.

'I can make worlds,' I told her. 'I can do without the missing bits of my personality. They'll come with me. Of course I'm fucking happy like this. This is playtime, all the time. If I'm two-dimensional, so be it. Come on then, you two. I'll sort a car out.'

'So long as this one isn't orange,' said Dermot.

The thing shyly held my hand.

We left Tina and Roger in Borth college. I haven't seen either of them since.

TWENTY-THREE

I

The car I created to go home in wasn't orange. It was enormous and had some strange controls – microwave guns, radar, pulse laser – but it was a quiet shade of blue, and as we drove home it didn't pick up any more attention than the Meriden 733t had.

'Do you want to pick up your car?' I asked Dermot.

'I'll go back for it,' he said. 'They won't have touched it yet.'

He turned to look at the thing, which was sitting up in the back seat with its face against the glass.

'You sure you want to take that back with us? Only it might not *like* the West Midlands. I mean, I don't like them much myself. And I fucking *live* there.'

'He's been there before,' I told him. 'He lives there too.'

'Oh?'

'Oh.'

Of course he did. I should have known that. Where else would he have gone? Just created, and with my memories, where else would he have gone? He was unable to speak, true, but he could write. He'd have tried to hitch, and then have ended up sneaking rides on lorries.

He'd have followed the route I followed, that being the only way he'd have known. He'd have gone to Machynleth, then on back to Newtown. On the hill outside town, he'd have waited for a lorry heading back to the Midlands, and he'd have been standing next to the sign I'd seen from Dermot's 733t on the way to Borth. The sign that read:

NEWTOWN
Twinned with
LES HERBIES

Like I said, he could write.

▌▌

Did I want to live in a fantasy world? Yes, of course I did. Me and the rest of the world. The alternatives were worse. Here is one alternative, one that I don't have a lot of trouble imagining:

Tina was understandably miffed that I'd – indirectly, as she thought – caused the death of Trish Newton. Tina and Roger were psychologists, and we know that psychology experiments are eight parts bluff and two parts cruelty.

So, what if they had been doing another experiment altogether? What if – for example, just for the sake of argument – they'd decided to kill me off in a way that'd give them a good case study?

In the mid eighties, cows began to have a bad time of it.

Tina used to cook meals for me.

Tina and Roger were always inviting me round, feeding me strange patés and pastes, freakish terrines, gristly pies.

A fantasy world is better than that version of things, which would also explain all of the known facts. Here is another version of reality: perhaps I'm now in a bed, unable to control my movements, unable to see or speak, inventing all of this as I go along. I could have been made that way by something composed of eight parts cruelty and two parts bluff.

I'll stick with the fantasy world, thank you very much.

III

'You're older than you pretend to be,' I told Dermot as we passed the Newtown sign on our way home. I saw him clock it, and knew that he'd worked out where our silent friend had got his name from.

'How old would that be?'

'The first song you ever heard was "Hobby For A Day",' I told him.

'Good song,' he said. 'You can get it on CD, you know. It's on a punk compilation.'

'But that wasn't the first time we met, was it?'

'Nope. I came to your house when you were a kid. You made me up. You wanted a friend and pop, there I was. You made a kitten too. Didn't look right.'

'It was orange. I remember that.'

'Then your mother comes home and you put us back inside your head. And it's *fucking untidy* in there, I can tell you.'

'And I didn't see you again until I really wanted something. If I really want something, I can get it.'

'You *really wanted* her not to be pregnant. You got drunk,

you got upset, and you got me out of your head again and *turned me loose.*'

'You got in the car with her.'

'You told me to. You made me, then told me to get in the car and wait for her. You told me to make it look like an accident. It *fucking hurt*, I can tell you that. I'm not real in your sense of the word, but it was a *mess* in that car. I had to heal myself when I got out. And then you just forgot about me. Charming.'

'I forgot about me, too. It was the guilt.'

'That or the contents of half the bars on the fucking peninsula.'

'Whatever.'

'And then that pair of *amateur shrinks* tried to sort you out with their stupid *modern techniques*. And the cheeky fuckers thought I turned up later. I'm the *original*.'

He looked at Les, who was drooling slightly.

'Which bit of you did he used to be?'

'Sarcasm? Bad manners? I don't know.'

'I like him. We can use him to *scare old ladies.*'

'We need him. He's the only one of us in proper employment.'

'His round then. Do they do a breakfast at the Slipped Disc?'

'They do in my world.'

'Breakfast it is then,' he said. I put my foot down and Wales became a blur. We crossed back into England as the sun came up. Dermot cheered. Our silent friend put a hand between the seats and gave us a thumbs-up.

EPILOGUE:
WHERE ARE THEY NOW?

I still live in Dudley, thanks for asking. I share a flat with Dermot and of course Les. Les now has columns in several dailies and one of the weekend glossies. He also ghosts columns for celebs who have columns but no vocab. He brings in a lot of money. Dermot does odd jobs for low wages. I don't work. After all, two parts of me are working more or less full time. I did make some money, though. Those old *Your Sinclair* magazines turned out to be worth a lot after all. A collector wanted the full set, and I had the full set.

Dermot sometimes lets me use the PC.

Roger and Tina are – as far as I know – still living in their overpriced little pretend world, bathed in an amber glow, drinking middling-good wine and watching out for floods from Wales.

Betts left Bright Harvest under a cloud following a break-in by a group of protesters. Police caught the protesters and convinced them to explain all.

The protesters claimed that a month ago they'd been standing about, peacefully waving banners, doing no harm, and suddenly something had happened.

They were sketchy about the event. Some said they'd been hypnotised. Others said that they'd been gassed. They all agreed that they'd suffered the illusion that they were two-dimensional figures, projected onto plywood.

They'd gone to their various homes, alarmed and upset.

They'd been afraid, and that had led to anger.

They'd regrouped and, after a month of preparation, stormed the building.

The guards had tried to prevent them, using the very latest crowd-control methods, which were based on research carried out in the building.

Something had thrown a spanner in the works. The new methods were unsuccessful. Months of research were invalidated. Four guinea pigs were liberated.

Betts now works at a small college somewhere in Wales.

Greg, Bob, Grant and Spot now live in a nice little house by the seaside. The exact location is secret. They have plenty of hay and are well supplied with foodstuffs. They are still confused or alarmed by everything they encounter, but are nonetheless always chirpy and cheerful. Their owners look after them well, and every now and then they are visited by a cat, which is very friendly, not quite in the right dimensions, and perhaps too bright a shade of orange.